Another Man's World

Previous Publications

Cold Fire, Calm Rage

Another Man's World

Joe Stein

Published by bluechrome publishing 2007

2 4 6 8 10 9 7 5 3 1

Copyright © Joe Stein 2007

Joe Stein has asserted his right under the Copyright, Designs and Patents Act 1988 to be identified as the author of this work.

First published in Great Britain in 2007 by
bluechrome publishing
PO Box 109,
Portishead, Bristol. BS20 7ZJ

www.bluechrome.co.uk
www.joestein.co.uk

A CIP catalogue record for this book is available from the British Library.

ISBN 978-1-906061-13-5

Cover photography by Tim & Cath French
© Tim & Cath French 2007

Printed by Biddles Ltd, King's Lynn, Norfolk

This is for those I have known who never had a chance.
Too many and mostly gone now.

Sweat freezing on the skin. Sitting bolt upright.

No dream. No memory of the dream, just the now familiar sensation of the heart pounding, blood racing, the traces of fear. No, of panic.

Still dark and the mattress on the floor is both refuge and jail.

Cold now, too cold to get up and pace the room, but sleep is gone. The dream is always unreachable, but the aftermath has become a known quantity. And the reason is known as well. By day it's controllable, but at night, the subconscious rebels and brings home the full implications of the road chosen.

Lie down once more, for there is nowhere else to go. Curl up. The body chooses the foetal position. For protection.

Protect yourselves at all times. A half and bitter curl of the mouth remembering another time. Referees' voices, trainers' voices. 'Protect yourselves at all times.'

Not now.

Not from the mind itself.

*

I should have brought the gun.

I should have brought the bloody gun.

Instead, I was caught cold like everyone else in the room, caught cold by these two punks in the Donald Duck masks. The masks could have been funny, but the shotguns weren't. Nor was the old man they'd thrown into the room to announce their entrance. He was doubled over behind them now, blood seeping from inside his mouth.

7

Everyone had stopped moving and it was a second or two before there was any response. Not surprisingly, when it came, it was from my American and directed at me.

"Well," he said, "aren't you going to do something, boy?"

The two masks turned to look at me.

The 'boy' bit grated. If I'd have been black I would have taken offence. And the last time I took offence, I hit someone with it. Okay, bad joke, but this whole thing had turned into a bad joke. A supposedly secret place for a high stakes card game. Five players, four minders, including myself, the organiser and the old man who let the place out and was here to make the tea.

And, of course, the two gatecrashers with the sack and the shotguns. One of them threw the sack on to the table.

"Well, do something!" The American was shouting now. "Shoot them or something!"

One of the two turned his sawn-off towards me.

"I don't have a gun," I said evenly, talking to the American, but looking at the shotgun. "And I'm too far away to do anything without one. And," I said pointedly, as he started in again, "I am now the centre of attention."

He shut up.

"Money. In the sack, now."

This was the one pointing the gun at me. A flat voice, but young. Didn't sound nervous though. The other was more jittery, couldn't keep still. He would be the one to pull a trigger because he lost control.

I didn't know if anyone else in the room was carrying, but I hoped not. If there was an enthusiastic amateur somewhere and he pulled a gun, there would be a bloodbath. The room wasn't that big that we'd all get out of the way.

Allingway, the American, spoke to me again.

"You can't let them take my money. You gotta stop them."

"You're paying me to mind you and to look after things," I replied, still looking at the man holding the gun. "You're not paying me enough to jump in front of a bullet for you and if I try to stop them, that's what will happen. If I were in your position, I'd give them the money."

"You bastard," he said, "you lousy bastard." But he started dropping his money into the sack.

So did two of the other men round the table and a fourth dropped his head into his hands and I thought it was going to be all right, when somebody had to get heroic. One of the minders suddenly jammed his hand behind his back under his jacket and grabbed at a small handgun. No diversion, no lateral movement, I don't think he even waited until a point when Donald Duck wasn't looking at him. He actually got halfway clear with the gun, before the shot hit him and his hero's chest exploded into little pieces. A shotgun blast at five paces doesn't leave much of its target left.

I'd started moving as soon as I'd seen the minder go for his gun. I was on the furthest side of the room from him, which helped, near to Allingway at the playing table and by the time the shotgun went off, I was across the American, taking him down to the floor and holding him there. The sound of the blast hadn't faded when there were two more. The nervous Donald, hopping from one foot to the other, had let two barrels go at someone or at nothing, I didn't know which. As the sound of those two shots cleared he was shouting, "Bang, Bang, Bang." A psycho, or high on something. From where I was on the floor, I could see the other one, having calmly tossed the last loose money into the sack, grab him and pull him backwards out of the room and down the stairs. My ears were ringing after the sound of the shots in the room, but I thought I heard a car gunning away.

I pulled Allingway up from the ground, grabbed his jacket and pushed him towards the door. He didn't say a word. Probably working out whether he could sue me for bruises as well as losing him his money. The old man was still doubled up on the floor, but now wasn't the time to be a good Samaritan. Someone would have heard the shots. Now was the time to run like hell. Pretty soon there would be police swarming all over the place. At the bottom of the stairs the door led straight out on to the street. I didn't think the Disney Duo would still be around, but I checked briefly before dragging Allingway out and half pushed, half ran him up the street to the car. I didn't think I'd left any traces behind. I hadn't leant on the table, I hadn't even sat down and I hadn't opened any doors myself, so with a bit of luck there wouldn't be any of my prints anywhere. Bloody science for you. It might be great for catching criminals, but it makes it hard for someone like me to earn an honest living. Allingway, as a tourist, would hopefully be clean. If the police got hold of anyone else from the game they might know Allingway, but if that led back to him, I'd speak to Mick who gave me the job and stop it before it got any further.

Once I'd got him into the car, he started.

"I want my money."

I was surprised that he'd been quiet as long as he had.

"I'm sure you do," I replied, "but for the moment, let's just be thankful you're not dead and you're not hurt."

"Not hurt!" he shouted, "I've lost my damn money. I'm not leaving this country until I get my money back."

He was a large man, probably still powerful, with a Southern States caricature of an accent and a tone that said he was used to getting what he wanted. This time it might be more difficult.

"You came highly recommended to me and you've screwed up. Now I want my twenty-five grand back and that's British pounds sterling, not dollars and I want it back before my pocket even realises it's gone."

I didn't say anything. From his point of view, maybe I had messed up. Maybe I should have been standing by the door with a gun in my hand, but I'd been more worried about the other players than about an attack by an outsider. Allingway was still talking. Client or not, he was beginning to get on my nerves.

"Mr. Allingway," I said, cutting across his sentence, "if you'd be quiet for a few minutes, I might be able to think about this."

"You asking me to stop talking, boy?"

That 'boy' thing again. I must be getting sensitive.

"No, I'm not asking, I'm telling you to shut up and let me think."

Amazingly, there was silence.

I tried to remember everything about the two men in the masks. They were both young, but one had been steady, the other nervy. The way the second one had shouted 'Bang, Bang' after he'd fired the shotgun sounded like he was either out of his skull on something, or a nutter. If he was stupid enough to yak about this, or to spend, then Mick might hear something about it, but London's a big place. It ought to be someone fairly local though, this wasn't a big enough game to be known all over the city.

I dropped Allingway at his hotel in Central London and promised to contact him the next day. He wasn't a happy man, but there wasn't anything I could do for him. Then, even though it was nearly midnight, I went to see Mick.

*

Mick buzzed me in through the block's outer door and by the time I'd turned into the corridor, the dog was in his usual place, barring the doorway of the flat. I gave him the back of my hand to sniff, fingers closed of course. He half gave way and allowed me to bump past him through to the hall and Mick's living room. Mick was up even though I hadn't called. He hates using the phone, thinks its bugged. That's what paranoia does for you, but then again, he's still on the outside.

"Lost the money," I said.

Mick was sprawled on his sofa, a smallish, wiry man with what some might call character etched into his face and what I would call too many cigarettes and too little sleep, but then no-one asked me. There were some papers in his hand and the TV was talking to itself quietly against the wall. Maybe he never went to bed.

"Is Allingway all right?"

"Yes, but not happy about his 'pounds sterling'. Thought I should have been armed and shot it out with them. Maybe he thinks he'd have had his money's worth then."

"Maybe he would have done."

Mick hadn't put the papers down yet, so I walked over and took them away from him.

"What's that supposed to mean?" I asked him.

No preamble with Mick, he cuts straight to the point.

"It means that for the past three or four months, you've been very quick to try not to go armed, or to get into any trouble."

"Bodyguards don't get into trouble, Mick, they avoid it," I countered. "And going armed when you don't need to isn't worth it."

He sat up and looked straight at me.

"All I know," he said, "is that something happened. You dropped out of circulation for three or four weeks and it might have been longer if I hadn't have got Tony to go after you and pull you over here. No, I'm not asking, but whatever it was, I hope it's over. And if it is, then you have to snap back into the land of the living. I'm not saying tonight was your fault, but a few months ago I'd have known it wasn't."

He had a point. I'd been avoiding trouble a bit, I just didn't want the hassle that could come with it. And he was right that it was directly because of the Smith thing. But tonight it wouldn't have made any difference, I was sure of that.

"You better tell me what happened and I'll put the feelers out," he said.

While I ran through the events, I tried to work out if there was anything else I could have done. There wasn't. I wouldn't have played it any differently if I had been armed and more people would have been hit if I'd pulled a gun from where I was. But still there was a niggling thought. Was I acting differently? No. And when I found these cowboys, Mick would see that.

"I'll find out what I can," he said "and I'll talk to Alling-way, get him to sit tight for a couple of days. You can do the same. Don't go chasing round after these guys like some bloody loose cannon. Just keep out of it until I get a handle on them."

"Okay, Mick," I said, "it's your client." I turned to go.

"Hold on," he said. "I've got something else for you, while you've got time on your hands. Not your normal stuff, but you can handle it. And," he carried on, as I started to butt in, "you owe me for this one, if I get you out of it. Your rep won't be too hot if everyone knows a couple of punks can take twenty-five grand off you. And I put you up for it as well."

I turned back. For one thing, Mick had got me the place I slept in, the rent collecting job that paid for it, as well as the bodyguard jobs that kept me going. We went back a long way, back to when I was a snotty nosed light-middle, not fully grown yet and he and Al were showing me how to get into and stay out of trouble at the same time. Whatever he had, I would listen to. He hadn't steered me wrong yet.

The second thing was the dog lying in the doorway of the lounge. I might have been a 'friend', but I didn't think he would let me out if Mick didn't give him the signal.

So I listened to a simple enough problem that a night-club owner in East London wanted help with. Mick was right, it wasn't the usual bodyguarding routine, but it wasn't difficult and it didn't sound dangerous.

Shows you how good my instincts are.

*

I drove the Mondeo back to Tony's car lot, parked it up, stuck the keys through the office letter box and got into the ten year old Cavalier that he lets me use. Tony's a useful bloke for me to know and we grew up together, so he puts himself out for me. In return, I make sure he doesn't get dragged into any trouble of my making. Not much of a deal for him, but it works for me. The Cavalier's on a sort of permanent loan from him. If anyone asks, I've got it on an extended test drive for a couple of days, but both Tony and I know it's staying with me unless he gets a buyer for it. In the meantime, I pay him a hire charge for the use of the newer cars I need for working and as long as he gets them back in the same condition, he's happy. There's a little wear and tear, but this is a used car lot and he can deal with that. I've never yet had a scratch on one of his cars, but if I do, he's insured if it's on the lot and we've got a couple of ready made witnesses lined up who saw someone nicking it, if I can't get it back there.

I drove easy back to Camden through a light London drizzle to my first floor hovel. 'Studio flat' an estate agent would probably call it, but luckily I can still recognise a large room with a kitchen, a shower and a toilet to one side behind a thin partition, for what it is. Obviously a damn sight easier than I can recognise a possible dodgy situation at a private card game. How the Disney guys found out about it was clear. Someone at the game had talked about it, but they shouldn't have done. These guys played for serious money and they knew enough to keep quiet about the games. The old man wouldn't have known how much money was being passed, besides which, that had been real pain and real blood on his face when they'd pitched him through the door. I parked up a couple of streets away from the flat and made my way up the stairs to the front door. Broken matchstick still showing out a few millimetres from the door-frame an inch above the ground. I've got one in the back door as well which leads out to the fire escape, but I don't check front and back anymore, only the one I'm using. Not unless I've got reason to.

The flat was cold and empty, the cat was out some-where, which was okay by me. I don't own him, he just happens to live here as well. We tolerate each other and he keeps the place clean of anything that crawls or scurries. When I moved in, I put a magnetised catflap into the small section of the window that was broken which he was using as an entrance. Now it doesn't rain in anymore and he still comes and goes as he pleases. Suits me. I don't use him for any kind of comfort and he wouldn't expect me to. The nearest I'd ever come to stroking him, was when I grabbed him while he was eating and sprayed a de-flea aerosol down his chest. About three seconds and a dozen scratches later, we resumed our non-tactile relationship.

I switched on the oil heater, went into the kitchen and pulled out a half bottle of cheap whisky from one of the cup-boards. I don't know why I insist on putting it away there instead of leaving it out on the table, but for some reason I do. I don't even like drinking and I don't get drunk, but after a while it does deaden the senses, which was what I wanted. Maybe leaving it out would have been too easy. Or an admission. I didn't want to eat and I didn't want to sleep, so I just sat and killed the rest of the bottle. I even found myself wanting the cat to come back in, which was a sure sign I was in trouble, so I went to bed. Prayed for sleep.

16

No, prayed for untroubled sleep.

*

'Snazz' was a flash nightclub in East London, part of a chain and run by Adam Hillier. Didn't sound like a hard nut name, but that's what he was and he had the muscle around him to back up his reputation. Hillier wasn't a fool and he'd decided that the problem he had was best sorted by an outsider and that was where I came in. He only knew Mick by reputation, but that was precious enough in Mick's game. If you had no rep, you had no business, so I had to make sure I protected that.

I turned up as requested at two in the afternoon, when all clubs like these look tired and shabby. There are usually a few people around cleaning up and someone working in the office. This time it was the boss, together with a couple of his 'boys', one of whom it seems had more than the obvious function of keeping trouble away from his employer, as he was on the phone, running through rates for booking some novelty act for the club. It sounded like mud wresting chimpanzees, but I might have heard wrong.

The office was large, but not too flash and Hillier sat behind a desk that was only just big enough to turn upside down and sail up the Thames in, but he seemed down to earth enough. He waved me into the chair opposite him at the desk, offered me a drink, noted I refused it, offered me a cigarette, noted I turned that down as well, lit one up himself, leaned back in his chair and then started circling.

"Garron. Didn't you used to be on the circuit a few years back?" His voice was rough, a barrow boy's tone, but a little quieter.

"Several years back." I said. I left it at that. I was becoming used to people with long memories. In some ways I should have been flattered, but the truth was, that was a lifetime ago and recognition nowdays wasn't always helpful.

"Yeah," he said, "I lost a packet on you, when you hammered that French bloke at Bethnal Green. Thought he'd be too much for you and dropped a load on that."

I didn't answer. I certainly wasn't going to apologise for it.

"Ah well," he carried on, "taught me a valuable lesson, that did. Never bet on something that you don't know the outcome of."

He laughed slightly and I smiled along. Why not, it was his office.

There was silence for a moment and then changing gear, he stepped right in.

"I've got a problem, Garron, someone is trying to ruin the club's reputation."

This time I tried not to smile. It was hard to imagine what could hit the reputation of a club like this. Unfortunately, I must have failed, because he said:

"Yeah, I know that sounds funny, but one or two things can and do hurt a club like this. One of them is if there's too much trouble. The word goes out and punters start to stay away. That's what's happening now."

"I wouldn't have thought you'd have too many problems here," I said, gesturing to the two other guys in the room. "They look like they can handle trouble and I'm sure there are more where they came from."

He shook his head at me. "Nah, you're missing the point, Garron. They can deal with it when it happens, but I need to stop it happening. Someone is targeting this club. And the worst of it is that it's so amateurish, I can't stop it. If it was professional I'd know what to look for, but what's happening is petty. Stupid stuff. But it is having an effect. Four out of the last six Thursdays, there's been trouble. Someone starting a ruck over nothing. A different person each time and not the type you'd think. And no connection between them that I can find out. But the result is that Thursdays are dropping now. The word is out. There might be trouble on Thursdays at Snazz, so stay away. And this'll be just the start. Once it happens on other nights, I'll really feel it."

"What have you done about it so far?" I didn't ask if he'd called the police. He wouldn't want them nosing around his clubs.

"I've had the lads take a couple of the troublemakers out the back and ask 'em, but one of them wouldn't say anything and the other just told us about it being a bit of a laugh, doing it for some woman he met in a bar as a dare. Couldn't get anything useful out of them and by then it's all got a bit public and your hands are tied. Bad enough there's trouble in the club, without having any of my staff pulled for it."

"And what do you want me to do?" I asked

"I want you to find out what's going on of course," he said, sounding surprised.

19

I looked at him. Mick had told me roughly what the job was about, but this wasn't what I did and I wanted Hillier to understand that I didn't really know how to go about it.

"Mr. Hillier," I said, "I'm a bodyguard, not an investigator. I can't just 'find out' what's happening. I wouldn't know where to start."

"I know what you are, Garron and I don't want an investigator, I don't want someone to go through my past and start looking for enemies, I can do that myself. I want someone on the floor of the club listening to what people are saying, looking out for what's going on."

I thought about it. I owed Mick anyway and I could do what this guy wanted for a week or so.

"Okay, I'll turn up for a few nights. I'll come in as a regular punter, no nods, no free drinks and I'll keep my eyes open. If anything happens I might get involved, or I might not, we can play that by ear." I looked at the heavy leaning against the office wall. "If I do get involved, try not to break anything while you're throwing me out, all right?"

He sneered at me, but said nothing. The one who had been on the phone though, caught the meaning.

"Don't worry," he said, "we'll make it look good, but it won't hurt too much."

I turned back to Hillier.

"Mick quote you a price?" I asked.

"All sorted," he answered and then took a few folded notes out of one of the desk drawers and passed them over to me. "Expenses," he said, "entry, drinks and so on. Should last you for a night or three. Whatever you don't use, you can add into the price."

I took the money and put it away without looking at it. I can be classy when I remember to be.

"All right, Mr. Hillier, I'll be here Wednesday night and we'll see how it goes."

I got up. Hillier didn't and as he hadn't offered his hand, I turned to go. As I reached the door, the man leaning on the wall straightened up.

"Smart casual, Garron," he said, "don't give us a reason not to let you in."

I couldn't think of a quick comeback to that one, so I just left.

*

I had nothing to do for the next couple of days, so I did nothing. I used to be good at that, sitting around, playing blues harmonica, doing a few exercises and generally killing time. Now though, I was finding it more difficult to spend time on my own without the prop of work. I knew why this was, but knowing that there was a problem didn't make it any easier to get my mind off the people that had died and why. I was having trouble concentrating and I ended up wondering what real people did with their time if they weren't working. I reckoned it wasn't by thinking about people they'd killed, why they'd done it and how many bridges they'd burned. Sometimes I'd just get out of the flat and run for half an hour or so, break the thought process, clear the head, but in the end the flat was where I went for refuge, where I ate and where I slept. And sleep was a different problem. I found myself looking forward to working, looking forward to possible confrontations and situations and that's when

I realised that I might really be beginning to lose it. And if I lost it on a job, that would be real trouble.

Allingway went home. He hadn't wanted to go, but nothing was happening and he had, in his words, a business to run. He extracted a promise from Mick to find his money, but I didn't think there was much chance of that. Mick had decided not to blame me for the loss, but it still hurt. I may not have much pride left, but there's enough to not want to be taken to the cleaners by a couple of cartoon characters.

*

Wednesday night was almost the first evening of the year that made it look like summer could arrive. Snazz was reasonably full and I dressed up enough to blend in. No jeans. No T-shirts. And no trouble. The usual night club crowd of people let out of their shops and offices for a few hours, some of them just after a bit of release, others trying to forge the contact that would make them feel the night had been worthwhile. I tried not to drink anything too fast, I could use the extra expense money. I made irregular circuits of the club and tried not to look like I was cruising for anything. When the crowd started to thin, I made my way out. The heavy who'd been leaning on Hillier's office wall, was on the door. As I walked past he pointed his index finger at me and stuck his thumb straight up. Then he dropped his thumb, shooting me dead. Gunman's goodbye. From a mate it would be OK. From him, it just got my back up.

*

It could have gone on like that for several days, but Thursday we got lucky. In amongst a group of half a dozen young guys was one who was looking for trouble from the first minute. It didn't fit the mould though, the previous problems had been from individuals, but I caught on to him when they were ordering drinks at the bar and he was hyped up and ready to go. A tallish, loud-mouthed, flash git, was how I would have described him. Greased-back hair, cut short at the sides and back, loud open-necked shirt, probably had a gym membership he didn't use too much and a couple of barbells in the corner of his bedroom. I stuck with them when they moved to the dance floor and thought about letting the bouncers know. But if I moved it might all kick off in the few moments I wasn't there, so I hung around. It wasn't long before Flash Harry had started bumping into a group that were dancing next to him and it was only a matter of time before one of the guys in the second group had words. Next thing, Harry's thrown a punch, someone's fallen into someone else and it was all off. The bouncers were on their way, so I had only a few seconds to get this right. I shouldered into the ruck, grabbed the guy holding on to my mate Harry, pulled him off and threw a nice looping right hand that connected somewhere on the guy's cheekbone. A big showy punch that no-one, not even a wally like Harry, could fail to notice. The guy went over, the bouncers arrived and my friend from the upstairs office pinned my arms to my sides, lifted me off my feet and wrestled me towards the emergency exit. I didn't resist and I think that disappointed him. I was looking for Harry and couldn't see him.

"Hold up!" I hissed at the guy, "I need to be with the others you're chucking out."

He took no notice and bundled me through the exit into a corridor that led to the fire doors, so I scraped my heel down the front of his shin bone. There was a grunt of pain and he threw me head first into the wall next to a fire extinguisher. I managed to put one arm up to take some of the impact and thought about reaching for the extinguisher, but then he was grabbing my jacket, turning me around and pulling back his right hand. I kicked him in the groin. His hands went down and his knees snapped together as what passed for a brain registered the pain and he dropped sideways on to the stone floor. I looked back at the emergency exit we'd just come through and swore. I had no idea where Harry and his group were. They had to be outside, so I turned to go out through the fire doors with the idea of running round to the front to try and catch them, when the emergency doors from the club burst open and Harry and one of his mates appeared, being manhandled out by two of Hillier's other tame wildlife. When the bouncers saw their colleague curled up on the floor and me standing over him, they dropped their charges and started towards me. This was all getting out of hand. I grabbed the fire extinguisher and fired the CO_2 gas at them at the same time shouting: "Run!" at Harry. To be fair, he and his friend did, aiming a couple of soft kicks at the two bouncers on the way. I dropped the extinguisher on the floor, turned and shouldered through the exit at the end of the corridor. Out into the car park at the back, with Harry and friend a couple of strides behind me. They wanted to go round to the front, but there would be more trouble there, so I shouted to them to follow me over the wall at the back of the car park, which left us in a service road at the back of a row of shops. Another couple of minutes hard running and we were round the back of a takeaway four streets away, leaning against a wall and trying to breathe again. For some reason, they were ecstatic.

"Did you see that guy I kicked?" Harry was almost shouting at his mate. "Did you see that? Whack! He's going to feel that for a week, he will."

Harry's voice was all cockney edge and youthful strut. Probably a car salesman.

I let them get it out of their system and waited for them to come to me. Which eventually they did.

"Owe you one, mate," Harry said to me putting out his hand. "You got us out of what could have been a kicking out the back there. What's your name?"

"Harry," I said, having been caught out by the most obvious question of all.

"I'm Dean," he said, "this is Ollie. Stupid name we all think, but that's what it is. Don't know why you were in that, but I'm glad you were."

"I just..." I said, still trying to get my breath back, "wanted to have a poke... at the guy you were wrestling with."

"Oh yeah, yeah, I saw you land a good one on that sod in the white shirt. Bet it's not white now, eh?" He started laughing and his mate joined in although a little more reluctantly. I wasn't having the same nervous reaction as they were, but I was more out of breath. Maybe he did use his gym membership after all.

"Bastard... knocked my drink out of my hand earlier... and then walked off," I said, finally getting my breathing into some sort of regular, if laboured, pattern. "I'd been following him around for about ten minutes, trying to get a chance at him."

"See," said Ollie, "there'd have been trouble there anyway, if you'd have held off. Then we wouldn't have had to get ourselves kicked out and you'd still have got your leg over."

Bingo.

I played it down, but I needn't have. Dean was so full of himself after what had happened, he wanted to tell the world. They were off to a place now to meet with the girl who had set Dean up to cause the fight at the club.

"That is just crazy," I said.

"Crazy, but true," he said. "Good looking girl too and it's no trouble to me. I'm up for a ruck every now and then. Come on with us to the pub, I'll buy you a drink and you can meet her as well."

"Drink," I said, straightening up from my knackered crouch. "That sounds good."

*

The pub was more of a wine bar, but as I was still dressed for the club, they let me in. The place was packed, but the girl was sitting at a table on her own and Dean went straight over, gave her a kiss on the cheek, which she didn't respond to and told her it was a breeze. He introduced me and Ollie and then said: "I'll get some in. Come on, Ollie, give me hand with them."

He and his mate went off to the bar. I sat down in front of the girl. She had a hard face, cold eyes, although she couldn't have been more than mid-twenties, but she was good looking, just in a slightly brittle way. It wouldn't be long before the two lads were back again. Time to go to work.

26

"Jane your real name, or are you just using it on Dean here?"

She took a long drag on her cigarette and blew out some smoke.

"Isn't this the bit where I say, 'I don't know what you're talking about'?"

"Are you actually planning on sleeping with him, or are you just going to fade when it comes to pay off time?"

"Does it matter to you?" she answered.

I'd just tried to push a few buttons, get a response, but she wasn't reacting. She also wasn't a fool though. She said:

"I thought you were trouble when you walked in with them. You're the wrong type to be hanging around in clubs."

"You don't think I can dance?" I asked

"I know you can't," she said and stood up.

"Sit down, lady."

She didn't, but she didn't walk off either.

"If you walk away, I'm not going to run after you, but I've got an idea now what you're doing and even without your name, I'll be able to track you down. I've got one end of this thing now and I'll keep picking away at it until I pull the whole thing apart."

She stayed where she was, but she didn't sit down.

"Or I could hand it over to Hillier as it is now, but I think you'd be better off talking to me than to his guys."

The thin, hard face for a second became even more set, but then she said:

"All right. Let's go now though, before 'city boy' and his mate get back."

We left. My new-found friend would probably think the worst and hate me for it, but I wasn't going to lose sleep over that. He could always go back to the club and try looking for me there.

She was parked on the road nearby, not in the car park. Whether by accident or design I didn't know and it might make a difference. I wasn't sure yet what I was dealing with here. Hers was a small Micra, six or seven years old, with a couple of small dents.

"You all right to drive?" I asked.

She didn't look at me when she answered: "I don't drink when I'm working," she said.

She didn't bother with a seat belt and the car was moving before I'd even closed the door. It was a short ride. About three streets later she pulled over, switched the engine off and turned to me. It suddenly occurred to me that I'd slipped up. I'd stepped into a confined space, into an unknown environment where she could have any kind of weapon stashed. And I'd thought that she was the amateur! If I got hurt now, I'd bloody deserve it.

"OK," she said, "you're not police and you're not one of Hillier's thugs, so what is this to you?"

"I'm an outsider," I said, "hired help, unknown face, no ties. Hillier wants the trouble to stop, asked around and got me to look into it. Now I know who's behind this, I can stop it." I paused for a moment. "Like to know why you're doing it though."

She ignored the last bit.

"If you don't hurt me now, or haul me into Hillier, how can you stop me?"

I looked at her hard face, the bleached hair and the heavy make-up and realised that she was just a girl who was getting out of her depth. There wouldn't be any gun under the seat; at worst it might be a nasty set of curling tongs.

"Jane, or whoever you are, I can probably find you again. You're most likely off your home patch, but I know what you look like and there has to be a reason why you're doing this to Hillier. If I work with him, we'll dig out what it is and who you are. Or we can wait for the next bit of trouble and work on the guys you've set up. Or track them back to you."

She didn't look too upset yet. None of this had struck close to home.

"Of course," I went on, "I don't need any of that, since I've got your car registration now. If it's not yours, then the odds are it belongs to someone you know and that'll be good enough. Any connection will do. I can work back from there."

She turned away to face front again and after a few seconds started the car and drove some more in silence. In a little while she said:

"Hillier killed my brother. Threw him out of a fifth floor window. The police did nothing. They said it was suicide whilst under the influence of drugs and Hillier and one of his 'boys' were witnesses that Stuart jumped."

She was staring rigidly ahead now.

"Bastards." She said it quietly and as I looked at her I could see her eyes were wet. Not rolling tears, but tears nonetheless. "He would never have jumped. He was a user, but he never got like that, never got that much out of control."

I could think of a few things to say to that, but it wasn't my grief.

"I know I can't hurt Hillier," she said, "I can't even get to him, but I started to hurt his business. Word's started to go round and as long as I was careful, I could get away with it." She stopped at a red light. "There are enough stupid jerks around who want to fight anyway." She turned to look at me and it was a bitter look. "Give them the prospect of sex and dress the whole thing up as a laugh, as a dare and it's easy."

The lights changed. She looked forwards again, but didn't move off. There was no-one behind us.

"What happens now?" she said. "I don't suppose you'd fall for the sex promise thing?"

I didn't answer for a second.

"I don't think, after what I know now, that I'd trust you in the dark."

The lights turned red again.

"Jane," I said, "I - "

"Nicola," she cut in. "It's Nicola."

"All right, Nicola. Do you know how someone like Adam Hillier will react when he finds out what you've been doing? It's not even about the money he's lost or might lose. It's about reputation. Ego maybe. He can't afford to be taken for a sucker. And even if I don't tell him and just bow out, he'll get someone else. It didn't take me long to get to you and the next guy will probably be better than I am at this." I paused for a moment. "Of course they might fall for the sex bit and get an ice pick through the brain, but sooner or later someone will get to you. So this has to stop. Now."

Someone hooted from behind. The lights were green. She drew forward, but pulled over as soon as she could.

"What are you going to tell Hillier?" she asked.

"That depends on you."

"What do you mean?"

"If this stops now, tonight, right here and I mean stops completely, no more trouble, no harassment, no bomb threats, no dodgy phone calls, then I'll tell him I've stopped the trouble and we'll leave it there."

"He'll want to know who was doing it."

"He will, but I won't tell him."

She shook her head. "He'll make you."

"No," I said, "he won't."

"He'll buy you then."

"No," I said again, "he won't."

"I can't trust you."

"Yes you can. You just don't know that you can. And you don't have much of a choice. Either it stops here and you're safe, or it doesn't and I shop you. It's up to you."

"No," she said, "there is no choice."

"Then it stops here. Now."

She stared straight ahead out of the windscreen.

"Yes," she said quietly, "it stops here and now."

"That's the right decision."

She turned and looked at me with a bitter smile.

"It's the only decision you left me with," she said. "Now please get out of the car."

I looked at the rain outside.

"I thought I might rate a lift to the nearest station at least."

"You've just made me give up what I promised my brother I'd do. Now get out."

"I just saved your bloody neck, girl!"

"And I'm supposed to be grateful and thank you? Get out!"

I sighed and got out. It was raining hard, but an hysterical girl driving me around maybe wasn't such a good idea either. The car was moving off before I'd shut the door again. Women drivers! I wondered what Hillier would have done in my position. Probably clipped her one, dumped her on the road and driven home himself. But then that was the difference between him and his kind and me. I hoped. I had no idea where I was. I could have gone back to the club, they would still be working, but I didn't. It would wait until tomorrow. I decided to go home. There were no shops and this wasn't a cab route. I picked a direction and started walking. My left shoe sprung a leak.

*

Look at the clock. Focus on it. Pull away from the subconscious. Don't stay there.

Sit up now, damping down the panic tide. What is wrong? What is wrong with me? I did what I had to do. I couldn't know anything else. I did it right.

Or was that the problem?

Al would've said I was right. But Al was dead and I wasn't sure. This is to do with me. I don't need anyone else's justification. I need my own. But I'm not sure.

Stand up and walk around, control the breathing and then, God help me, reach for the bottle. Bloody cliché. I've become a bloody cliché. But it's a truth. Someone said when you feel you need it, is when you shouldn't take it. But I will. Only at night though. Just to chill. Just to sleep.

*

Hillier was in his office, in the same place behind his desk, but this time there were no heavies. I'd called first and he'd diplomatically removed them.

"You're not flavour of the month round here, son, I can tell you that. Bobby might be a loud-mouthed git, but he's one of the team and you hurt him pretty bad."

"Shouldn't have tried to take my head off then," I said.

"Yeah, well maybe, but I wouldn't hang around here too much if you can help it. You may be able to take Bobby nine times out of ten, but he's not usually on his own."

He leant forward and rested his arms on his desk. "Now, any news on my little problem?"

"Yeah," I said, "it's finished."

He stared at me.

"You're pissing me," he said. "Two days on the job and it's sorted? Not possible."

"Or it could be that I'm good at my job."

He ignored that.

"Who was it then, what was it about?"

"Well," I said, "here comes the tricky bit. I can't tell you who or why, only that it will stop now."

I don't suppose many people told Adam Hillier he couldn't have what he wanted and it wasn't easy for him. I could see him controlling himself and to be fair, with the exception of going a deep red under his tan, he did pretty well.

"Garron," he said, "don't fuck with me. You may be a hard nut, but I am far tougher than you and I didn't employ you to find out what was going on and then refuse to tell me." He slammed his hand down on the desk and some papers scattered. "Now, if you know what was going on, you have to tell me."

And the funny thing was, it didn't mean anything to me. I was detached, like I was seeing this - hell, like I was analysing this - from afar. Hillier was a bastard and a professional bastard, but he wasn't as hard as Al, although he had more power, had more people working for him. So maybe he was like Julot, but Julot had class and efficiency, he would never have raised his voice, never have let me see that he was anything but in control. No, Hillier was dangerous, but compared to those two he was second string.

Still, the objective thought popped up that he could probably have me killed if he wanted to, but the point was, I didn't care. And that was when I realised I was in trouble. Not with Hillier, but with myself.

"Well?" he demanded. He was still staring red-faced at me.

"Mr. Hillier, you employed me to find out what was behind the trouble and I have done that. I've also stopped it happening again. The price of that was no retribution and if I let you have the details, there would be retribution. There'd have to be, 'cos your rep would be on it. Now, I gave my word to the…people involved, that if it stopped, that would be the end. Now I'll give my word to you. Any more trouble that's similar, you get in touch with Mick and I'll give you chapter and verse. But there won't be."

He sat back in his chair, his hands resting on the desktop.

"Christ, you play a dangerous game, Garron. I don't expect people to sit in my own bloody office and dictate terms to me. I don't even have any proof that what you're telling me is true."

He looked at me for a few moments longer, trying to make me think that he was deciding whether to shake me by the hand, or have someone else shake me by the neck, but it wasn't convincing and I knew I'd won this.

"OK." He stood up. "I don't think you're stupid and I don't think Mick is either, so I'm going to take it that you're not bullshitting me, but any hint of trouble and I'll have someone straight round to Mick and you'd better have the answers if that happens." This time, he put out his hand. "If this is all true, then I know I'm paying you, but I still owe you one. If you need to collect, I'll stand up."

I shook his hand and moved to the door.

"I mean it," he said, "you've done a good job and done it quickly."

"Not only that," I said, opening the door, "but I also had the satisfaction of kicking Bobby in the balls."

I closed the door after me.

*

Sunday was rent day, not for me to pay, but for me to collect from the weekly tenants and drop round to Mick. Four houses in North and North-East London split into bedsits, four a piece in three of them, three in the fourth. None of the houses were up-market, but they were in working order and the rents were bringing in good money for whoever owned them. I didn't know who that was. Mick was not only the contact, but the cut-out as well.

I had the keys to all the front doors and usually I just had to pick up envelopes out of the hall or kitchen, check the money was right and leave. Sometimes I'd see one of the tenants, most times I wouldn't. So far there'd been no short payments and no defaulters, but Mick hadn't got me the job out of charity. Sooner or later there would be trouble and then I'd be expected to clear it up. The house in Edgware was a medium sized semi-detached, three tenants upstairs, one downstairs in a larger room. Shared kitchen and a locked smaller room downstairs that had to be some kind of storage. I'd been there three times before with no trouble, but this time there was no envelope on the table in the hall from flat four, the downstairs tenant. A young, thin man with long hair was in the kitchen, so I asked him if he was flat four.

"Nah," he said, "I'm upstairs, but I think she's in."

That was unusual. I would've expected anyone else in the flat to cover at least minimally for someone who hadn't paid the rent. This guy gave her straight up.

"You could always kick her out if she isn't paying," he said as he walked past me carrying a plate of spaghetti and went up the stairs, "and get someone in who isn't such a moody cow."

I knocked on the door of the downstairs bedsit. There was some music playing quietly inside, but I couldn't tell what it was. No answer, so I knocked again.

"Come on, lady," I called, "at least open the door."

After a few seconds the door did open, but only about four inches. As far as the chain would allow.

"Or what," a low, quiet voice said, "you'll kick it in?"

The face that appeared was only partly visible, but I could see it had serious dark eyes, high cheekbones and was framed with dark black-brown hair. The voice had no real accent and may have been quiet, but it did have an edge to it, a tone that was somewhere between resigned and challenging. As though she expected the worst, but wouldn't just take it.

"I try not to kick in more than one door a day," I said, "quota's been used up this morning already."

She didn't say anything for a short while, so we stood looking at each other. I could hear the music clearly now. Janis Ian, *At Seventeen*. Then she said:

"I don't have the rent this week."

I tried for a reassuring smile, if that's possible on the face of a rent collector.

"You got a reason why not?" I asked.

"Is that your business?" The voice was still quiet. "I haven't got it. That's all you need to know."

I sighed. Out loud.

"Look," I said, "I don't suppose we could have this conversation face to face, instead of face to half-face behind a chained door, could we?"

"No."

"Why not?"

She almost smiled then, a sort of ironic curl at the corners of her mouth.

"The chain's supposed to keep people like you out. People who might want to get inside to, for example, take goods to the value of maybe a week's rent."

She was right of course.

"OK, leave me on the outside then, but it is my business why you can't pay this week. It will help me," I said deliberately, "*determine*, whether you might be able to pay next week."

After a moment she said: "I was sick last week. I couldn't work and I didn't get paid. I'm better now. I'll be able to work this week and I'll pay next Sunday. I'll have to pay this week's rent off over the next few weeks."

"What if you're sick again?"

"I won't be," she said and there was a hint of the smile again at the corners of the mouth. "Quota's been used up this year already."

Second score to her.

"All right," I said, "where do you work?"

"What, you don't trust me?" she said.

And then I did something that went against all the reasoning that I worked by. The right thing to do was to take the employer's name and details and check the story. Instead, I said:

"I'll see you, or rather your money, next week then."

I took a step back and turned to leave. I'd gone another two steps down the hall before I heard the low voice say:

"It's the Mexican restaurant on the High Street. I wait tables there most days."

Trusts begats trust, I thought, feeling pleased with myself. I didn't turn round though, just paused for a couple of seconds, knowing she was watching me and then continued out through the front door.

*

Mick was not pleased.

"You're short of money on the rent and you think, you *think*, it'll be made up over the next few weeks."

"Ahh, come on, Mick, what was I supposed to do, kick the door down and evict her? It's not a lot of money - "

"The money is not the point. The point is that people contract to pay rent. You can't have people deciding when to pay and when not to."

He was standing in the small kitchen of his council flat and I was sitting on the sofa in the lounge. The TV, as ever, was quietly going about its business in the corner and the dog, as ever, was in the doorway of the lounge just in case I decided to leave and Mick didn't want me to. Mick came out of the kitchen, pushed the dog's head to one side with his foot and stood just inside the lounge. He looked down at me.

"Jesus, Garron, what is happening to you? You get rousted by a couple of kids in masks, you piss off Adam Hillier, okay," he said, as I started to protest, "I know you say you sorted it, but you didn't exactly give him what he wanted and now you're handing me short rent because some girl tells you she can't pay. I don't know if you're losing your edge because of all the good Samaritan stuff you're doing, or you're doing the good Samaritan stuff because you're losing your edge."

"Hey, if I'd have just kicked the door in, it would've cost more to repair than the rent."

"Yeah, but you know how it should have been done, how Al would've done it, if he'd ever collected rent. He'd have had a pair of bolt-cutters, snipped the chain and removed the stereo, or the TV or whatever. Then at least we'd have had some security."

I stared at him. "You're throwing Al at me?" I said incredulously. "*You* are throwing what Al would have done at me? Al's dead. And you still won't tell me exactly how he died - "

"I don't *know* exactly how he died," Mick shot back.

I took a deep breath. "He taught me a hell of a lot, but Jesus, Mick, half the time you tell me not to do what he would have done and half the time you're telling me he would have done it better." I stood up. "I've got things to do, I'm going. If you're dog lets me out."

"I'm taking the rent money out of your pay from Hillier when I get it," he said. "You collect it back from the girl, you can keep it."

I couldn't really argue with that one, so I let it go. I didn't want to leave in the middle of a ruck with Mick, but I didn't know how to bring it down from there. He did though. He caught my arm as I walked past him.

"Hey, was she at least good looking?"

"You know something, Mick, I don't know. I think so, but she only opened the door enough to talk."

"Christ, don't tell me you fell for her voice?"

He was joking and the edge had gone out of his tone, but I didn't let him follow up.

"Stranger things..." I said and walked past.

"Garron," he called after me, "don't take me too seriously, I'm just pissed 'cos you're short on the money, but I might have done the same thing...and been wrong as well. You did a good job with Hillier, but you aren't right. You're not thinking straight for this kind of work. You can't always do what you think is right. Sometimes you got to give people what they're paying for. Sooner or later, if you're not thinking right, you're going to make a mistake. You don't straighten your head out, you better hope the mistake doesn't matter."

And the hell of it was, he was right.

I did pretty well. I lasted until Wednesday and then decided that I'd shown enough self-restraint and drove to Edgware, parked up behind Sainsburys and wandered down the High street to the Mexican restaurant. I walked in and sat at a table for two. A short blonde waitress with a ponytail started over, but stopped when the girl with the serious eyes and the high cheek-bones cut across her.

"My table, Jill," she said and came over, stopping the other side of the table facing me.

"Just happened to be passing?" she said, the low voice still holding the ironic tone from three days earlier.

Snap decision, I thought, play the game or just tell it like it is. Last time I'd sat down to talk with a woman, I'd messed it right up. Be nice to do a little better this time.

"No," I said, "I wanted to see you and I didn't want to wait until Sunday."

For a moment it seemed that I'd disrupted her poise, but only for a moment.

"Can you talk for a few minutes?" I asked.

She stood looking down at me as though weighing up the question and the consequences and then turned to where the blonde girl was standing and said:

"I'm gonna take five minutes, Jill, is that okay?"

Without waiting for an answer, she pulled out the chair opposite me, sat down, leaned forwards with her elbows on the table and looked straight at me. It was a frank, direct look and I held it, feeling something in the pit of my stomach and a slight

41

light-headedness that I hadn't felt in years, that I couldn't even remember feeling at any time since I was a teenager.

"So," she said, "you want to tell me who you are and why you want to get into my life?"

"Thing is," I replied slowly, "I'm not too good at answering questions, but I'm trying here. My name's Garron and the answer to the second part is...I'm not sure."

She carried on staring straight at me, a look of faint amusement on her face.

"Well, Garron, I don't think that's a hell of an answer if you're trying to pick me up. You're supposed to tell me how great I am, or how good I look, or maybe play it cool and say how you were just walking along and saw me through the window, you know and isn't it a co-incidence, or something like that."

"Yeah," I said, "or I could say I was checking your story to make sure you'd have the rent money this week, but that wouldn't be true either." I stopped for a second and then said, "And if we're going to start at all, we should start with truth."

There was silence. A heavy silence that held us together, but as it went on, threatened to stay between us. The air of amusement had vanished from her face. It suddenly occurred to me that I didn't even know if she was with someone, or ever wanted to be. I shot an involuntary glance at her left hand. No ring on the fourth finger, no mark of one having been there.

Defining moment, I thought.

"What?" she said.

I'd spoken out loud. Go on, I thought to myself, just for once get it right.

"Defining moment," I said. "Truth is, I just got a feeling from you on Sunday. It may be wrong, or it may be...misleading, but it's rare and I owe it to myself to follow it."

Another silence, then she took her arms off the table, sat back on the chair and broke the spell.

"Jeez," she said, "I don't know if you're genuine, or just a real smooth talker, or some kind of mind expert, but you've said some stuff here. I've damn near got goose-bumps listening to you. I'm almost believing you're genuine, because you didn't come across like a con-man when you were collecting the rent and I haven't yet met a thug who is that much of a psychological genius. That is what you are, right? A thug of some description?"

"What gives it away?"

"Oh, the movements, the scar tissue and the fact I've seen thugs before. Some of them are a little wider than you are and mostly they come across as louder and more aggressive than you do, but it's there somewhere."

"Yeah, well, I'm one of the new breed of quiet introspective thugs. We're into gentle thuggery."

She got up abruptly and I wondered if I'd said something, been too flippant, pressed the wrong button.

"Okay, Garron. I take it that's your last name, right? No-one could have a first name like that, not even an introspective thug. If I'm in when you come for the rent on Sunday, you can take me out somewhere."

"Fine, provided you tell me what the 'J' stands for?"

"What?"

"I collect your rent, I've got your last name and an initial. I wondered what the J is for."

"Jenny," she said. Then she pushed the chair back under the table and looked back at me and there was almost the faint beginnings of a smile. "You just got a feeling, huh?"

"Just a feeling," I said.

I got up as well.

"And, I wanted to find out what you were like without a door and a chain in the way."

The ironic tone was back in her voice again immediately and I realised then just how much of a defence it was and maybe, just how scared she might be.

"Do I pass?" she said.

"Oh yes," I replied. And left.

*

I spent Saturday transporting cash for one of Mick's contacts and I took the gun with me. I wasn't expecting trouble, but I couldn't face the possibility of another embarrassment. A shooting I could face, but not another embarrassment. It's a pain in the arse though, because it's a Smith and Wesson with a six-inch barrel and I don't have a holster for it. I just never thought I'd need one. But carrying it around wasn't easy until I stitched a small leather strap into my outside jacket pocket. For stitched, read botched. I had to cut out the lining of the pocket, which is OK until I forget sometimes and stick my keys in there. There were no problems though on the job and Sunday came around soon enough. I'd like to say that I put on my Sunday best, but I don't have anything that fits that description. I was, however, shaved, showered and unarmed. I half expected her not to be there, but when I knocked she answered with a small bag in one hand and the rent in the other.

"It's not all of last week's as well, but there's some there," she said. "I thought we'd get business out of the way first. Isn't that how it works?"

"Very funny," I answered, "anywhere in particular you want to go?"

"Yes. You're taking me to the National Portrait Gallery, on a boat up the river, ice cream at Greenwich and back in time for me to go to work tonight."

I looked at her.

"The National Portrait Gallery?" I said. "Art?"

She smiled at me.

"You're going to tell me that the only culture you have is growing on your dishes at home, right?"

"No, actually I wasn't," I muttered, not following at all.

She was already locking up her room and she looked up.

"Hey, this is my choice. If I've actually got a guy taking me out somewhere, I'm gonna make the most of it." She walked past me to the front door. "Come, on, what are you waiting for?"

And we had a nice day. No awkward silences, nothing too heavy like our previous conversation in the restaurant. I even liked the pictures and after a while I realised that Jenny had relaxed. Until it happened, I hadn't really noticed she was nervy. Well, not nervy, just a little tense. Maybe she wasn't used to going out places with a guy. I sure as hell wasn't used to being out with a girl. But I was enjoying myself.

Sometime around five, when we were eating the promised ice creams, sitting on a wall near the Cutty Sark in Greenwich she said:

"I looked you up. You know, on the internet - found out about the boxing and stuff."

"I'm flattered," I said, trying not to look stupid whilst saving the ice cream from dripping out of the cornet.

"You were supposed to be pretty good. Did you really have to stop because of your hand?"

Then before I could answer, she said:

"Sorry, I shouldn't have asked you that. If it was your career, it can't have been easy giving it up. We'll change the subject."

"No," I said, "it's okay. I don't usually talk about it, but I don't mind." I took a deep breath. It was true, I didn't usually talk about it. But I did think about it. "Yes, I stopped fighting because of my hand and wrist - " I showed her the operation scar - "and yes, it was tough stopping. It was more than tough really. It wasn't that it was my career; it was my life. Everything went around boxing and in some ways I'm still trying to fill the gap even now. And," I said, turning to look at her, "I was good. Maybe I wouldn't have become the absolute best, but I was very, very good. I think sometimes it's difficult for me to realise that I'll never be as good at anything else that I ever do."

There was a moment's silence when I think she wondered whether she'd touched too raw a nerve, so I smiled at her and she tried to lighten things up again.

"I'm sure you're one hell of a good thug," she said.

I went with it.

"I'll let you into a secret," I said, "I'm only a part-time thug. The rest of the time I'm a bodyguard, which is, in my humble opinion, a much nobler profession."

And while I was saying this, a part of me noticed that I was opening up to her, that I was talking about things and trusting her with things that I didn't give out to people, even the few people I was still in touch with. And I wondered if that was down to her, or a comment on what my mind had decided that I needed.

"Hey," I said, "we'd better get you back, you're supposed to be working soon."

"Oh," she said, "actually, no I'm not," and there was that ironic look again. "I just said that in case I wanted to cut the day short and get away from you. Which I don't. I'm not at work until tomorrow on the lunch shift."

"So you don't want to, uh, 'get away' from me?"

"Well, not yet. So you can buy me dinner now. Unless you want to get away from me?"

It was meant to be funny, but there was still that underlying vulnerability that she tried so hard to cover.

"I can stand dinner," I said. "What'll it be?"

"Anything. No, anything except Mexican," she said and she took my arm as we walked away from the dock.

I dropped her home around eleven. She didn't ask me in and I hadn't expected her to. She was working Monday on the day shift and I was working Monday night, but I said I'd call and she knew I would. There were no games being played here. It was too important for that.

*

47

Tuesday evening I got a text from Tony to go see him. Pete was sitting outside Tony's little office on the car lot with his feet up on a second chair and the inevitable cigarette between his lips. I remembered that he only ever used to take a smoke out of his mouth to talk or to drink and sometimes not even then. I couldn't recall what he did about food. Come to think of it, I'm not sure I'd ever seen him eat, at least not anything that required a knife and fork. He was still rake thin, the untidy light brown hair was still the same and despite several years up north, the 'Sarf' London accent hadn't changed. He got up when he saw me.

"Here he is, Ladies and Gentlemen, the best champion England never had! Old Broken-Hand himself, - "

"Ah, shut up, you old fart," I said, "all this time and you're still playing the same record."

And with that we were right back where we'd been three or four years earlier. With some people it's like that, you just pick up where you left off. We talked about the places and the people we'd known and the same jokes and the same situations that we'd talked about before came around again, but as the evening drew on, I began to think that this wasn't quite as it had been. The three of us sat around Tony's office talking and arguing about the different ways we each remembered things happening, but there was something about Pete that wasn't right. Maybe he thought the same about me. I certainly wasn't the same person I'd been, but I could hide it, or at least I thought I could. Pete couldn't. He'd always been a bit manic, sometimes wired, but he was always genuine. Now he seemed occasionally forced, sometimes nervy.

48

After a couple of hours, Tony said he had to go and I asked Pete where he was staying.

"Right here, mate," he said. "Tony's office has all the comforts of home and it's free. Unless you've got room wherever you are now?"

"Might have in a few days, Pete," I lied smoothly, "but I've got someone crashing there at the moment and it's only one room."

Even as I said it, I wasn't sure exactly why I was lying to him, but something wasn't right with Pete and nowdays my own security was so ingrained that it kicked into gear and covered me automatically. But I gave him my mobile number and we agreed to meet up in a couple of days.

Tony left Pete a set of keys and walked down with me to where my car, well, his car really, was parked outside the lot.

"So you noticed it as well," he said, when we were far enough away from Pete.

"What do you mean?"

"A few years ago, you'd have let him stay with you, now you don't want him. And don't," he said, as I started to reply, "tell me that you've got someone staying there. I only know where you live now because Mick told me. And having seen the way you've been over the past few months, I don't reckon anyone else knows you're there. But leaving aside your own weird behaviour, you think there's something up with Pete."

"Yeah, you're right, Tony, he's a little different, but everyone has the right to change a bit in three or four years. How come he's in the office and not staying with you at home?"

"You think Marie would let him in?"

I made a squelching sound and ground my right thumb into my left palm.

"Ah, shut it, Garron," he said, "I agree with her. Don't like saying it, but I'm not even really happy with him staying at the lot and I don't even know why." He looked back at the office. "If you need anything from the lock-up, he's going there tomorrow, I'm lending him a van for a couple of hours."

Pete and I shared the cost of a garage lock-up in Finsbury Park. When he'd moved up north and I'd been struggling, we both stashed some stuff there, but I didn't go there much.

"He didn't mention that," I said, "but I don't think there's anything I need right now from there." I got into the car. "If you really think there's something wrong with him, give me a bell. I've got to go now, or I'll be late."

"You working?" he asked.

"No, I've got a date."

"What? A real one?" I heard him say, but I was driving off by then.

*

And it was a real date. In fact it was a series of real dates and I started to do the things that real people did. We saw films and went to museums and ate takeaways and the only odd point was that I never went inside her bedsit at the house. It was like that would have been too close. And then I realised that I never took her to the flat in Camden where I lived. That was just basic security. But a strange thing started to happen. I discovered that I wanted to let her in. I wanted to trust her. To show her that I felt I could trust her. And then one evening, four or five weeks after that first Sunday, I went round to pick her up and when she opened the door, on the chain as usual, she said:

"I thought maybe tonight we'd stay in. Casablanca's on..." she sounded nervy and her voice trailed away a bit, "...if you like old movies."

"Sounds good to me," I said. I tried to make it sound easy, but for whatever reason, for her it wasn't. And I didn't think it was anything to do with me.

She unchained the door and let me in to a longish, fairly narrow room, with a table set against one side wall and a straight backed chair slid underneath it. There were three bookshelves crammed with books in no particular order, a small sofa covered with a bedspread and at the far end of the room, a single bed. The walls and carpet were a dark blue and the carpet was showing its age. A CD/tape player was standing on one of the bookshelves and a small TV was on the table.

"Black and white," she said, pointing at the television, "but it doesn't matter for Casablanca."

I didn't move too far into the room. I waited to be invited. This was her space and I knew enough to be careful of it.

There was a wardrobe near to the bed and stacks of CDs and tapes next to it on the floor. She was over there now, picking one out.

"Film's not on for a few minutes, Mary Coughlan okay for you?"

"Sure," I said. "Janis Ian, Mary Coughlan, bit of a pattern emerging here?"

She turned and smiled at me. "And Judie Tzuke, Rikki Lee Jones, Katie Melua. You got your blues guys, I got these girls." And before I could answer, she held up a couple of CDs.

"I got Motorhead and the Chilli Peppers as well if you like, so no pigeonholes, all right?"

"It's fine by me," I said. "Heavy rock's good. Sort of blues, but faster and heavier. And the girl songwriters, they're doing the same thing the old blues singers were doing in their time. If you had boy bands, or techno stuff, then I'd be worried."

She pulled a face and stuck the tape in the player.

"It's all right, you know, you can come in and sit down."

I did, on the sofa, but on the way I noted the lack of photographs, or of anything really personal in the room. There were a couple of glasses on the table and Coughlan was singing one I knew, about living in a hologram and wondering who she was and I sat back on the sofa and put my head back and closed my eyes and felt myself relaxing. How long had it been since I'd really chilled out? Since I'd not been watching the next street corner, or the next face in the crowd? For the most part there was no reason to be that hyped up, but it was how I'd started to live and it was the only way to live if you were to be ready for the one time it mattered.

When was the last time I'd seen Casablanca? Maybe in the old bedsit, maybe with Linda. She'd liked old films too. I said:

"Apparently they were still writing Casablanca while they were filming it, the cast didn't know what was going to happen in the end."

"Yeah, I read that. I also read that apparently, you never marry the person you first see the film with."

There was a pause, while she realised what she'd said. I could let her off the hook, or push it.

"I've seen it maybe ten times," I said. "How about you?"

"At least a dozen."

She picked up a bottle of whisky from the bottom of the wardrobe and brought it over, picked up the glasses and sat down next to me on the sofa.

"Scotch, right?" she said.

She'd splashed out. A small bottle, but malt.

"Oh, it's the right stuff," I said, "but I don't drink at all if I've got to drive later."

And she put her head on my shoulder and looked up at me and said quietly:

"If you want to stay, then you don't have to drive."

And it didn't take me by surprise, because she was no fool, this girl and a little scared though she might be, she knew what she was doing.

So, I said that I wanted to stay, but only if...

"Yes," she said and put the glasses down.

*

And later, in the dark, when the tapes had run out, the quiet, hot tears fell onto my chest and I didn't ask, I just held her. And maybe that was the right thing to do, for in a while, the tears stopped and the breathing regulated and though I didn't sleep, my own demons slid away for a time, confronted as they were, by someone else's ghosts.

*

"I got a possible lead. Come round as soon as you can."

Mick on the voicemail and it could only mean he'd got a line on Allingway's money. The dog let me pass grudgingly, still playing his usual game of making me push past him, but with a bit more menace this time. As I walked into the lounge, he took up his usual station in the doorway to the hall with a short growl.

"Don't mind him," Mick said from his prone position on the sofa. "He's been grumpy all day. Couple of kids threw stones towards him in the park and I wouldn't let him off the lead."

"I'm not bloody surprised," I said, "what would he have done to them?"

"Nothing much, except chase them down and scare the shite out of them, which they deserved, he's too disciplined to attack properly unless he's been given the command. Or unless he thinks I'm threatened. But you can never know for sure. Dogs aren't that different from humans. You can push them too far, or press the wrong button. Anyway, there were too many people around in the park to complain about him if he took a run at those little sods. And they'll be there another day when it's quieter."

He swung himself up and around so he was sitting straight and started making a cigarette while he spoke.

"Now, a little birdie tells me that one elderly man, Patrick Briscoe, who can be found at an address you well know, has had a couple of visits from the old bill. Which means - "

"Either he knows something and is telling, or they think he knows something and he isn't," I finished for him.

"Right. Given that our police are not usually too far wide of the mark in murder cases, which remember is what this is, our Mr. Briscoe may be a way in."

"I can feel a 'but' lurking," I said.

"Yes, well, here we go. At the least, Briscoe may be a link to whoever organised the game. If they were good, they may have used a cut-out, if not, the trail could lead to the players and then to us. Except I'll keep you out of it, if it gets that far. Otherwise, Briscoe may have been in on the job, in - "

"Whoa, Mick! Wait a minute. That was real blood on his face, not fake stuff. He was in pain."

"Yes and a better alibi couldn't be established. He maybe didn't even know he was going to be hit. Or maybe they've turned him over as well after promising him a share. So if you see him, he could tell you anything. Anything from genuine info to get at the two bastards who sold him short, through to a cock and bull story that sets you up to walk into a couple of shotguns the wrong way round."

I thought about this for a minute. There was, of course, something else besides not knowing what Briscoe might do.

"What if he denies everything?" I asked Mick.

"Good lad." He looked up from rolling his cigarette. "You got there. How good is your judgment and what are you prepared to do to back it?"

I knew what he meant. If Briscoe denied all knowledge of everything, I'd have to apply 'pressure' to get anything out of him at all. I wasn't sure I could do that. Or wanted to.

"Mick, I'm not sure that being a bodyguard and beating the crap out of an old man for information, sit in the same camp."

He half-smiled at me. "Good," he said, "then there's hope for you yet. But that means I'm going to have to give this to someone else to follow up and that will mean money, 'specially to keep it at arm's length. That'll be your share of the original job."

"That's fine by me," I said and got up. I wasn't happy though and I wasn't sure whether it was at the thought of the old guy being threatened, or because I wasn't prepared to do it myself.

"Look," I said, "whoever you get, if they do find where these two guys are, I want to be the one to go get the money back. I want to do that myself."

"We'll see." Mick was already getting himself comfortable lying back down on the sofa again. "You can't always pick and choose, Garron. There's a reasonable amount of money here and not everyone's as trustworthy as you. Someone taking this on, might insist on the bigger job for a bigger piece. We'll see how it goes."

"Yeah," I said, "I can see that." And then as I moved towards the hall, Mick said:

"Garron, don't waste time wondering if you're 'soft' for not doing this. You're not. And don't think about Al and what he would have done. He's not here. He's dead and gone. And yes, he would have done it himself, but that doesn't make it right for you. I've told you before, you're not him and you're not like him and you're all the better for that. He taught you a lot, but he didn't tell you what to be. He left that for you to work out."

I nodded, although Mick wasn't looking. Mick was one of my closest friends, along with Tony almost my only friend, but it was still freaky that he knew what I'd been thinking.

*

Outside and driving back home to Camden, I had to think about it some more and I tied myself up in knots. I didn't want to consider myself 'pressurising' someone, as Mick had said, which meant, put bluntly, hurting them until they told you what you wanted to know. That was something other people did. Sick people who got a kick out of the hurting, or out of holding power over others. But at the same time, this had been my mess and now I was asking someone else to help me out of it. 'Careful,' I thought, 'don't go down that road.'

I'd had a kind of conversation with Al about something like this, years before. I don't know what sparked it, maybe a news item in the paper, but I'd made a comment and he'd replied that if he needed information from somebody that would, for example, save his child's life, he'd do whatever it took to get that information. So I asked him if he had any kids and he gave me a look that shut me up and made me drop the subject before I'd finished asking the question. But he had said that his attitude wasn't necessarily right, it was just his attitude. Then he kind of backtracked and said that it wouldn't apply in all cases and there were people around the world who would torture and kill just for the thrill of it and that was different and it suddenly struck me that for the first time that I knew of, Al was trying to justify something he'd said.

And now sitting here, years later, that was scary. Al did questionable things at the least, some would say bad things without bothering about the questionable bit. He certainly hurt people, I know he'd killed people, but in his mind these were all people who deserved it. Either they were scum, or they were trying to hurt him, but somehow whatever happened to them by his hand was justified.

"Christ!" I said out loud, "an avenging bloody angel."

Which brought us back to Briscoe. If he was involved, then he was partly to blame for at least one person dying. I was there. If I asked him questions, I would know better than an outsider, whether he was lying or not. Maybe he wasn't involved. Maybe there would be no pressure necessary. At least if I was there, then I'd be in control of what went on. I could minimise any trouble. And I could always walk away. But even if I wasn't there, I already knew what might happen. That made me as guilty as whoever struck the first blow. If there was to be a first blow. I pulled over and called Mick on the mobile. I'm not always that careful about driving and being on the phone, but this conversation needed concentration.

Except that it didn't.

Mick answered on the second ring and before I could say a word, gave me the bottom line.

"Two days, mate. You've got two days. Then I give it to someone else."

He hung up and I drove off thinking about the fact that he'd known what I'd feel I'd have to do. If I was there, at least I'd know. At least I'd be in control.

*

I called Jenny and said I couldn't make it that night and I didn't know about the next couple of days. There was a pause on the line. Then she said:

"You letting me down slow, Garron?"

"Don't be a silly cow, Jenny," I said. "I've got one, maybe two days work and I have to take it. I can't stop working, just because you've got a complex."

I could have been more tactful, but I thought I'd earned a bit of trust over the past month.

"You're right," she said, "but being the day after the night before, I was kind of hoping you wouldn't be running off."

Okay, I could see her point now, but that was just how it had worked out. Bad timing, but necessary.

"Is it dangerous?" she asked.

"It's no more or less dangerous than anything else I've done. This is what I do. You know that already."

"I know," she said, "I'm not complaining and I'm not asking you to stop, or to change what you do. But if something happened to you, how would I know? Or would you just never turn up here again, or answer your phone?"

I hadn't thought about it, but it was a fair question. We'd been moving into a relationship and now each time we met, we were getting more involved. She had a right to some kind of reassurance.

"Listen, you got a pen? I'm going to give you home and work numbers for someone called Tony. For Christ's sake if you call him at home and his wife answers, make sure you explain who you are and that you're with me, otherwise she'll be off the handle before you've finished a sentence. Tony's a legit guy, but I've known him for years, since we were kids. If anything happened to me, he'd know about it soon enough. But it won't, so don't worry. And don't give the numbers to anyone and certainly not in connection with me."

As soon as I'd said the last sentence, I regretted it. She wasn't in the life, but she knew instinctively what to do and what not to do. Telling her not to give out the numbers was treating her like a child. She took it well though. Only called me an arse a couple of times, before saying she'd see me whenever and that she loved me. Then she put the phone down. It wasn't until after the connection was broken that I realised what she'd said. I called her back, but the phone was off the hook.

*

I really needed to know whether anyone, police or otherwise, but mainly the police were watching Briscoe's house. I could sit outside myself, but if I were pulled, it would be difficult to go there again. And I'd need a good excuse for being there. I thought who I could ask. Not Tony, I couldn't bring him into anything even remotely dodgy. Not that he wouldn't do it, but he had too much to lose. Pete was a possibility, but the few times I'd seen him over the last couple of weeks he'd seemed flakier than ever, certainly not reliable.

I could ask McGuire. As a cabby, he could have any number of reasons to be almost anywhere and as a driver he was totally reliable, one of the old school from Al's days. I'd have to pay him for his time, but it would be worth it. I called his mobile number, but it was no go, he was in Dublin and not due back for a few days. I was reluctant to call Mick. I'd taken this off him, I didn't want to go and give some of it back.

So I called Hillier, but from a call box, not from my mobile. The hired help didn't seem too pleased to hear from me. I couldn't tell from the voice whether it was the one I'd put down, but they were a team and none of them would need a second excuse to take a pop at me. When Hillier took the phone, I came straight to the point. Polite, but no pleasantries.

"I'd like to call in the favour, Mr. Hillier, I need some help. Nothing too tricky, just a few hours of one of your lads' time. No rough stuff, just a pair of eyes and ears."

Maybe he'd never expected me to come back to him, but he stood up for it.

"Okay, Garron, what do you need?"

"I need a body in or out of a car on a street, watching a door. He needs a reason to be there and I need to know if he's approached by the police or anyone else. If he is, he just walks away. If not then I need him to knock on a few doors, maybe with a survey, maybe ask if anyone needs their windows cleaning, that sort of thing. Then he just leaves, but I need to know if the police check up on him afterwards."

Hillier wasn't a fool. He knew what I was doing and he knew I would give his man fifteen or twenty houses to knock at, to cover the one I was interested in.

"How long do you want him for and when?"

"As soon as possible 'till the end of the day."

There was a slight pause and then he said; "There's a certain risk in this, Garron and I don't like setting my lads up in any way."

I'd been expecting this and there was only one answer.

"Mr. Hillier, there might possibly, but only possibly be something at the end of this. If there is, I'll pay you for your man's time. Not much, the pot's someone else's, but I'll pay something."

"And either way we're square?"

"Either way, we're square."

There was a pause, like he was considering, but we both knew he'd already decided.

"All right. Where do you want him?"

"I'll meet him on Granville Road, the far end from where it hits Lordship Lane in one hour," I said. "And Mr. Hillier, send someone who isn't going to try to take my head off."

He laughed. "You're not very popular with my staff, Garron, but I'll find someone who can control his natural urges."

"One hour," I said, hung up and wondered what I'd done. With people like Hillier it paid to stay as far away as possible unless you actually had to deal with them. He owed me, he'd stick to his side of the bargain and he wouldn't learn anything from what I'd ask his man to do. But I wasn't happy about it.

*

The man was on time, gave me the leery look like he was superior, but did what he was told and sat in his car for a while. I didn't hang around there as well, but from what I could tell, no-one paid him any attention. Then, at the time I gave him, he got out and started knocking on doors. I took a walk down the other side of the road timed to be in the right place when he reached the house. No-one approached him. Briscoe answered his door, but on the chain and I noted that and also how high the chain was on the door. I walked on, waited again 'till the guy had finished the section of houses I'd asked him to cover and then watched as he got back in his car and drove off. I drove to my lock-up in Finsbury Park, struggled for five minutes with the old rusty padlock and then cursed as the light didn't work. I had a torch in the car though, but when I came back and took a look round, most of my stuff had gone. The box with photos and newspaper cuttings was still there and a couple of black plastic sacks, but the odd pieces of furniture, an armchair and a cabinet had gone. It didn't look like the place had been broken into, so maybe Pete had been there and thought they were his. But I dismissed that thought. We'd divided the place into two long ago and it was pretty clear which was which. Most of his stuff had gone as well, there were only a couple of boxes left, but I didn't understand why he would have wanted a few pieces of furniture. If it was him that had taken them. Maybe he'd given the key to someone else and asked him to clear the place and the guy had taken the wrong stuff, but I didn't think so. Meantime, in the far corner under some old thrown away newspapers, was a plastic bag with a couple of tools of a trade in them, including bolt-cutters. I picked them up, tucked them under my jacket, wishing I'd worn a longer coat and locked up again. I walked to the nearest phone box and called Hillier.

"Your man back?"

"Yes," he answered "and he wants to know what it was all about. Said you're nuts."

"I'm sure you can explain it to him, if you choose to, but I don't think you will. You won't want your lads understanding how these things work and thinking for themselves."

He laughed. "Like you do?" he said and I let it go. He carried on, "we're all square now then, I take it?"

"All square," I replied and put the phone down.

If the police had been in touch he would have said. It looked like Briscoe's place was clear.

I had a little time to kill before I headed back there and now that I was thinking about it, I was fairly pissed at Pete taking my things. Even if it had been a mistake, Tony had my number and Pete could have let me know. I could sit here for the best part of an hour until it was a little darker and time to head back to Briscoe's neck of the woods, or I could shoot round to the car lot and sort this out with Pete.

No contest.

*

I pulled up outside Tony's car lot and realised I was still pretty angry. Whichever way you looked at it, Pete had nicked my stuff. But being angry was unusual for me. I wasn't usually worked up enough about anything to get angry. Hey, maybe I really was getting better!

Tony was with a customer, so I left him to it and walked straight into the office. Pete was lounging in Tony's chair with his feet on the desk. He looked up when I came in.

"Where's my gear, Pete?"

He looked genuinely startled for a moment, then recovered himself.

"Nothing I can say, man. I was in real trouble cashwise. I thought you never went there and I'd be able to get you some new things, before you even knew the old stuff was gone."

I looked down at him sitting there. Same old Pete. He hadn't even said he was sorry. Years ago he might have got away with it, just because years ago people liked him and somehow responded to him, but not now. Now the wide-eyed charm had gone. I said:

"Why didn't you just ask me for money if you needed it that bad?"

"Ah, come on, man, would you have subbed me?"

I leaned down and put my face in front of his.

"So, you stole my furniture."

"Hey, I said I was sorry!"

I pushed his feet sideways off the desk, hard and he sat up in the chair as they hit the floor.

"No," I said, "you didn't. I want my furniture back. It's not much, but it's mine."

He didn't say anything.

"Pete, I want my things back."

He still didn't answer.

"Pete, I want - "

"I can't get them back," he said quietly. "I sold them."

"You sold my stuff? Not pawned, but sold?"

"Yeah."

"Where's the money?"

"Gone."

"Gone? Just gone? How did it go? Did it get up and walk?"

"I spent it."

"All right. You spent it. On what?"

He didn't answer me and the slightly odd reaction he'd had when I'd first asked him where my gear was, registered at last with me. It wasn't that he was surprised at me asking, it was my choice of words that had thrown him.

"You're using, aren't you?" I said.

He looked up at me with a half smile on his face.

"Well, whoopee," he said quietly, "give the man a medal. He's only three steps behind everyone else."

"How bad are you?"

"I'm hooked, man, through the bag and back again."

"Does Tony know?"

He sat back and sighed.

"Yeah, Tony's figured it out. He hasn't said anything though. Just makes sure there's no money lying around, you know, little discreet things like that."

"Well, he hasn't told Marie, or you wouldn't still be here."

He actually had the sense to look worried at that.

"So," I went on, "you've got until the weekend to work out how I get my furniture back, or the money for it, or I'll go straight to Marie and tell her myself."

He sat up in the chair at last.

"You wouldn't do that, mate, I'd be out on the street."

"Oh, I would. And I think you can stop calling me 'mate'. Mates don't hock each others' furniture, even to fuel their habits. You've got till the weekend."

*

I got back in the car still fuming and used the drive back to Briscoe's house to calm down. I parked up a street away and thought about what I was going to do. I was about to break a golden rule. I knew how to get in, but I was going in not sure what I was going to do once I was inside. Winging it may be okay in certain instances, but it also means that things can get out of hand.

It was getting late and I waited a while until it was not quite, but nearly dark. Not so easy for someone to see me going in from a distance and less chance of anyone remembering my face. I put on an old balaclava, but turned it up so it looked like a docker's hat. The eyeholes weren't visible and in the gloom no-one would notice the difference. I got the bolt-cutters out of the boot and tucked one end of them inside my jacket. Best I could do. I'd blindside them when I rang Briscoe's bell.

I didn't want any possible comeback. I wanted to make sure that there was no possible way of Briscoe realising that I was one of the guys who was at the game, so when I rang the bell, I half turned away from the door as though I was looking back along the street. Through the spy-hole I wouldn't be recognisable.

He didn't answer the door, but called out: "Who is it?"

"D.I. Taylor, Mr. Briscoe," I said, flashing my wallet up to the spy-hole and back, like it was routine, but too fast for him to see what it was. "I've got a couple of follow up questions I'm afraid."

Most people are stupid. Even when they know they haven't seen ID properly, they don't ask to see it again.

"I've already been through everything ten times with the others," he said irritably.

"Believe me, Mr. Briscoe, I want to be here even less than you want me to."

"I want to see that warrant card properly," he said. "Hang on."

He opened the door on the chain and that was all I needed. As he put his face round to see the ID, I shoved my foot in the gap, slammed the bolt-cutters against the door jamb low down and slid them fast up the edge of the wood until they caught on the chain. Briscoe had reacted quite quickly for an old man, taking in what was happening and putting his weight against the door, but I had the bolt-cutters and my foot there and there was no way back for him. Pressure on the cutters, the chain snapped and as I shouldered the door inwards, he went flying back onto the floor at the foot of the stairs. I pulled the balaclava down over my face as I stepped in and kicked the door shut behind me. It was a small space between the door and the stairs and I was standing right over him. Intimidating at the least. Probably terrifying.

"Don't touch me!" he shouted. "What are you going to do? Don't touch me!"

He was cowering away from me. I'd never had anyone be as scared of me as this man was. And it was sickening. I stood there, all the stuff you read about pensioners being beaten up in their own homes going through my head. Thoughts about bullied kids and people living in fear and how much it always made me sick to read about it and now I was doing it. And I thought of Jenny. She knew what I did for a living and had accepted it. But not this. Not this. In her eyes, I was one of the good guys. But she wouldn't stand for this. Bolt-cutters! Christ knows what the man thought I was going to do to him. And I didn't even know myself. I'd failed on one of Al's basic principles. Always know what your objective is. Always know what you want out of a situation and how you're going to get it. And how far you're prepared to go, in order to get it. But this time I hadn't thought it all the way through. All I'd done was terrorise an old man. Maybe it was just that even if he was guilty, he wasn't guilty of doing anything specifically to me. Not specifically to me. Or maybe, when it came to it, I hadn't fallen as far as I thought I had.

Listen to yourself, I thought. You're a fucking killer and you're worrying about hurting a guy who may have set you up.

It didn't help. I didn't want to hurt him. He was too vulnerable. He didn't have a chance. I couldn't see myself damaging someone that viciously. I didn't want to see myself doing that.

I backed away slightly, which wasn't easy in the tiny hallway.

"I'm not going to hurt you, Briscoe," I said. Not the best opening gambit when you want information from someone, so I tried again.

"I think someone might have turned you over, not kept their end of the bargain." I leant the bolt-cutters against the wall. "I can help you get even. I don't know whether you got your cut, or whether you got hurt when you weren't supposed to, but my guess is you're not happy and you'd like to straighten things out."

He was still curled up on the floor, but his dark eyes were wary now.

"I told the police everything I know," he said.

"Yeah, that's exactly what you're expected to say, but I'm not a copper at the moment and you're not an innocent victim."

"You said you were police!"

Lord help me from idiots, but if he wanted to believe it, I could use that.

"I'm not looking for information for the police now, Briscoe, I'm looking for the two toe-rags who broke up the game and your dentures. Did they pay you out, or not even that?"

"Don't know what you're talking about."

"Briscoe, what do you think will happen when your two friends hear the police are hounding you? What if they hear that you're actually helping the police?"

It was the oldest trick in the book, but he was thinking about it, so I thought I'd help him along a little.

"One of two things will happen, Briscoe. Either you can't hurt them, because you don't know anything about them that could help the police, in which case if they have any sense, they'll sit tight. Or they think you do know something that could touch them and they'll have to do something about it."

The penny was dropping somewhere in his head.

"Unless of course you really are completely innocent of complicity in this matter, in which case you're in the clear. Aren't you?"

I was laying it on a bit thick with the police talk, 'complicity in this matter' and so on, but I didn't rate Briscoe as brain of Britain, so it wouldn't matter. In fact I knew he wasn't too clever or he wouldn't have got mixed up in anything like this in the first place. But if he just blanked it, I'd be in trouble. I was already on plan B, I wasn't sure I could think fast enough for another one.

He pushed himself up to a sitting position.

"They paid me," he said. "They paid me what they said they would. But they didn't have to hurt me. They shouldn't have hurt me like that." He looked down at the floor. "Time was they couldn't have done that to me. That wasn't right. They hurt me just because they could. Bastards. They paid me, but they shouldn't have hurt me."

I looked at him then, not as point man in a set up, but as an old man who'd been hurt, not just physically, but even worse, in himself, in his pride.

I squatted down in front of him.

"Mr. Briscoe," I said, "how about we pay those bastards back, for taking that liberty?"

*

I came away from his place and took the balaclava off as I walked to the car.

I had the name of a pub and a couple of first names, but the descriptions weren't too good. Couldn't be worrying about that though. At least this was progress. I wanted to move fast in case Briscoe had a change of heart and let the two guys know there was trouble on the way. I didn't think he would, but I couldn't be sure. But I had to call Jenny. I needed to. Not good, part of me said. Or very good, the rest of me screamed.

I used the mobile and she answered on the third ring. About as fast as possible from her room to the phone. Once she had answered, I didn't know what to say. 'I'm okay', seemed stupid, I hadn't done anything dangerous yet, that was still to come. Besides, I wasn't sure that I was okay. I'd been close to doing something, to falling into something that I didn't want to think about. But she wanted to know, so I said yes, I was all right. Physically, I was all right.

"Which means what?" she said.

"I'm not sure, I'm just checking in. I wanted to check in."

"Will you come round?"

"I can't yet, I'm still in the middle of it."

"Has something happened? You sound like something's happened."

Intuitive people are a pain in the butt. Or maybe she was just getting to know me better than I realised. I took a breath.

"Yeah, something happened. Not good, but I'm all right. Could have been a disaster, but it's okay."

"Come round," she said.

"Not yet. I'm not finished yet."

"When you finish, come round."

"No, it'll be too late."

"It won't be too late. Whatever time it is, I'll be up. I'll wait up."

I hesitated and she heard it.

"Is there a reason why you wouldn't come?" she asked.

"No," I said, "not from me. Maybe from you though."

"If that happens, I'll decide it," she said. "I'll expect you later."

She cut the connection and I realised I was sweating.

*

I was sitting in the car now and not moving, which was dumb. I had to move quickly, sitting around wasn't an option, but with Briscoe I'd just come close to crossing a line that I'd always imagined I couldn't cross. Or was I just more reflective now, losing that edge because for the first time I had something, someone, to lose. I took another deep breath and switched on the engine. Whichever way, if I didn't get after these two guys, I might not get another chance. Before I drove off, I called Mick. He answered as he always does, no name, just a short 'yes'.

"Got a name and a frame," I said.

I didn't expect a comment back, Mick hardly ever says anything over the phone. I was just leaving a trail in case something went wrong further down the line. But this time there was a question.

"You want help?"

"No, I'm on a roll," I said and hung up.

*

Without a decent description and with only two first names to go on, I was relying on the pub being the right place. There was no guarantee either of them would be out this night, but the pub was fairly close, only about fifteen minutes drive and I thought I'd give it a go. I was sure that when I got there it would turn out to be one of those quiet pubs with regulars only, where you couldn't go in and move around without standing out a mile, but for once I really was on a roll. The place was modern and crowded. Bright lights and potted plants. Problem was, I wouldn't know either of my two guys, but they might recognise me. Of course, they wouldn't know whether I'd recognised them or not, so if I got a reaction from someone that might be one of them. It was a bit risky, but the best I had. If I waited I could lose the opportunity. Unless I used someone else. I called the car lot. Tony was still there. I told him to put Pete in a cab and send him down to me. And if he argued, to tell him that this was the first instalment on my furniture.

*

Pete wasn't happy.

"What am I going to say to them?" he complained.

"Don't know, don't care, mate," I said. "Just ID them and let me know who they are. They probably go around together and Lewis isn't such a common name, so if there's a Lewis somewhere with a Gavin, then you've done your bit."

"This is mad and it'll probably get me beaten up in the bogs or something."

"Don't go in the bogs then," I said. "Look, it's not rocket science, you go up to the bar and ask if Gavin and Lewis are in tonight. Tell the bar staff you're an old mate, or you've got a message for them...anything you like. If it doesn't happen then it doesn't happen, all right?"

"What if they *are* there though?"

"Then tell them you've got something to sell, get them out the front for me to look at and then tell 'em the local police are on to them, but you don't know what for."

He went off and I could hear him mumbling as he went:

"Don't go to the bogs he says, that's the first place I'm going when I get in there."

I didn't have too long to wait, but most of the time was taken up in thinking about how many different ways Pete could mess this up. By the time I'd reached nine, he was coming out with a medium built teenager following him, dressed in a combat jacket and with long blond streaked hair. They stood outside the door of the pub, the kid shifting from foot to foot, hands thrust into his pockets, looking like he was almost unable to keep still. After about a minute, it was clear that Pete was asking for money and the kid was telling him to take a hike. Pete wasn't having any of it and eventually the kid pushed him away hard, sending him back a few feet and went back into the pub. Pete turned and started towards the car, but I'd thought he'd be thick enough to do that and I already had it in gear, pulled away and drove off. I stopped a hundred yards up the road at which point Pete, realising I wasn't leaving him, legged it up the road and got in.

"Bastard wouldn't pay me a thing!" he said.

"And you're surprised." It was a statement not a question. "Which one was that?"

"That was Lewis," Pete answered "and he's a dopehead, no question. I know one when I see one."

"And you see one every day in the mirror," I put in.

"That's not fair. I found out what you wanted."

"Tried to make a profit out of it as well," I said.

"If I hadn't have argued, he'd have thought there was something wrong. Anyway, his mate's not with him tonight, but he's the one."

"Good, here's your bus fare, you're going back now."

"What! On the bleedin' bus?"

"Yep. You still owe me for furniture, there's no first class travel until that's paid off."

I turfed Pete out and reversed down the road to where I'd parked before. I'd assumed Lewis would try to contact Gavin now, but he'd gone back into the pub. Of course, he could call him from anywhere, but I'd thought he'd try to meet him. I'd have to wait.

It was thirty minutes later that the blond haired kid came out of the pub alone and started up the street. I had no way of knowing whether he had a car, took the bus, or was going to carry on walking, but here I had a safe parking space, so I got out and started after him, a reasonable distance behind. Tailing someone easily, Al always said, was to a large extent determined by whether the subject expected to be tailed or not. Lewis clearly didn't. He strode boldly forwards, oblivious to anything other than himself. He turned left once, crossed the road, took a right and then jogged up a short set of entry steps to an old house that I could see was converted into flats, or bedsits. I had no way of knowing if anyone else was in there waiting for him, but it would be easier going in with him, than after him. As he fumbled for his keys and put them in the lock, I came up the steps behind him and pushed through the front door with him.

"Hey," he started to shout, but then I stuffed my sleeve in his mouth with a fair amount of arm behind it and he fell over. He looked up at me from the floor and then as I put my finger to my lips and mimed 'shush' to him, a look of recognition came over his face. I was conscious of the fact that anyone could come out of any of the flats in the house and I had to get him into his room quickly. I took his keys out of the door and said:

"Quietly and no-one gets hurt. Noise and you get hurt, plus the police come to call in about ten minutes time, once one of your neighbours phones it in. Then you'll have more explaining to do."

Lewis nodded and I realised that he was slightly drunk, but fortunately not enough to blow the situation. I stepped back, ready for a possible move as he got up, but it didn't come. I think he recognised the fact that the police might be more trouble than me in the long term.

He walked a little unsteadily to the stairs and started up to the first floor. He stopped at one of the two doors there and tried to find his keys. I reminded him that I still had them.

"Is there anyone else in there?" I said.

He shook his head, but I kept onto his keys after I opened the door and pushed him inside just in front of me. I hadn't forgotten that these guys had had shotguns at the game and even if they'd got rid of those, there might be other weapons in the flat. I put my arm partway around his neck and gripped his windpipe right at the top between my thumb and third finger. Gripped, that is, not just held.

It wasn't a flat. It was, I saw as I followed him in, a bed-sit, which made it easier to check for other occupants. I man-handled Lewis into the kitchen unit area and past the wardrobe, which I opened. The bed was a mattress on the floor. Home from home, I thought. I sat him on the floor in the middle of the room, away, I thought, from any place where a gun might have been hidden. But the place was a mess and it was just as likely that the gun was on the floor under some old Back Street Heroes magazines, as anywhere else.

"Where's the gun?" I said.

"Man, Gav's gonna kill you," he replied, his voice a little high pitched. He crossed his legs and was rolling slightly as he looked at me. "He's gonna fuckin' kill you, man. He's really tough and when I tell him about this, he's gonna kill you."

"Well, let's make it easy for him, then. Tell me where he is and I'll go see him now."

Lewis' face worked its way into a frown and he sobered up slightly.

"Oh no, man, then he'd kill me."

For a minute I'd thought this might be easy, but Lewis was drunk more than high and enough in control not to give it away.

"Where's the gun, Lewis?"

"Not here, man. Gav wouldn't let me keep it. Said I might blow my own head off."

He might be lying, but it wasn't a problem getting him to talk. Maybe he was far enough gone to be just spilling everything.

"Where's the money?"

"You'll never find it."

Not that far gone then.

"Lewis," I said, "you are a drunk junkie who stole money from a card game. I am a guy you stole money from. We are in your bedsit and I doubt if there are many other places you would have to hide anything. I am going to take this place apart to find the money and when I've finished it will be a mess." I looked at the mess around where he was sitting. "Even more of a mess," I said. "And it will be my mess, not yours. If you tell me where the money is, I'll just go."

"Fuck you, man!"

I suddenly remembered that this guy had fired a shotgun right next to me a few weeks ago and now he was swearing at me so I kicked him very hard on the outside of his leg half way up his thigh. It was a good kick and as well as hurting like hell, it would keep him from running off anywhere soon. He did scream though, which might bring someone, but I figured that his neighbours would be used to some strange noises from this room and it was worth the risk.

I leant down, grabbed his collar and dragged him to one wall. I propped him up there and told him to shut up. There was no weapon near him and he wasn't going to be moving too far too quickly.

Then I ripped his room apart. After three or four minutes I'd taken the sofa apart, pulled up the carpet and emptied the drawers. I didn't want too much noise, so I was careful, but thorough. I didn't find anything. I threw the bedclothes off the mattress and upended it. Nothing. It wasn't impossible that he'd unstitched the mattress or sofa and stitched the money back inside them, but it wasn't likely. This guy would want to be able to get to the money whenever he felt like it. I grabbed a t-shirt that was lying on the floor, took it over to Lewis and stuffed it in his mouth. Then I kicked him hard in the leg again in the same place and as he tried to scream, dragged him with me over to the kitchen area to carry on with the search. There was a cupboard under the sink. In it was a black bin liner stuffed with cash. As easy as that.

I looked at him.

"Lewis, did you really think I wouldn't find that? A kid of five would find that. Why didn't you just tell me where it was? Then your leg wouldn't hurt and you wouldn't have all this mess to clear up. How much money is left? Sorry," I said, taking the shirt out of his mouth, "forgot you couldn't answer. How much money is left?"

He was curled up clutching at his leg, shaking. I was a little surprised he hadn't been sick, but then if he had, he'd probably have choked on his own vomit with the shirt in his mouth. Should've thought of that really.

I obviously wasn't going to get an answer, so I looked for myself. Without counting it all, I couldn't tell, but there was a lot of cash there. I tied a knot in the bag and took it with me while I looked over the rest of the room. It didn't take long. I did find a tin of change which I emptied into the bag and his stash of drugs, which given the amount of money he had available to him could have been bigger. Pills, twists of paper, pre-torn pieces of tin foil. I left them where they were.

Then I went and stood over Lewis until he looked like he could speak.

"Broken my leg, you bastard," he mumbled.

"No, I haven't. But it'll hurt like hell for a while. Where do I find your mate, Gavin?"

"Can't tell you." He was still shaking and his voice was little more than a whisper. He sounded sober though.

"Can't tell me because what?" I asked.

"He'll kill me."

"If you don't tell me, I might kill you."

He raised his head for the first time and tried to look at me.

"Yeah, I know," I said. "There's a difference between kicking someone and killing them and your Gavin's killed at least one man that I know of, but then," I squatted down in front of him, "so have I. Look at me, Lewis, look right at me. I need to know where Gavin is and if I have to, I'll take it out of you."

He couldn't hold my gaze and, objectively, I didn't envy him. He'd lost the money and he knew that. Probably, the only way for him to safely get more was with Gavin, he'd never manage on his own, although why Gavin was using him I couldn't work out. But if he gave Gavin up, there'd be no more quick money and possibly no more Lewis either. I thought I'd make it easy for him.

"Tell you what, Lewis, have you got his address written down somewhere, then you could say I just ransacked the flat and found it. You wouldn't have told me where he is." I smiled at him. "Easy way out," I said.

No answer.

I stood up and put my foot at the side of his head, pushing it so that he was face up. Then I put my heel on his nose and started to push down. He started to cry out again and his hands came up to move my foot, but there was no strength in them.

"It's going to break in a few seconds, Lewis. It's not necessary. Just tell me where he is. You can call him when I've gone and tell him what's happened. He'll appreciate that you've called him. You're going to need surgery to correct this, Lewis..."

I think he was about to tell me when I felt the bones split under my heel and the blood started to run out. I held my foot in place for a few seconds more and then took it away. His nose was a mess and for a second I told myself that this guy would have shot me dead a few weeks ago and that this was less punishment than I would have handed out in the ring to a fighter. Then I realised that I'd gone beyond a certain point and that I hadn't needed to remind myself of anything in order to do this.

"Where is he, Lewis?"

There was no answer, so I stepped towards him again, but this time he jerked away and said something. There were tears running down his face mingling with the blood and he couldn't stand up, but he wanted to say something. I leant down to try and work out what it was.

"Pen."

I found him one and tore the cover off a book that was on the kitchen worktop for him to write on. His hands were shaking, but he managed. It was a local address.

"Good man, Lewis. Tell me, what is he to you, this Gavin?"

"Shister's 'oyfriend," he managed.

"OK, Lewis, I'm going to go now and if you want to, you can call him and let him know what's gone on. I'm sure he won't blame you. And of course you're going to have to get your nose seen to when you can walk, but if you do go to hospital I'd stick with a simple mugging story if I was you. I wouldn't go on about card games and robberies and shotgun killings and stuff. It might all get too complicated. I reached down and he flinched, but I was just taking his mobile phone away from him and his wallet, which I emptied and put back in his pocket.

"Sorry, but if you want to phone, you'll have to use the payphone down the hall. And I've nicked your small change out of the tin there as well, so you might be knocking on someone's door to borrow some silver. Maybe best wait until you've cleaned up a bit, eh?"

I checked the corridor was clear and closed the door behind me. I saw no-one on the way out of the building and once round the corner I dropped the mobile into a drain. There was some blood on the heel of my shoe which I would have to clean properly later, but for the moment I wiped it off with a paper tissue, wrapped it in another one so that the blood wasn't immediately visible and dropped it in someone's outdoor bin. Even if anyone did see it, it just looked like the result of a nosebleed. The bin liner with the money was heavy, but that was good. I looked at the address and thought about whether to continue the roll. It might be pushing it. But if I left it, sooner or later Lewis would get in touch with Gavin, who was probably altogether a tougher proposition and would then be prepared. I turned over the torn book cover. Lloyds TSB's guide to starting your own small business.

Wrong business, Lewis, wrong business.

*

Back in the car, I decided to count up the money. If there was enough for Allingway, I'd call it a night. I'd got by so far on a wing, a prayer and some improvisation, but you can only push things so far like that. For someone a bit tougher, possibly with a girlfriend in tow, I'd have to think it through. I didn't want to be counting money out of a sack in a car, so I drove round to Mick. He would still be up, knowing that I was into something and in any case, the money had to go through him in the end.

At the flat, the dog stood in the doorway as ever and allowed me to push past him only after he'd sniffed at me. I'm not sure that the sniffing meant anything from a guarding point of view. The fact that Mick had buzzed open the door may have been enough for him to let me in, but I wasn't going to rub my hand in aftershave next time to find out. Mick was stretched out on the sofa.

"How'd it go," he said.

"We got some money, cost us delivery on a broken nose and a very dead leg."

I dumped the bag on the floor and sat down next to it. Mick stayed where he was. I'd worked out in my head that with five players at about twenty to twenty-five grand apiece, if Lewis had a quarter of the cash he could have up to £30,000 in bag. If he'd spent five thou' of that, I would have been surprised. It took me a little over ten minutes, but maybe Lewis had been on a third of the take. Or maybe one of the players had been carrying more. There was a little under thirty-three thousand pounds in the bin liner.

"Allingway gets twenty-five grand, plus I'll send him the cost of his hotel for the extra few days he stayed. We turn a profit of over six and a half thousand. Not bad for a night's work. Finder's fee to me, plus the hassle of dealing with Allingway and couriering the money. Three and a bit thousand to you. You okay with that?"

I was. Now I knew how much there was, I decided to throw £500 at Hillier. I'd said there'd be something small in it for him and it doesn't hurt to keep your word to people like that. What I wasn't sure of was what to do about the rest of it that was with Gavin. Mick left that up to me.

"Your call, Garron. If you go get it then let me know, just as a back up and I'll take something on it as a fee. Keeps you legitimate." He didn't quite smile as he said that. "If you don't, that's up to you. Seems a shame to let it go though, could be another 35K or more sitting there, but we've covered ourselves with this and in the end, we're not thieves, that's not our game."

I let that go. Mick was a fence. Sort of. Whatever else he was involved in that didn't come to me, I didn't know. And didn't want to know. But I understood what he was saying. There was a real score sitting there and we knew where to start looking for it. So what was stopping me?

"If he's got any sense," I said, "he'll have it spread around and either he'll be ready now, or he'll be running."

"If your dopehead has told him. He might be too scared to."

"There's something else, Mick."

Something in my tone made him sit up. "Go on," he said.

"I'm still working it out, but I think I need to stop this kind of stuff. Tonight, I nearly did something to someone that wouldn't have been right and I'm not sure what to do about it. It's kind of stopped me short."

"Bollocks!" Mick said. "You're talking about putting pressure on old Briscoe, right? An old lag who set you up, lost you a load of money and could have ruined your rep. And you're worried about putting a scare into him. And then," he carried on as I started to butt in, "you go straight round to someone else, bust him up and don't give it any weight at all. You think too much, that's your problem."

"You always told me I wasn't a thug, Mick. You always said I wasn't like Al and I shouldn't be like him. Now you're saying I am."

He shook his head.

"First thing, Garron, Al wasn't a thug. He was a class and a half above that. Second, I never said you weren't a thug, I said you weren't a killer, or you shouldn't be because it would change you. Well I think you've changed now. I don't want to know and I'm not asking, but I'm not an idiot and I'm the one got you the gun, right?"

I sat down on the upright chair, thinking back to the night I'd asked Mick to get me a gun and to all that had followed.

"All right, Mick, maybe I've changed, but I want to change back. I've found something out in the last few months, which is you can't pick and choose what you get involved in. If you're living it, things just come up and drag you in. But I don't want to be in a position where I'm standing over a scared old man with a set of bolt-cutters in my hand. How the hell did I get to that? Even if he's scum, that's not what I want to be doing."

"But it's OK to do it to a younger guy?"

"It's different. He nearly shot me, could've shot me. And he stole the money."

Mick sighed and sat back on the sofa. "I don't understand you, Garron. You're an ex-pug, you're a good bodyguard, you're capable of beating someone to within an inch of their life, you own a gun, which you may or may not have used," he said carefully "and now you want to stop. What are you going to do, go mini-cabbing?"

"If I had to, I would and I could, but there are a lot of other things I can do."

"You tried before; you ended up back here."

He had a point. As usual. I got up to go.

"Sorry, Mick, I've got to think about it. I nearly lost it tonight and I didn't like it. I'll keep on collecting the rents, but just give me a couple of weeks off from the bodyguarding jobs."

"Talking about the rents, has this got anything to do with that girl you've been seeing?"

I looked back at him. "Yes, Mick, I think it has. Maybe not, but I think it has."

He swung himself back onto the sofa and stretched out. Gave the hand signal to the dog to let me out of the room.

"If this is serious with her, then you go with it, Garron. But you are what you are. You're not some kid who can get a job and change just like that. You'll have to work at it. Maybe you can do it. Or maybe you'll end up back here again. Because it's not just what you do. It's what you are."

*

Sitting up again. 4:20 am. Jenny is asleep, but not me. Not me. Dozed maybe, but then jerked upright and found my hand reaching, but there's no bottle here. I haven't moved in, so there's no bottle. 'It's what you are,' he'd said. What I am.

What am I?

*

We hadn't spoken much when I'd arrived. Jenny was good like that. Knew when not to say anything. I needed to rest and to let things work themselves out of my head. The next morning we talked.

"Was it as bad as you sounded?" she asked.

"Yep." I said. Mr. Communication at his best.

"I'm glad you came round though."

And that opened me up, because I realised that it wasn't that I had nowhere else to go. Before Jenny I would have gone back to the flat and been happy to close the door on everything. But last night, I'd wanted to come here. Not to talk, not for sex, but just to be here, where she was.

87

"I'm glad I came here as well. Couldn't have been much fun for you, having me turn up in the middle of the night, say two and a half words and go to sleep."

"Except you didn't sleep, did you?"

"Not much, no."

"You think you'll sleep tonight?"

I smiled at her. "I doubt it, but it doesn't matter. I'm going to change a few things around, I think. I'm not sure I want to carry on doing what I'm doing."

"Because of last night?"

"You're carefully not asking are you?" I took a deep breath. "Last night, I nearly hurt someone who I shouldn't hurt. Maybe he deserved to be hurt, but I didn't like being in that position."

"But you didn't do it." She picked up my hand and held it. "You didn't do it."

"No," I said, "but then I went straight round to someone else and beat him up."

She looked at me, but didn't let go of my hand. I carried on.

"You see, that's the truth of it. That's something of what I do. But that's not how it's supposed to be. That's not how it was ever supposed to be, but you get carried along with it. You get pulled into a situation where that's the right thing to do. It still seems like the right thing to do and that's crazy. I'm living in a world where the right thing to do is to stamp on a guy's nose. Not in a ring, not even in a fight, but just because he's stupid enough to have it happen."

She kissed my hand.

"But you still think it was right to do what you did," she said. "Which means you didn't do this out of malice, or because you're evil, or because you're stealing from someone, or mugging them, or anything like that. You did this for the right reason."

I sighed out loud. "You're missing the point. The thing is, I might be completely wrong. Just 'cos I think I should do something doesn't make it right." I took my hand away. "It's going to change though. I'm going to move out of bodyguarding for a while, see if I can do something else. I'll keep collecting the rents otherwise I'd lose my flat, but if I can keep out of the rest of it, I'll maybe stay out of this kind of situation."

She sat back and looked at me.

"Is this what you want?" she said.

I remembered what Mick had said.

"Yeah, I think so."

"You're not doing this in any way for me, then?"

I looked up and held her gaze. "Maybe," I said, "maybe you're in there somewhere as well."

There was silence for a moment and then she said:

"You see, I don't want you to change yourself because you think I want you to. I'm falling for you as you are. I don't care what you do as long as you're okay with it. Does that sound stupid? I should care if you're a criminal, but I know you're not. What you've said just proves that. The fact that you're sitting here tearing yourself up about this, proves that. So I only care that you don't get hurt. And if you don't get hurt by stopping this kind of work, then that's fine with me. But I'm not going to ask you to do anything, or to change anything. Which makes me stupid, right?"

"No," I said, "it makes you bloody wonderful."

*

So there I was. Stepping away from it all. I had a woman who for whatever reason wanted to be with me and who I wanted to be with. I had a job collecting rents, which in effect paid for my flat. I had two and a half thousand pounds in my pocket and I had the chance to look around and see what I wanted to do next. I only had one obligation to discharge...

I took Pete with me to Hillier's club. He hadn't wanted to go, but I was still furious with him for stealing my furniture and I didn't give him a choice.

"All you have to do is take this into the man in the club. I'd go myself, but I'm not overly popular there and it's not worth the hassle."

"You're not overly popular here either, mate," he mumbled. "What's in it?"

"Five hundred pounds cash. And before your thieving junkie hands get on it, this guy plays very rough and I'll be calling him as you go in, telling him you're on the way and how much to expect. If you don't behave, I'll tell him there's supposed to be five-fifty and you'll take a kicking for what's missing."

"You're just a bastard, you are. I make one mistake and you're right on my case."

I let that go. I was never going to get my furniture back and I knew that. It wasn't worth anything much anyway, but the thought that Pete had stolen it still hurt and I was going to make him pay for that. He'd spotted Lewis for me and now he was going to pay off Hillier for me and all this was useful. Not vital, but certainly useful. I was sure I could think of some more little jobs for Pete, to help make up for what he'd done. It was an easier revenge for him to take than breaking his head open, which was what I'd first thought of doing.

"How'd you get hooked, Pete?" I asked, "you knew enough about drugs to stay clear."

He didn't answer for a minute and then sort of shrugged and said;

"I'd always had a few smokes and stuff and then I just got caught up in it. I was with some people up north and they were all chasing and I just went along with it. I'd like to say I'm sorry I got into it, mate, but you know, what else have I got?"

"You had the music, Pete, more than any of us, you had the music. And you know, that's what really makes me think you're out of control with the stuff. I can't imagine there ever being a time when you would have sold your guitar, but you have. That was your life and you've hocked it for a hit."

"For a week of hits, mate, it wasn't a cheap guitar."

I gave up and then thought, sod it, he was a good friend once, you've got to try.

"Pete, don't you ever - "

"Garron," he cut in, "I know what I am. I know what I'm doing to myself. You can't help me. No-one can do anything to help me unless I want to be helped. And I don't."

Last time.

"You hate yourself that much?"

"If that's what you want to think."

We lapsed into silence for the rest of the drive and I found myself thinking of the times years ago when a group of us would sit in his Mum's flat on the estate with a couple of cans listening to him playing. It didn't matter what he was playing, he was that good we'd be listening. Long time ago, more than just years. And now he was a restless, edgy junkie. All those dreams, all those efforts, of all of us, not just Pete. All of us and especially me. Because in the end he was just destroying himself. I'd branched out to destroying others.

I pulled myself up at that thought. I had done what I thought was right and I was moving on now, away from the life, away from the brink. But as we drove along, I wondered why I was so keen to judge Pete for his actions.

We pulled up outside Hillier's club, but on the other side of the road and I left the engine running. Really I should find a call box to phone Hillier, but I didn't. I just wanted to get this last bit over and done with, so I called through using my mobile and told him I was outside and had something to deliver.

"There's five hundred and I want you to count it when you get it," I said, aware of Pete listening to every word, "'cos the delivery boy's a crackhead and I don't want any misunderstandings here. This is what I promised and now we're square. I'm going to watch him in and then if he ducks out a side door, he's your responsibility."

"Wise man, Garron, not coming in. My boys might not want to let you out again. It's a shame really, 'cos I think you're a useful man to know."

"Not any more, Mr. Hillier, I'm taking a break for a while. As long a while as I can handle."

I killed the call and Pete looked at me with real venom.

"You really are a bastard, Garron, a real five star bastard!"

"Yes," I said, "I am. And I'm going to carry on reminding you about it until you remember that I'm the friend you stole from. Now piss off in there and give him this. And don't do anything stupid with it, 'cos this guy's a professional bastard, not just a part-time one like me who only shits on people that cross them. This guy'll do it to anyone. Put your fingers in that packet and he'll cut them off for you. Now go on and you can find your own way back."

"What! I'm skint! How do I get back from here?"

"You know something, Pete, I don't care. I've had enough of sitting next to someone I can't trust. Forget the furniture, forget paying me back, just get out of the car and deliver the packet. You want to get back, ask Hillier for a delivery fee."

"You can't leave - "

"Get out of the car, Pete. Now."

He got out and after slamming the door, which would please Tony no end, crossed the road and rang the buzzer at the front of the club. As soon as the door opened I drove off. It wasn't Hillier's heavies I was driving away from, it was Pete and the life I'd been leading. I headed back to Camden and hit the tape on in the car. Robert Johnson, *Hellhound on my Trail*. I should have known then.

*

I didn't think I'd sleep that night. I sat up on the mattress at my place, deliberately not having a drink and wondering what the hell I was going to do next. I hadn't burnt any bridges, but in my own mind I'd made the decision. At about half midnight the cat came in through the flap in the window and sat in his corner in the dark, eyes glowing at me.

"What d'you think, cat?" I asked him, "do you think I can make a go of it this time? Get a job, pay taxes, buy you tuna with legitimately earned money?"

The cat sat there staring at me for a minute and then vanished out of the window again.

"Some bloody help you are," I called after him. The mobile rang. Jenny.

"I'm home. You coming over?"

"How did you know I wouldn't be asleep now?"

"You don't sleep much. And you'd have switched the phone off if you'd really wanted to sleep."

I thought about going over there and then realised I could start changing now.

"Tell you what, pack a toothbrush and I'll bring you back here. You can meet the cat."

There was a pause.

"You don't want to come over here," I said.

"No, I do. I...just never figured you for someone who had a cat."

That hadn't been what she was going to say, but I let it go. It would come out later if it had to.

"I didn't say I *had* a cat, I just said you could meet him." I didn't wait for the question. "I'll be round soon, I'm leaving now."

"I'll be waiting," she said.

*

"I know what you were going to say on the phone before."

We were in the car driving back to Camden.

"You were going to ask me why I wanted you to come back now, why I hadn't asked you back before."

She didn't say anything.

"And the answer," I carried on, "is that I've decided to change what I'm doing. I'm going to cut out the bodyguarding, I'm going to carry on with the rent stuff like I said, 'cos that pays for the flat, but I'm going to do something else. And I want you to be part of whatever that is. And I can't ask you to do that unless I let you in more to my life. And since I don't intend being at risk in the future, I can start with my flat. Which is here," I said, pulling up.

"That was quite a speech," she said. "What was I before you decided to change you life? A security risk?"

I'd thought she'd get the hump with that idea, but it was basic tradecraft. The fewer people that knew where you lived, the safer you were. And the safer they were. I hesitated and then told her that.

"Yeah," she said, "I thought so. It's okay, I'm not mad at you. It's just the way it is. Quite an achievement really, being a security risk without even knowing anything."

We walked up the stairs and along to the front door. The match was still there, but I didn't point it out. I may have decided to make a change, but I wasn't going to cut out the basics for a while yet.

"What are your neighbours like?" she asked.

I turned to try to explain that I'd never met them and found her smiling at me.

"Don't worry, I'm just teasing you."

I think I managed to smile back. Bloody women for you. Always hitting the nerve.

I put the light on and the fact that the room was nearly empty jumped back at us. There really was very little here, just the mattress, a small TV, one table, one chair and the cat's food and water bowls in the far corner. There were a few dishes in the kitchen area through the doorway to the right, but very little food and everything was put away.

"Well," she said, "at least it's clean."

"And it's tidy," I put in.

"I think that's because there's nothing here."

She moved in and sat on the chair. There was another one, but the TV was on it, so I leant back against the wall. There was a silence which dragged a bit.

"You're the first person to have been in here since I moved in. The cat's going to do his nut."

"You mean, you really do have a cat?"

"No, he just lives here as well. He was here first and he comes and goes as he pleases. He's not a very, er, touchy-feely kind of a cat."

She sat in silence again for a while and then said:

"This is ridiculous, I feel like I'm intruding here."

I looked at her. "I know, but you're not. Look, I'll get you a cup of tea and shift the telly so we can both sit down and then maybe we can work out what we're going to do with the rest of my life."

That broke the ice a bit and we were okay from then on. She relaxed, I relaxed and we got back to where we should be. And it was quite touching really, that she thought that I could be anything that I wanted to be.

"Well, okay," she said, "you're not going to be a brain surgeon, but you could do a lot of other things."

"I don't know, I tried before. When I stopped fighting I tried sales repping and didn't get very far."

"Why not?"

"The driving did my head in, I got bored and the truth is, I wasn't very good at it. I think the company I worked for were trading on my name and then when they found out I couldn't actually produce any real sales, they got fed up with me. Quite right really."

"But you've got a brain, you could train up for something. What about training fighters, or teaching sports in schools, something like that."

Yeah, I thought, maybe, but it didn't grab my interest.

"What about you?" I said. "Why is it you're waiting tables and not pushing yourself somewhere else?"

After a moment she said: "How come you haven't asked me that before?"

"I didn't think it was my business, but since we're discussing moving forwards, I thought I'd include you. Do you mind?"

"I probably would've done if you'd asked me earlier, but you've got as much right to know what I'm doing as I have to know about you. I'm waiting tables because it's safe. Because although you have to deal with dick-brains sometimes, everyone else leaves me alone." Her voice was quiet now, but with an edge to it and she wasn't looking at me. "I don't have any pressure to be anyone or to have anyone relying on me. If they don't like what I'm doing or the way I work, they can just fire me." She looked up at me now. "Is that good enough?"

Dangerous ground for some reason and I backed away.

"If it's good enough for you, then that's fine with me. Doesn't solve how I earn some money after this couple of grand runs out, but I guess we've got a bit of time to work it out."

"And," she said, getting herself together again, "you're going to have to get back into the system. Address, taxes, National Insurance, all that stuff."

At which point I nearly gave up and went back to bodyguarding.

We threw a few more ideas around and then decided it was late enough. The problems would still be there in the morning, but tonight wouldn't be. It was the first night Jenny had stayed in my flat...so we went to bed.

*

I woke up before five. I'd slept and not dreamt. Not a miracle, but worthy of note. Jenny was sitting up on the bed wearing a sweatshirt of mine and leaning against the wall.

"Hey," I said quietly, "I'm the one who's supposed to not sleep, remember?"

Then I noticed her eyes were wet.

I reached out to take her hand, but she didn't move.

"The reason," she said in a low whisper, not looking at me, "that I wait tables is that I don't want any responsibility. I don't want to be in charge of anything or anyone. I don't want anyone relying on me and I know it's a waste of a life, but it's my wasted life."

I opened my mouth, but for once had the good sense to close it again before I said anything. Instead I sat up, put my arm around her and pulled her into me. She carried on talking, although into my shoulder as though she could talk to me, but not if I was there directly, not if she had to face me.

"My sister was a drug addict, started sniffing glue and smoking dope, went on to crack. She was younger than me, got hooked early on in her teens and never got back on track. My Mum couldn't handle it. She ended up leaning more and more on me. Most of the time I couldn't go to school, I had to do the shopping, sort the bills out, collect her benefits and of course, deal with my sister and her friends. And the dealers and the police and the social workers. When I left school I got a job, but I had to keep leaving it to get back to the flat because my sister had done something, or not done something. My Mum couldn't believe she was a drug user. She loved her so much and she got nothing back from her. And I couldn't reach her either. I tried. I really tried, but she ended up stealing money from me and from Mum, she even sold some of my books and CDs. And it just got worse."

I didn't say anything, none of this had come out before and she'd never mentioned family before, other than she'd never known her Dad.

"When she was a kid we'd got on really well, there was only two years between us, but by the end she wasn't the same person. There was just nothing there anymore. But my Mum couldn't see that, it was always, 'when Amy's got herself sorted out', or 'when Amy's better' and sometimes I'd say, 'it's not going to happen', but then she'd really round on me and I guess for that she was right. We couldn't give up on her.

"And she'd have her user friends round, no respect for our place, no consideration for us and Mum would just take it. I thought it was because that was all we could do, because Amy needed our help and I tried to understand that, I could live with that, but eventually I came to think it was because it was Amy. If it would've been me, she wouldn't have been the same. I know, I know that's not rational, but then Amy died. It was while she was shooting up, but it wasn't an overdose. Heart failure they said. Her heart gave out. And then Mum went to pieces, just couldn't handle it, although it had been coming for over four years. And maybe it sounds callous, but that was when I needed her. I couldn't keep supporting her, I wanted her to give something back to me."

Her voice was a little louder now, but breaking up, there were tears on her face, on my shoulder and chest.

"Not much, I didn't want much, just some words, just some signal, something to say that she loved me, even that she appreciated me, but it never came. And then the ultimate kick in the teeth, she killed herself. Committed suicide. She even left a note, not to me, but to the police, saying why she'd done it. She never mentioned me in it at all."

She suddenly pulled away from me slightly and stared right into me.

"You see, in the end she didn't love me. If she had, she'd have carried on living for me. In the end, I wasn't enough for her and I never knew why."

She kept staring at me and I put both my hands up and held her face gently and looked right back into her eyes.

"Maybe you weren't enough for her. Maybe, for whatever crazy reason, she'd tied herself to your sister, but you can't go back to something like that. You can talk about it, you can think about it if you need to, but you can't go back. Whatever it was, you've got to understand, it wasn't to do with you, it was down to her, not you. And you've got to know that now, going forwards, it is to do with you. And that you are enough. You're enough for me."

She looked at me like I was crazy, but I wasn't and given time, I'd be able to prove that to her.

*

About a week after I'd last seen Pete, he gave me a call. He said he had the perfect way to get the money back for my furniture and much more on top. I'd spent the time trying to chill out and think about what I could do. Jenny had stayed at my flat most nights and I was even beginning to sleep better, I thought maybe because I'd made a decision to change things. Or maybe, because with Jenny at least, I was moving forwards. I didn't really want to hear a proposition from Pete, but he was so up for it I told him I'd listen.

"No, mate, come round to the car lot. I want to go through this face to face."

"You're not still crashing there are you?" I said, "Tony must be going mad."

"No, I've got a place. Just a room, but it's fine for the moment."

I didn't ask him how he could afford rent and I didn't want to know. I had thought of going round to Tony anyway, to find out if he had any thoughts on driving work that I could do, so I said I'd see Pete later and then spent the drive over there wondering what stupid plan he'd come up with.

It was even more stupid than I'd thought.

"You've got to be joking, Pete," I said. "I don't fight anymore."

"Yeah, but this isn't a twelve round title fight, it's unlicensed, four rounds, you can still do that."

I'd arrived to find him sitting behind Tony's desk with his feet up and a joint in his hand. I'd told him to put it out before Tony came in, but he didn't, he just said Tony was out for a while and had left him in charge. Then he'd started in on the fight thing. Hillier had a fighter, put him into unlicensed fights and put up a purse for the winner, with something for the loser as well. The real money was made on the bets. Sometimes the fights were open with admission charges, sometimes closed for the high rollers. And Hillier had suggested that I might want to take on one of his boys, thought it would be a real attraction.

For a moment I was almost tempted. I don't know of any fighter who hasn't at some time had that thought of getting back to it, but then reality kicked in.

"Pete, this guy will be training regularly if he's Hillier's boy and he'll be very fit and probably pretty good. I'm not up to it anymore. I don't train much now, just some exercises. I'm not in the gym hitting the bags or doing any sparring, I run maybe once, at most twice a week and don't forget I lost my license because my wrist was knackered and had to be pinned for a while. If I hit anything, or anybody, it might fall apart. So no, there's no way I would even consider doing this."

"You've got to, mate," he said, "I told him you would."

"*You* told him, I'd do it? You can't do that, Pete and anyway, why didn't he come to me himself about this? He can get to me through Mick any time he likes."

He didn't say anything, just sat there, looking like he was caught in the headlights.

"Wait a minute," I said, "he didn't mention this to you at all, did he? You brought this to him. You told him you could get me to fight his man and it would be a real crowd pleaser and I'm right up for it and you'll have me there anytime he likes. Is that how it went?"

"Man, it just sort of came out, you know." Pete's voice had squeaked up an octave, something I suddenly remembered used to happen to him now and again when he was put under pressure. Then he started gabbling a bit. "Hillier was talking about his fighter and how good he was and I said I'd bet you could take him and he said, no you were out of training and I said it wouldn't matter 'cos you were a pro and he said his man was as good as a professional fighter and it kind of went from there."

I didn't know whether to believe him or not. Whether it really had been a conversation that had got out of hand, or he'd just gone in with the proposition cold. And that was the problem with Pete now, you just couldn't trust him, you couldn't believe anything he said. And there was something else I didn't understand.

"How come you were just sitting there having a chinwag with Adam Hillier, Pete? Is he your long lost uncle or something?"

"I'm working for him, Garron."

"You! Working for Hillier! As what, his food taster?"

"I'm working in the club, bit of cleaning, stand-in barman, you know."

I couldn't believe it. "That's amazing, Pete. I drop you off there as a low life junkie delivery boy and you land a job. Takes some doing."

"Yes it does and yesterday I moved into a room that one of the staff there wanted to rent out, so I'm doing all right. But I need you to take this fight. It's only a short fight and you'll make money even if you lose. And if you win it's bigger money and side bets - "

"You'll be telling me it's fixed next and I've got to take a dive in the third. Come off it, Pete, I'm not fighting. That time is over."

"Garron, I said you'd do it."

"Well, you'll have to un-say it. I don't fight now unless I have to and if I was going to, then I wouldn't want to fight unlicensed. If I did ever want to get back into managing or training a fighter, I couldn't do it if I'd been involved with unlicensed fights, so I'm not going down that road."

Pete had taken his feet off the desk and was sitting now in the chair, elbows on his knees and head in his hands.

"Garron, you don't understand. I told Hillier you'd do this. I told him I could get you to do this, I could persuade you to do it. I need your help here, you can't turn me down."

He sounded really desperate and I was almost sorry for him, but not enough to get myself into this much trouble.

"Pete, you can't persuade me, I don't owe you anything -"

"We were friends once, Garron, doesn't that count for anything?"

"It did, once, but now I don't see the same person, Pete." I was starting to get annoyed about this. "There was a time I would have stuck my neck out for you, but there was also

104

a time when you wouldn't have asked me to do something like this, because you would have been worried enough about me getting damaged not to get me into it. That time has gone as well, hasn't it, Pete?"

"I told him you'd do it."

"Well, tell him you were wrong."

"I've taken his money."

"Give it back."

"I can't give it back, I don't have all of it now."

I made the most of the next line. "Where did you lose it then, Pete, up your nose or in a vein? Either way, it's your problem, not mine."

I left the office and bumped into Tony on his way in, juggling some car keys around hand to hand.

"Don't look too happy, Garron, what's up? Pete annoying you again?"

"Tony, get him out of your life, mate. He's mixing in bad company, he's an addict and he's going to bring seven kinds of hell onto everyone around him soon."

"Easy now, he's not that bad. He's got himself somewhere to live now, just drops in occasionally to use the phone, which is the least I can do for him. He looks like he's sorting himself out a bit."

I put my hand on Tony's shoulder and looked straight at him.

"You're a good man, Tony, but you're too trusting. Pete's got himself involved with Adam Hillier, who is a - "

"I know what Hillier is," he broke in.

"That's where his money has come from, that's probably where his supply is coming from and that's who he's going to be in hock to. So throw him out, change the locks on the office and the main gate and watch yourself, 'cos I don't know which is worse. To be hooked by the drugs, or to be hooked into Adam Hillier."

"You don't think you're overreacting to this, then?"

"No, Tony, I don't. Hillier is a villain and a well set up one at that. Pete's taken his money and that means he's in hock to him. Hillier won't do anything to you, but Pete will if he gets desperate. You just watch things for a while."

Tony nodded, trusting my judgment on this.

"You going to help him out of this?" he asked.

"Not this one," I said, "not this one. I just got out of the life, I'm not getting back in it again."

*

I'd got so wound up at Pete, that I'd forgotten to ask Tony about any work. Well, it would wait, I wasn't going back there again. I couldn't believe that Pete had thought I would just say, 'yeah, sure, no problem, I'll fight whoever you want'. The best unlicensed fighters were very tough guys who worked at it and I reckoned that Hillier would have one of the best. Like I'd said to him, all fighters think back to being in the ring, for most of us it's the time when we were most alive, when we were somebody, when we felt like our lives had possibilities. Most of us recognise that that time comes to an end, like it or not and if you try to push it, you can end up badly hurt. But Pete didn't care about that. Christ knew what his deal was with Hillier, but he'd promised to deliver me as a fighter and that wasn't going to happen. Even given the fact that I still had the basic skills and could still whack hard, I wasn't in training, my reflexes would be shot, my stamina low and of course my wrist might break with the first punch. And the bugger of it was, that there was still that little voice...

 - *Well, the wrist might not give out and you were a British title contender before you had to give it up...*

Shut up. Don't be stupid. I might have had the skills, but these guys are hardened streetfighters.

 - *So are you. You're a killer. There could be money in it. That two and a half grand won't last forever.*

Time to step on the voice and walk away. There's no future in this. And there could be a weight difference to contend with. Hillier might put in someone bigger and heavier than me and tell everyone it was to help even up the skills mismatch. I'd seen that happen before. I'd even seen a big man and a bantamweight matched up with bets not on who was going to win, but on how many rounds the little guy would stay on his feet. So however much you think you're at a loose end, however much you recognise the wish to be in the ring again, use your head. You got out in one piece. Your brain still works. You don't and can't trust either Pete or Hillier. So leave it.

And then I started to get it. Even if this had come up in conversation, as Pete had said, Hillier would've come to me. And he hadn't, so Pete really must have gone straight in there and pitched it to him, told him he could deliver me to fight and then asked him for some cash up front. Hillier probably wouldn't give him money, but he might give him a job around the place to keep him around. Or would he? Would Hillier want a user working in his club? Or maybe Pete had just pitched for the job to keep himself around the place there while he set me up for the fight. Perhaps he hadn't actually talked to Hillier about it yet. I gave up. It didn't matter. I wasn't fighting, not for Pete, not for Hillier, not for anyone.

The phone rang and I answered it. Illegal of course, while I was driving, but then I was working on everything else, I couldn't be completely clean. Mick, being his usual talkative self.

"Problem, get here soon as."

I was going to say I'd be straight round, but he'd hung up already. One day I'm going to get an expert in to convince Mick that his phone isn't bugged, but it probably wouldn't be worth it. He'd only think the guy had been bribed. On the way to Mick's flat I ran through the things that I could work at. I was sure I could get some driving work, couriering, or even cabbing if I had to. I knew I wasn't cut out to be in field sales and I couldn't see myself working in a shop, but maybe I could get into an office somewhere, do some admin work, maybe into a council job somewhere. I had a fairly logical mind and it would be a start. The prospect didn't exactly fill me with joy, but I wouldn't be getting calls like this from Mick and wondering what I was going to find myself involved with next. I ran over the kinds of problem that Mick might be talking about. Allingway had his money. Hillier was happy with the job he passed to Mick and Mick wouldn't know about Pete's hair-brained idea, so I didn't have a clue what might be up.

When Mick pressed the outer entry buzzer of the block for me, the dog was already waiting in the doorway of the flat inside. I gave him my hand to smell, as ever with my fingers closed and pushed past him inside. Mick wasn't stretched out on the sofa in his usual pose, but sitting up with papers all around him.

"Okay, Mick," I said, "where's the fire?"

"Briscoe's house," he answered. "He's dead."

That stopped me short.

"Killed by the fire, or killed before the fire?"

"You catch on quick, Garron, you always have. It seems like he was beaten to death and then the place was torched. Not a nice thing to do in a terraced road, the whole row could have gone up."

I sat down and tried to work it through. I was sorry Briscoe had died, but not anything more than that. He'd chosen his road and it had caught up with him.

"Mick, I left his cover intact, I never mentioned him and there was no trail to him."

Mick shook his head. "I'm not worried about Briscoe, I'm worried about you. If someone beat him up before they set his place alight, then what did he say about you?"

"Nothing. He had nothing to say. He didn't see my face. He thought I was Old Bill checking up on his story again, until I got in and as far as I know he still thought that I was police when I left. Just police that was interested in the set-up." I ran it through again in my head while Mick waited, realising what I was doing. "No, there's nothing, nothing for anyone to follow up."

He stood up. "All right, but I had to check. I didn't ask for details on how you got the money back and I don't want them, but I needed to check there was no way for anyone to connect you."

"Mick, how do you get all this information? I know I shouldn't ask you, but when things happen, you get to know about them."

"No, you shouldn't ask, but since you have, I'll remind you that I'm a fence. Unlike you, who think of yourself as one of the good guys, which is at the least debatable, I don't have any such illusions. I'm a criminal. I buy and sell things, goods, services, such as yours in the past and I've no doubt again in the future and sometimes information. I also cut people in when I sell things and they get to trust me. If they give me information and I use it, I'll pass something on to them. Occasionally, I'll pay out to someone even when I haven't used the information, keeps the sense of trust going. Since I'm trustworthy, people volunteer information to me. End of explanation and don't ask me again."

I took the hint and filed it away. Some things were off limits and that was the first time I'd ever heard Mick talk about what he did in any detail.

"You've got to remember something, Garron," he went on. "This is a murder investigation. People have died, at the game and also now separately, but connected. The police aren't going to let this go. They'll have statements from Briscoe, maybe from others who were at the game. It looks like they haven't got to Allingway, otherwise there's a possibility they might have tracked back to me."

I noticed he didn't say 'me and you'. Reminding me that he would have kept me out of it.

"Now, I'm careful and I've got cut-outs between me and the people who want my services, but the possibility is always there and the police will keep digging at it. Briscoe's been killed, probably by your man who had the cash, or by the partner. Question is, what happens now and is there anything we need to do about it?"

I thought about it for while. I didn't rate Lewis with the brains to connect my visit with Briscoe, but Gavin may have thought of it. And if Gavin had wanted information out of Briscoe, he would have been the one to go and see him. It was possible he hadn't wanted to kill him, but things had gone too far, or it was possible that Gavin was a sick bastard and happy to close off any loose ends. If he'd thought Briscoe had led someone to Lewis, then maybe he'd thought that Briscoe could lead someone to him. Which begged another question; had Gavin done anything to Lewis? Was he another loose end? Mick was asking something.

"Did Lewis know who you were?"

"Not by name, only that I was at the game. He recognised that."

"So his partner will know that."

"If Lewis admitted that he knew me, which he might not have done."

"Why not?"

"Embarrassment, fear, shame. He could have told this Gavin bloke that he was jumped by five gorillas with tyre irons."

Mick worked that one over for a moment.

"And," I said, thinking it through, "even if he did tell Gavin that he recognised me, there's no trail back to you. At the most it would be back to Allingway, who's in the States."

"Okay, you've got a point, but keep your head down for a while. Not so much from Gavin, as from the police."

"All right, Mick, but I haven't done anything that they would be looking at."

Mick shook his head almost pityingly.

"There you go again, thinking you're one of the good guys. Assault, GBH, threatening behaviour, threats with menace, theft of the money, material witness at the game. Not much, eh?"

"That's not what they're looking for though."

"Garron, whenever there's a police enquiry, there's all sorts of extra stuff that they dig up that's related, but not primary. They don't just forget about it. It all comes out."

I shut up and thought about that for a bit. It always gets so bloody complicated. I take a job, nothing illegal in the job itself, but it goes wrong and then I'm caught with things just getting out of hand. I'd been here before, but this one I could have walked away from. Maybe I really should have left the money with them, not gone after it. What was that about? Pride? Ego? Reputation? Dress it up as justice? Justice for who? I'd kept the excess money and it hadn't bothered me at all. My due for getting the cash back, I'd thought. It was lost to the owners anyway. And now it was getting bigger and out of hand. Someone else had died. Maybe Briscoe would have died anyway, maybe Gavin would have felt the police were getting too close and that Briscoe was a danger, but I had got in there first and perhaps speeded that up. I'd been worried before about the fact that I'd scared an old man, but maybe I'd killed him too.

"You're not thinking of going after the money from this Gavin, then?"

"No," I said, "I was leaving it."

"It's the right thing to do, leave it alone." He paused for a moment, then said, "you got anything lined up now?"

"No, but I've got enough cash left from Lewis' stash. I'm okay on that."

Mick sat down again on the sofa and then lay back on it, a sure sign we were coming to the end of the business talk.

"Garron, you didn't do anything wrong here, I mean in the way you did things, not what you did. So don't torture yourself about it. There weren't any mistakes, it just sometimes happens like this. Keep your head down, just like you want to and you'll be all right."

"Yeah, just like Briscoe was all right."

"Different. He was a victim, you're not."

"No, I'm the opposite, aren't I?"

He looked sideways at me.

"You want to sit here and moralise about this?"

"No," I said, standing up, "I want to go home."

*

I started seriously looking for jobs. Problem was, of course, I wasn't qualified to do much, so I was limited to the general vacancies section. I answered an ad in the Evening Standard for a stores operator. I wasn't entirely sure what sort of store I would be operating, but I assumed it was a warehouse job. I didn't even know what sort of company it was for and it certainly wasn't the best job in the paper, but I had to face the fact that I wasn't a very good salesman and I wasn't going to be in the running for managing a hotel, cooking in a bistro, or even servicing hoovers. An ad for a software developer confused me, since I didn't know my SQL from MySQL and I thought C# was the note between C and D. I couldn't see myself answering the ad for working in the fashion industry and all that was left was telesales. So stores operator it had to be.

The interview was to be in an office in West London above a curry house. I waited in a small reception room with a tired looking girl who in between typing up letters at twenty words a minute, told me that Mr. Barton was very busy, really very busy and I was really lucky to get to see him today. Since I'd made the appointment with him, I didn't think that luck had much to do with it, but Jenny had warned me that sarcasm should not be on the agenda at job interviews, so I shut up and smiled instead. I wore my suit and I had even bought a new dark blue tie. I didn't really see the point in this, as the ad stated there was a uniform for the successful applicant, but again, Jenny had said this was the done thing, so I did it. I was there early, but Mr. Barton kept me waiting twenty minutes. He then strode out of his office, no jacket, shirt sleeves held up with those metal arm bands that I've never understood the use for and asked me if I resented being made to wait. It was a long time since I'd been to an interview and I had no idea if this was part of the process or not. Truth was, I didn't mind, as there was nowhere else I had to be, but at the same time I thought it was a little unfair to keep someone waiting that long, so I said so.

"But I was on a call," he said, "an important business call."

I wondered if there were ever any unimportant business calls for this guy, but I didn't go that far.

"In that case," I said, "you could always apologise for keeping me waiting. It doesn't even have to be sincere, just polite."

He looked me up and down and then told me he didn't think I'd suit his organisation and strode back into his office. I hadn't even got into the interviewing room.

I looked at the receptionist and started to ask her something, but she cut in.

"Well, Mr. Barton is a very busy man. Really, *very* busy."

She looked almost apologetically at me, but didn't say anything else. I wondered how many times she'd had to tell people just how busy Mr. Barton was. I had a vague thought of kicking his door in and telling him what a jerk he was, but there wasn't much future in it. He'd only call the police after I'd gone and he had my name and mobile number, so that was the last thing I wanted. Instead, I nodded to the girl and walked out with as much dignity as I had left. I still didn't know what the company did.

*

Mick called and said that Adam Hillier had been in contact with him, wanting to know if he was interested in a side bet on the fight.

"I played dumb, mate, said I hadn't seen you for a while." There was a pause and then when I didn't fill it, he carried on. "You want to tell me about this?"

"Nothing to tell."

"You're not jerking Adam Hillier around, are you?"

"Nope, someone else is though." I thought for a moment. "You want to do me a favour?"

"Not if it gets me involved."

"No, just get back to him for me and tell him, I didn't know what you were talking about, that as far as I'm concerned our business together was concluded and everyone went away happy. Will you do that for me?"

"Yeah, I'll call him, but that's as far as it goes. He's not a lightweight, Garron, don't mess about with him."

"Mick, that's exactly what I'm trying not to do."

*

Next, I answered an ad in the local paper for a vending operator. I had no idea what a vending operator was, but I thought it must be one of those guys who install and then refill the chocolate machines on the underground, or in pubs and clubs. At least this time I would know what the company's business was.

This interview was to be in a shoddy office above a dry cleaners in Tufnell Park. This time I did actually make it into the interview room and even sat down. Mr. Chopri was wildly enthusiastic about vending machines, asking me if I was familiar with Westomatic and Zanussi and a couple of other makes and quite disappointed when I said I wasn't. He seemed quite upset that I might have to start as a Junior Service Engineer rather than a full Service Engineer, given that I was 'getting on a bit to be a junior', but was convinced that I would soon get my City and Guilds to become a Qualified Vending Engineer. I'd worked out by now that I'd have to service the machines and not just refill them, but that was okay with me. The trouble started when he asked me about my previous employment. I told him about the sales repping that I'd done, but that since then I'd not been employed. I had my P45 from the repping company, but he was more interested in the fact that it had been a long time since I'd worked.

"Well, Mr Chopri, I have been doing a bit of part time work, collecting some rents and doing some security work. But

I've not been signed on or anything while I've been doing that," I added quickly.

"Security work," he said, "and before that I see you were a professional boxer. So tell me, Mr. Garron, if someone approached you and demanded the money while you were emptying a machine, what would you do?"

I thought about this for a moment and said:

"Whack him one and make a citizen's arrest."

"No, no, no!" he shouted, getting up out of his chair. "That is not correct at all. The correct thing to do is to give him the money and make a note of all the details, then call the police and we report it to the insurance company. This is an occupational hazard and every now and then we need to make our insurance payments worthwhile."

I thought his reaction to me getting the wrong answer was a bit over the top, but I said I understood, although I wasn't sure I did. He'd already moved on to another question.

"So, if some kid grabs a chocolate bar and tries to run when you're working on the machine, what do you do?"

"Let him go, take note of the time, place and description and report it," I said confidently.

"Rubbish," he shouted. "You clip him round the ear and take the bar back. You think we and the insurance company are going to do all the paperwork for one bar of chocolate? You have to think on your feet here!"

And there I was, thinking that I was quite good at that.

I got the feeling that he kind of lost interest after that and I left with the promise that he would be in touch if they wanted to take it further. I wasn't going to hold my breath.

I began to understand how dispiriting this could be. I was lucky. I had a couple of grand to spare and no-one depending on me. But I wasn't sure what was worse; not being offered the jobs, or thinking that I might have to work for one of these idiots.

*

Voicemail:

"Garron, it's Tony. Need to know if you've seen Pete at all. He said he was doing something with you and he hasn't been around for a few days now and that's not usual. If you've seen him, let me know. Cheers."

*

Tried an admin job at a business school. The advert said they were looking for someone who they would train up, which was good, since I didn't know what would be involved. It also said it would suit a school leaver, which didn't sound so good. Mind you, I had left school, just early and a long time ago. This place was really smart and set in the docklands, which is a cruddy area with some really up to date offices built in it. The technological centre of London apparently. I wore the suit again and this time it nearly blended in. The guy taking the interview was at least ten years younger than me, very polite and was fascinated by the fact that I'd been a fighter. He genuinely seemed to want to give me the job, but he did point out that I wasn't computer literate and I hadn't been through an education college, so I wouldn't really know what the students' problems were.

"You see," he said, "there's a bit of guidance work here and it's easier if the administrator has some experience of the student life."

"What," I said, "you mean beer, relationships, gigs and having a laugh? I'm probably qualified on most of those."

He did laugh, but it wasn't going to work.

"I know that's the image, but there is a bit more to it than that. Or at least we need to make everyone believe there is. I'm sorry, Mr. Garron, but there will be other candidates with better experience for the job and I'm not sure if you might not intimidate one or two of our students if they find out who you were."

He suddenly must have realised what he'd said, because he flushed a bit and added: "are, I mean. Who you are, not who you were."

I looked steadily at him and then got up. It wasn't his fault and he was right. It would be nice to work in a bright clean office like this, but it wasn't going to happen.

"Thank you for your time," I said and turned to go.

"You could always enrol as a student," he called after me, "that might be a way to get a better job."

I looked back at him. "You may be right, but I don't know that I could do that. I'm not sure I have the time, or the money, or the inclination to do that. Besides, I might intimidate the teachers."

"Think about it," he said.

So I said I would.

*

"How come you never use your first name then, it's not that bad?"

We were sitting on the little sofa in Jenny's bedsit, Billie Holliday in the background and the local paper open at the job section on my knees. I looked round at her.

"It's the information age," she said, smiling, "I looked you up in the boxing records, remember?"

"Yeah, I remember," I replied. "Truth is, I haven't got anything against the name, it's just that no-one ever used it."

She looked the question at me, so I carried on.

"I didn't exactly grow up with parental care and everyone called me by my last name. It stuck."

"You could use it now, though."

I shrugged. "Wouldn't feel right. It's like..." I struggled to think of a way of explaining it, "...it's like some people with their middle name. No-one uses it, so it becomes just a label. It doesn't mean anything. I had that with my first name, that's all. No-one ever used it, not even on the rare occasions I was at school, so I got no...I don't know, no...ownership of it. It's just a word. Doesn't relate to me."

There was quiet and then she said, "You know, that's really sad."

I hadn't thought about it like that at all.

"Not really. It is what it is. There's no point in worrying about it."

I circled a couple of possibles in the 'general' section and when I looked up at her, I thought for a moment that her eyes were wet, but it could have been a trick of the light, because her voice was steady as she said:

"That's worse than mine, I suppose, although I always thought my name was a bit duff."

"Nothing wrong with Jenny," I replied, "it's a good name." I smiled at her. "I like it anyway."

"It's okay, but I only got it because my mother had been reading a story where this nutty girl jumps off a roof."

"All right," I said, closing up the paper. "So you're named after a heroine in a book. Is that so bad?"

"No, I'm named after a psychotic, suicidal addict in a two and a half page short story. Not quite the same thing and nothing to brag about."

She got up and went over to one of the stacks of books, pulled out a blue paperback and brought it over to me.

"Here, you can read it. There's a bookmark at the right place," she said, showing me.

I glanced at the title, '*Listen*' and noted the fact that the bookmark was a child's drawing of a toy bear, cut round almost to the bear's shape and covered with protective plastic. I opened my mouth to say that I didn't read much and then I shut it again. There was a determined tone in her voice, almost a challenge. If you thought about it, keeping the page marked and all was a little over the top, but for whatever reason, this was important to her. Her mother had committed suicide, her sister had been an addict. Apart from that one time and a couple of minor comments, she hadn't talked about her family at all. Maybe this was a link, a way for her to look back in a manner that she could deal with.

I took the book from her. It was another step.

*

Tony called. "You better get round here."

"Problem?"

"Not for me, mate, but maybe for you."

"I'll be there."

On the way to the car lot, I thought about what Tony had said. And what he hadn't said. There was no mention of an emergency and if someone had been there with him who was a problem, he'd have put something into the conversation that didn't fit. Called me 'Mr. Garron' or given me the address, something like that. So whatever it was, it wasn't trouble in the next ten minutes.

The car lot's on a corner site and I drove past once, just to clock anyone who maybe shouldn't have been there, but it was clear. I parked up and walked through to the hut. Inside Tony was standing over Pete. Pete was a mess. His face was bruised up badly and there was a stitched cut above his left eye and another below his right eye. It hadn't just happened though, the bruising was a few days old.

"Couple of ribs as well, Pete?"

"How did you guess?" he said, without moving his mouth too much.

"Usual way of things. Bad but not terminal. They want you to remember the kicking even when you're not in front of a mirror."

"He says it's - " Tony started to explain, but I cut him off.

"It's my fault, right? If this was Hillier, then it's my fault. That's what he says." I was talking to Tony, but looking at Pete. I didn't feel anything. Years ago, I'd have been burning, a mate beaten up, what were we going to do about it and when. Retribution. Revenge dressed up as justice. But I didn't feel any of that now and I didn't know whether that was because of me, because I'd changed, or because this was Pete. Lying, stealing, set-you-up, Pete.

I sat down and sighed. This wasn't my fault, although in the back of my mind I'd known that when I'd asked Mick to pass on to Hillier that I didn't know anything about the fight, it could rebound on Pete. If I was honest, I'd thought this would be a way out of it. Blame Pete. Forget the fight.

"Where've you been hiding out the last couple of days?" I asked Pete.

"I haven't been hiding anywhere," he said. "I'm renting a room from this girl at the club and they know exactly where I am. I don't have to run from this. I've still got a job there."

Tony shook his head.

"So this is what?" he asked. "In lieu of wages, or did you put your hand in the till?"

"This, Tony," I said, "is because Pete told Hillier he could deliver me to fight his boy in an unlicensed bout. And he didn't ask me first and I said no."

Pete sat up a bit straighter. "You told him you didn't know anything about it, you bastard. And he believed you."

"Yeah," I said, "I did."

"Ah, shite," Tony said. "So you're playing silly buggers as well. And now he's been hurt and where do we - sorry, you two - go from here?"

Pete looked at me. "He says he's told some high flyers about it. He's got some bruiser, not been beaten in two or three years or so and they're queuing up to see the two of you."

"I'm not fighting, Pete. I'm not fighting in some circus for rich guys to bet on whether I can lift my head up after three minutes."

"You did it before," Tony put in.

I rounded on him. "That was professional, that was my job, don't put it down, Tony. This is unlicensed. I'm not physically up to it, I don't want to lose whatever credibility I might still have in the game and I'm not some gangster's wind-up toy. I've seen these fights, you haven't. Do you want to come and pick up the pieces if I screw it up?"

He looked down and then back at me. "Yeah, okay, I was out of line. But are you going to leave it like this? Do you think Hillier will leave things as they are?"

"I don't know what he's going to do. But I'm asking you now, in front of Pete, am I supposed to put my head on the block for someone who I haven't seen in years, who turns up, sponges off you, steals my possessions and sets me up for a kicking without even telling me? Would you do it, Tony? Would you?"

There was quiet for a moment and then he said:

"Put it like that and no, I wouldn't. But then you don't have to put it like that. You maybe don't owe him anything for now and he's been stupid and you're right he stole your stuff, but we go a long way back together and I can't help him with this sort of thing, but you can. I can give him somewhere to crash out and I can give him a small stake and if he snorts it up his nose or he jabs it in a vein, that's up to him, but I can't help him with people like Hillier. But you can. This is what you can do. Work a way out of this. And maybe not because you owe him anything, but just because you can."

124

"That's not a very compelling argument for getting myself beaten to a pulp."

"Well, maybe then because you owe something to us. To the three of us and to the others. To all of the things we used to be to each other, not what we've grown into. Maybe you should help him just because he has screwed up and he can't help himself."

"You want me to get myself involved with a known hard nut and definitely hurt, so that you can feel better about it?"

"I didn't say take the fight, Garron, I said work something out."

And with that he walked out of the office and slammed the door behind him. Tony's a fairly unemotional man. This was the equivalent of a normal person smashing all the windows in his house and burning it to the ground.

I moved some papers to one side and sat on the edge of the desk.

"Pete," I said quietly, "I can't fight now. I was a professional, I can't start in on unlicensed fights. There's no way for me to win. Even if I win the fight, it's not going to help me. All that it would do is put my name out there again and that's the last thing I want. There'd be no point to it and it could even hurt me. I couldn't carry on fighting, even if I wanted to, I'm not physically up to it, even four-rounders. My wrist probably wouldn't take it and I'm not doing any real stamina training."

"I thought you'd be pleased. I thought it would get you some money in."

"No, Pete, you thought I wouldn't do it if you asked, but I might if it was all set up."

He didn't say anything and when I looked, he had his head in his hands staring at the floor. I thought about him, I thought about what Tony had said, about what we and a few others had meant to each other all those years ago. We'd been more than just friends. We'd looked out for one another. On the estates where we'd lived you had to have someone watch your back and there'd been a group of us who had done that for each other. Not a gang, we didn't have 'gangs', but some good people, most of whom were just memories now, hardly even images. But Pete wasn't a memory. I didn't want to go down this road, but maybe Tony was right. Maybe I should simply because I could. Because this was more my sort of thing, even if I didn't know why it was.

"Let me have a think about it," I said, "maybe there's something I can do for Hillier that'll get him off your back. Have you got somewhere you can go until I've spoken to him?"

"I'm not going anywhere. I've got somewhere to live and I'm staying there."

"Pete, he could have someone do this again to you any-time."

"I like where I am. The girl I'm renting off, the one who works at the club, I like her as well and I'm not running off. If I do, he might send someone round there and push her around, or even come here to Tony. I can't have that."

I looked at him almost in disbelief. "You're close to sounding responsible, mate, what's happened?"

He didn't answer straight away and then, still looking at the floor, he did.

"I've let a lot of people down, Garron, not just you with your stuff, but a lot of people over the last few years. I'm not being stupid about this, I can't just stop taking the drugs and I don't want to, but I can start to try to do things better. Maybe in time this girl will help, maybe not, but I've got a job, of sorts and a place to live and I don't want to run this time. I've been in trouble with people in the past and before you say it, I know Adam Hillier is a bit bigger than most of them, but I want to see this out."

I almost felt sorry for him. Or maybe what I felt wasn't that, but in fact was something for the friendship we once had. I reminded myself just how angry I'd been with him before, but then I thought I was being unfair. I'd been given the chance to turn things around. Pete deserved the same chance.

"You got a mobile now?"

"Yes."

I keyed the number into my phone and I remembered that he had mine already.

"Okay, sit tight and check in with Tony in a couple of days. He'll let you know if I've come up with anything, or I'll call you direct, but don't call me unless you have to." I didn't want anyone else knowing he was in touch with me or picking up my number off his phone.

He looked up. "I appreciate this, Garron, I really do. I know you think I'm a pain in the arse and I am, but I want you to know I appreciate you doing this."

"I haven't done anything yet, mate, save it for when I do. If I do."

I didn't know what I could think of that would help, but somehow I felt better for saying that I'd try.

*

"So let me get this straight. You don't want to fight, this Pete guy stole your things and you're going to put yourself into trouble in order to help him."

It wasn't a question, so I didn't answer. Jenny was standing in my kitchen area cooking up some pasta dish. Lots of herbs and spices and chicken pieces as well. The kitchen wasn't used to it and neither was I. Even the cat was interested, sitting outside the doorway to the kitchen far enough away to run if he had to, but near enough to see and smell what was going on. If you ignored the missing bits of ear, the scarring and the mean attitude you could almost imagine him as being domesticated. Come to think of it, the same sentence could apply to me as well.

"I think you're daft. You could just walk away from it now and there would be an end to it. That's what you said you wanted."

She dropped a small piece of chicken, swore once and flicked it with her foot towards the cat. It landed this side of the doorway though and he wouldn't be drawn in.

"Dopey animal, what do you think we're going to do to you? Leave it if you like then, I'm not picking things up off the floor for you." I pushed myself off the worktop where I'd been leaning, bent down and picked up the piece of chicken.

"He can't help himself," I said. "He works in a particular way. He can no more wander into range of us, than you or me can change the way that we do some things, like maybe the way we talk or the way we think."

I walked into the main room, the cat skedaddling away from me. I dropped the meat into his bowl in the corner and moved back to the kitchen. He was on it before I was back there.

No grateful glance, no mew of thanks, just accepting it as his due. A few seconds later, he was back at his post outside the open doorway.

"Scavenger," I said.

This time he did react to my tone, a little sneer as his mouth curled up for a second from his teeth.

"What's it called," I asked Jenny, "when you give human characteristics to an animal?"

"Don't know," she replied. "Drain the pasta please and tell me why you have to help this man."

"It's not something I can really explain. It goes right back to when we were kids growing up."

"Long time ago," she said, stirring the sauce.

"Yeah," I agreed, "a long time ago." I poured the drained pasta out of the sieve back into the pan.

"I think you're doing this for you, not for him."

I got a sudden chill. I'd heard those words before, or something like them. But that was a different girl, a different time.

Jenny scraped the last bit of sauce out of the pan and mixed it in with the pasta. "You all right?" she asked, "you've stopped moving."

"I was just waiting to hear what you were going to say next."

"Oh. Well, I was just going to say that I'm happier if you're going into this because it's something you think that you ought to do, rather than because you feel like you owe something to somebody. I mean I'm not happy that you're getting into stuff with this Hillier, but it's your call." She stopped and turned from the electric hob to face me. "I meant what I said,

Garron, I'm not one of these people who change too much as they go along. I'm not someone who says 'do this', 'don't do that'. This is your business, you understand it. Just don't get hurt." She smiled. "Or if that's too difficult, then at least try not getting hurt too much."

I don't know what it cost her to say that, but it meant something to me. I was thinking of what to reply, when she steamrollered that with a demand for the plates and cutlery. We didn't carry on the serious talk until we were sitting down eating what I have to say was a fantastic chicken pasta dish. The cat had retreated to his corner.

"One day," she said, "you're going to walk in here and he'll be sitting on my knee, purring."

"Anyone would be purring, sitting on your knee," I said and got a half laugh for it. "But," I went on, "I don't think you'll get anywhere with this cat, whether you feed him, or give him toys and a basket. He's too far gone."

"We'll see."

"I doubt it, but good luck to you. The iodine and the plasters are in the bathroom."

We ate in silence for a while and then she said: "I've been thinking about what you said, about needing to give Hillier something in return for getting out of the fight and getting your mate out of trouble."

"Go on."

"It's got to be something that's got enough money or prestige about it and something that he can't do unless you give it to him. Otherwise it's not a trade."

"Yep, you're getting the hang of it."

"Don't be sarcastic, I'm trying to help here."

"Sorry, it's tough to take someone seriously when they have pasta sauce on the end of their nose."

She wiped it off and carried on talking. "So, you haven't got anything that Hillier would be interested in? No information, instead of money, no knowledge of his business you could use against him?"

I sat back, opened a can of Strongbow and looked out of the window at the fading light. The thought came that it would be really nice if we were just discussing where to go the next day, or even what was on telly that night. But we weren't. We were discussing dealing with a very dangerous person with several tough men around him who expected me to take part in an unlicensed fight against an even tougher man. And in spite of all that I was quite relaxed. Maybe I still hadn't worked out the dead streak from my head. Or maybe I just liked being here with Jenny, more than I worried about the future.

"Are you listening to me? You look like you're miles away."

"Mmm, yes, I was just enjoying the moment."

"Which one?"

"The one where I'm sitting in my flat with my beautiful girlfriend, eating amazing food, with the sun going down in London and the sounds of Camden filtering in from outside."

She shook her head. "Given your circumstances, I don't know if that's the dumbest sentence I've ever heard or the nicest thing anyone's ever said to me."

We looked at each other stupidly for a moment.

"You going to answer my question about Hillier?"

"Yes, but it kind of brings reality back into it. Even if I had anything I could use against Hillier, I wouldn't. I'm not a blackmailer and he's not the sort of person that would stand for it."

"I'm not talking about blackmail," she broke in, "just forcing some kind of truce."

"A stand-off? Possibly, but I don't think so. He's more likely to have me killed for it. That would be his response. If I've read him right, he couldn't have someone do that to him. A trade he might do. That would be a case of giving something for getting something, but not a stand-off. Trouble is, I don't have anything to trade."

"What about Mick? Would he have any information that he could let you use. Something that would help Hillier, not threaten him?"

I turned and lobbed a couple of pieces of the chicken into the cat's bowl. One missed, but landed on the mat underneath the bowl and the cat was onto them before I'd turned back.

"Possibly, but you can never tell with Mick what he uses his information for." She looked the question at me. "What I mean is," I went on, "he wouldn't refuse me something that would help unless maybe he'd promised it elsewhere already. Then he wouldn't go back on that."

"Even to help you?"

"That's his code. He wouldn't expect me to ask him to do anything like that and I wouldn't."

She got up and took the plates back into the kitchen.

"Am I going to meet Mick sometime?" she called.

"Yeah, I'll take you to the pub he goes to, maybe at the weekend."

"Not to his flat?"

132

"No," I said, thinking about the dog and Mick's attitude, "it wouldn't be personal, but he wouldn't want to meet you at his flat."

She came back into the room. "You have strange friends," she said.

"And not many of them," I added. "I'm sorry, it's the world I live in."

"The world you're trying to move away from," she said quietly.

"But first there's Hillier and Pete."

"And what you're going to do about them."

"There you go," I said, "reality butting in again."

She came over and sat down on my knee.

"No," she said, "this is reality. You and me."

And for a while I thought she was right.

*

Again! The bastard won't let me be! Off the mattress and standing up in the dark, sweat on the skin, break this, break this, break thi -

Break it.

Jenny stirring now, I didn't think that I'd made a sound, but she leaned herself up on one elbow and asked me what it was, what was wrong. I couldn't answer for a while, something still running round in my head, heart rate still up, breathe, breathe easy...

" - you were better with this."

Didn't catch what she said, asked her to repeat it.

"I said, I thought you were getting better with this, sleeping better."

"I was."

"What?"

I hadn't said it out loud.

"I was better, I've been better with it. I don't know why it happened again tonight."

"Do you want to tell me about it this time?"

I was pacing now, standing still wasn't helping to bring me down, the adrenaline needed somewhere to go.

"I don't need to talk about it. I'm not a 'talk about it' person."

She sat up. "I know that, but wanting and needing don't have to be the same thing."

Somehow Jenny always seemed to have the right word, the right phrase to bring me back. I carried on walking, but slower now.

"I'm not putting anyone down if they need to open up, if they need to talk through something with someone else, it just isn't for me. I don't get any release, any help from that. What I need is to work things out in my own head. And if something's bugging me, I need to work out why. Break it down into pieces until I can figure out why it is that it's doing this to me. No-one else can do it for me, it's got to come from me. "

"But it's not working with this?"

"No, I think it is, it's just that there are some things that you don't get past, you just learn to live with."

"I know" she said quietly, "they don't go away, you just kind of adjust your mind to fit around them. If you don't, you go crazy."

"That's it. That's it exactly. You control how you think about them when you're going through your life, the day to day things, at least for most of the time, but when you're asleep you can't. That's when whatever's buzzing around can get loose without you being able to push it back into the box."

She lay back down again, pulling the duvet up and staring up at the ceiling. "But you've been better recently, been sleeping better. Do you think it's because of the Hillier thing? Do you think that's making this surface, whatever it is?"

I walked back to the mattress and sat down. "No," I said, "I just think it takes time. Things don't go away, they become easier to deal with, or to live with. Bad things become absorbed into your way of living, they're still there, but your head learns to deal with them better."

"But it doesn't happen overnight."

"No, it hangs around in the background where you've put it and then sometimes when you're not concentrating it comes out. Then you shove it back again for a while, maybe a bit further this time." I looked down at her. "I don't talk about things, not because I don't trust you, but because I just don't talk about things. It's how I am. I was always taught that the fewer people knew the bad stuff, the safer you were and that's - "

"It's okay, I understand."

"Yes, I think you do, but maybe you should know this."

She didn't say anything. Then: "Do you think it would make a difference?"

"I don't know. Maybe that's what I need to find out."

She sat up now and faced me. The faint light from the street-lamps in the service road behind the block was enough to see her face by and she was faintly smiling.

"You don't realise, do you?" she said. "You don't realise that it doesn't matter. Whatever it is, you haven't hurt me, you haven't betrayed my trust and I don't think you would. So what are you going to tell me?"

I took a deep breath and stepped off the edge.

"I killed a man. In fact I killed two men, but one is sort of okay in my mind because it was in a fight, him or me, but the other one wasn't. And however much I try to justify it, I know I was looking for it and that sets me off, because I don't know how I got to there."

She didn't flinch. She didn't move. She didn't change her expression. She just put her hand up and touched my face gently.

"Maybe, I should be worrying then."

"What? I wouldn't - "

"No, I mean because it doesn't bother me, because I don't look at you and see a killer, I see you. You wouldn't do something unless you thought it was right. You wouldn't hurt someone for no reason, or because you wanted their money, or their car, or their property."

"That's a dangerous thing to believe. My judgement might be wrong, I might do something because I'm angry, or upset, or jealous, or - "

"Except you're not like that. I know you well enough by now to know that."

I looked at her hard. Maybe this was what love was. Unconditional. Unquestioning. Terrifying.

"You can't be sure," I said, "you can't be sure of that."

"Sure enough for me," she said.

*

The thought came to me the following morning and I was going to run it past Mick to get his view and then I thought better of it. He'd told me it was my decision to go for it if I wanted to. Mick would lose his fee, but the truth was that if I could get Hillier to buy into it, I might get him off my back, keep clear of trouble and close several things off at once. I didn't want to get involved with the police or with any more of the money from the spiel, but if I could get Hillier interested in the 30 or 40K that this Gavin might have left, then I could maybe trade that information for Pete's neck.

I phoned Hillier from a call box and got one of his lads. Given that there was no back-chat, no comments at all and he put me straight through, he must have been in the same room as his boss. Question was how to play this, but I needn't have bothered with the thought. This man wasn't used to being played and waded straight in.

"You going to fight, or what?"

This was a different Hillier, blunt, harsh and to the point. He no longer needed my help, he no longer felt he owed me. Instead, he felt he owned me.

"No, I'm not going to fight," I said evenly.

"You're old mate's not going to like that."

"My old mate is exactly that; an old mate, who I haven't seen for years and owe nothing to. If it comes to it, I'll stand back and watch you break his bones."

There was a brief pause while he considered that. "That could be true, you might be cold enough for that, or it could be load of bullshit. He's made me a promise and I've gone out and put the word in a few of the big punters' ears. If this doesn't come off, then I'm going to lose face here."

And that was what it was all about again - face. Hillier had spread the word, he now had to deliver. It made my offering less likely to please. But it was all I had.

"I can't fight, Mr. Hillier and you know that. You probably knew that as soon as Pete came out with this crap idea. You'll have checked up. You'll know about my hand, you'll know I'm not in training and you'll know I can't fight unlicensed and have any hope of doing any training, or of having any connection with the legitimate game again. So what do you have? A junkie with a story that he can deliver me and you're pinning the chance of this happening on my old friendship with someone who isn't even the same person anymore. Not going to happen."

"It's going to look bad, Garron, I'm going to have to blame someone."

"Well, you can blame me if you want, but I'm not so easy, am I? To do that you'd have to pressure Mick to find me and he wouldn't just give me up, so it would be more than pressure and no-one's quite sure what Mick's connections are these days."

This was dangerous ground, telling someone like Hillier what he could and couldn't do. I hoped the call wasn't on a speakerphone where other people could hear it and he might feel he had to save face again.

After a while he hedged, not backing away, but acknowledging the point. "Well, that Shapiro bastard's dead, so it's not him anymore."

Yes, Al was dead, but Al hadn't been Mick's protection, just his friend. Then again, if you were Al's friend, people left you alone, so I didn't comment. Al had been my friend too and was good enough that he might even have been able to get me out of this situation with Hillier. But he'd been dead a good year and a half now and I had to rely on myself. On the other hand, it was the first time I'd seen Hillier hesitate and I noted it, even if it had been Al that had forced it rather than me. I carried on with the pitch.

"So you blame Pete and he ends up in a ditch somewhere and you go back to your high rollers and tell them there's been an unfortunate error, the man setting up the fight couldn't deliver, but he's now out of the picture and you're on to the next thing. Well, I can't stop that and I won't try too hard." Now was the tricky bit, shifting tack without making him think I would actually fight to save Pete. Which I wouldn't. "Do I care what happens to Pete? Yes. Do I care enough to fight? No. So, Mr Hillier, I had a think about whether I had anything that I was prepared to trade for him, something that wouldn't hurt me as much as your fight, but would interest you enough to give him a break."

"And you think you've found something, do you?"

"Don't know. That's up to you."

Silence. Then:

"Your buddy, Mick. His local. Tonight. Eight 'o' clock. One chance to convince me."

He rang off.

*

I had some time, so I called Jenny's landline. Someone else answered and sounded so pissed at having to go get her that I wasn't sure he would. I didn't explain that I was the guy who collected the rent. He might not have bothered at all then.

After an age, she came on the line.

"I read the story," I told her.

She didn't say anything.

"I'm not so sure she was a psychotic suicide," I went on, "she could have been a victim. She could in fact have been murdered."

After a while she replied. "Depends on how you read it."

"How you read it," I countered, "depends on what you bring to it yourself."

"Good point," she said, sounding satisfied, "but a little scary."

"From whose perspective? Yours or mine?"

"Touché."

*

This wasn't going to be easy, I thought, as I headed to Mick's local that night. I wanted to be there early and I wanted to drop in on Mick and tell him to stay away. Hillier was no fool. He'd not even bothered arguing about where to meet. He'd known I wouldn't want to go anywhere near his club and he was showing me that he could go anywhere, even to what he considered would be home ground for me and it didn't bother him. The implication was clear. I couldn't hurt him. He might bring some muscle with him, probably would, men like Hillier thrived on their image, but there'd be no trouble. Adam Hillier didn't get into pub brawls.

Mick's local was fairly innocuous. You could see in through the windows and there was enough light to see people inside. Any non-local walking in off the street wouldn't have any problems, provided they drank up and didn't bother the regulars. You had to look closely at some of the faces to realise that you'd been clocked as you came in and that there were people here you wouldn't want to cross.

After the quick stop off at Mick's flat, I got to the pub a good half an hour early. That was okay. I was a known face here and I could sit in on a conversation if I chose to. This time I didn't. I could have a game of pool, that was something I could be doing without implying that I was friendly with the people I was talking to, but other than that I wasn't going to give Hillier any other points of contact that I might know. The pool table was busy, so I settled into a seat in a corner facing the door with the evening paper. I was still scanning the job sections, but I knew that until this was over, I wouldn't be applying for anything.

Great set of news items. Something on the latest Big Brother z-list celebrity, a film star divorcing her fourth husband, the funding for an NHS hospital being 'redistributed' somewhere else, a shooting in Iraq and another suicide bomber in Tel Aviv. So far this year, there had been car bombs in London and Scotland, but as yet no-body had killed anyone in the mid-section of a London bendy bus with a full size military flame-thrower. It couldn't be long in coming though.

Property pages. Loads of them, full of London flats and houses that nobody could afford, unless you were a city broker spending your million-plus bonus, or a foreign bank buying accommodation for your staff. I was lucky, I didn't pay for my flat in cash, just in work collecting the rents, but how anybody managed to buy anything was beyond me. I was comparing the salaries offered on the job pages with the amounts you'd have to borrow to buy any of the properties on the housing pages, when Hillier walked in. He had two of his 'lads' with him and they'd entered first. To his credit, Hillier came in and walked straight up to the bar. He wasn't theatrical or anything like that, didn't pose in the doorway and look around, but all the same, you knew someone had arrived. So did the barman, but that was his job. Hillier ordered a drink and two for his employees. I doubted if they would be drinking, but he was playing by the rules. He was in someone else's yard and he'd buy a drink with all the rest of the punters.

I waited until he'd had his first gulp and started to look around and when his gaze passed to my corner, acknowledged his look. He walked over and sat down opposite me. His two minders stayed at the bar. If there'd been a table closer I'm sure they would have taken it, but as it was, they were close enough. There was background music, but not the kind you had to shout over, so in volume at least, the conversation was quite civilised. The subject matter of course, was not.

He took out a worn gunmetal lighter and lit a cigarette. Blew the smoke out of the side of his mouth. There was no small talk, that wasn't why we were there.

"All right, Garron, what do you have?"

"There was a card game in West London a while ago. Someone held it up and walked off with something in the region of a hundred thousand. Rumour has it that some of that was recovered, maybe thirty to forty thousand. Given some discreet spending, there's probably 40 to 45K left. I think I can give you a link to it."

He sat still for a minute blowing smoke out. I found myself in that detached state again, wondering, but not worrying,

142

about which way he would go. I hoped he might have too much class to start any kind of discussion on this. Question was, if he turned it down, would I have any comeback that would help Pete. Or would I just think, hey, I tried, I failed. Tough shit.

"The point is," he said, sitting back on his seat, "from a purely financial point of view, 40K is not really enough to make up for the fight. It's kind of borderline. By the time I've taken entrance fees, either at a big place or for a select few punters at a higher rate, then taken the house percentage on the betting, then laid a few bets myself, I could make that and a lot more."

"If you win the bets."

"Oh, I usually win my bets."

He paused again and I let the silence grow. It's an old police interrogation technique. Leave a gap in the conversation and too many people feel they have to fill it. Usually they fill it with information they'd rather not have given out, or an idea that doesn't help them, or something that the other party can use, just for the sake of filling that gap. I just kept quiet and after a while he continued.

"It's also fair to say that if it's the game I heard about, then there was a man killed, which means the police are going to be looking at it pretty hard. I can do without getting involved in that."

He was still thinking, so I stayed silent.

"No, sorry, Garron, it's not worth it to me. The police would love to have me mixed up in something that they can get their teeth into and this is too well known. It's not worth the risk to me."

It was slipping away. I said:

"Forty thousand, Mr. Hillier, sitting with a guy who has no support, nowhere to hide it and if he loses it, he's got no-one to tell. You're not tempted?"

"Tempted, yes. But not enough to risk stepping into someone else's mess. I think that's more your game. What I do is create my own situations and control them, not step into other people's." He shifted slightly on the chair and took another swallow of his beer.

"Good stuff, this American beer," he said. I didn't answer, I wasn't so keen on it myself.

"I can't take the risk," he said, "too much unknown." He held up a hand as I started to speak. "No, don't tell me anything, I don't want to know. If I'd been in this from the beginning I might be interested in taking it on, but now I'm not."

He sat back and looked at me. I had nothing else to offer. I'd thought he would go for this, I'd give him Lewis and the note with Gavin's address and he'd have a couple of his lads take it from there. Forty thousand, minimal effort. But as usual, I was guilty of projecting onto someone what I thought I would do in his position, instead of actually knowing how the other guy would see it. Hillier sat forwards again.

"Tell you what," he said. "You came to me looking for a deal, but this is not my sort of thing. Like I said, I like being in from the beginning, I like being in control. This is more your kind of game, you know, think on your feet, react to the situation, so I'll tell you what I'll do. I'll let your mate off responsibility for this fight, if you follow your deal through yourself and deliver me the forty thousand." He smiled a big false smile at me. Or maybe it wasn't false, I think he was enjoying himself now. "I'll even be fair. You can keep anything you find over the forty thousand, well, up to say five grand anyway. How's that? Fair deal?"

He leaned right forwards over the table and his voice suddenly became hard.

"Your mate dropped you in this, Garron and I don't envy you for that. He's a stupid bastard. But you think you can put me into God knows what and then walk away? I don't know you at all, Garron, not past some fence vouching for you and you clearing something up for me. You could be anything from an informer to a one-man disaster area and there's no way I'm going to get myself into anything dodgy on your say so." He sat back again. "You think about our new deal, Garron and when you're ready, you call me to tell me. But make it inside the next day, or I'll take your mate's stupidity out on him and I'll add a little something extra for your stunt here as well."

He got up. "You want to play with the big boys, Garron, you've got to learn to think like them." He turned and walked out, not even looking at his minders. He didn't need to. He knew they would be where they were supposed to be.

I sat there for a minute.

I'd been here before. Sure that I'd covered all the angles and realising too late that I didn't think like these guys. I could make that into a virtue, but right now it just left me feeling stupid and out of my depth. I had been going to get out of this life and now I was right back in it. Either I left Pete to his fate, which is what I'd intended to do not so long ago and somehow found myself moving away from, or I had to find the spiel money whilst the man who had it was killing people and the police were looking for him. I wasn't sure what to do next. Years ago I'd have gone to Al, but he was dead now, so I could go home and talk to Jenny, which would be nice but might not get me to the right answer, or I could go to Mick and run it past him. Or I could sit here and try to work it out myself. My state of detachment was long gone and I'd done about as much thinking as I could on this. All it had done was land me in even more trouble. I went to see Mick. I was in such a hurry, I nearly didn't finish my drink.

Nearly.

*

Mick wasn't too impressed.

"You stupid shite-head! Of all the people to pull an angle on, you have to pick Adam Hillier. And for what? For a burnt out ex-musician junkie."

"Who used to be a friend of mine," I said. He had a point, but I had to say something.

"If he was any friend of yours, he wouldn't have got you into this. And before you say anything else, I know who Pete is, I know you grew up together, but at some point anyone can forfeit the right to friendship and he's hit that point."

I was sitting in an armchair facing him. For once the TV was off, but otherwise everything was as it always was. Mick and his flat and his ways never changed. He was on the sofa, sitting this time, not sprawled out and the dog was in the doorway of the lounge blocking the way, just in case I was someone who decided to leave when his food supplier didn't want me to.

Mick ran his hand through his hair (how come he wasn't going grey and I was, even though he had nearly ten years on me) and spoke again.

146

"What does your new girlfriend think about all this, or haven't you told her you could be dead or beaten to a pulp in the next few days?"

"She kind of trusts me to work it out for myself."

"Then what are you doing here asking me for advice?"

"I thought," I said as sarcastically as I could, "I'd benefit from the vast experience at your disposal. If Al was still alive, I'd have asked him and not you."

"Al would be just as pissed with you as I am."

"But what would he do?"

"He wouldn't have got himself into this in the first place!" Mick exploded. "It's just stupid. You said you wanted to get out of this way of living and now you're becoming Adam Hillier's arm's length operative."

He stood up and the dog, alert to his movements, raised his head and watched as he paced a bit. "Al would have left Pete to whatever would happen to him. He would say that he'd brought it on himself and he'd give him the nod to run like hell, but he wouldn't take on Hillier for Pete."

"No," I said slowly, "you're right, he wouldn't have done it for Pete, but he would have done it for me, wouldn't he? Or for you?"

He didn't answer.

"So what we're saying," I went on, "is that it's the old rule. There's some people you stick your neck out for and there's some that you don't. How many people would you go to the wire for, Mick?"

He looked down at me.

"Careful, son," he said, "dangerous ground. I've kept you safe more often than you know about and some of the time, when you act stupid, I'm not even sure why."

I let that go. It was probably true and it was no good antagonising Mick, just because I was pissed off with myself.

"Yeah, I'm sorry, Mick, I was out of line. I'm not sure what to do and I'm starting to feel it."

"Oh, I think you know what you're going to do and I think I know why. I've told you the sensible thing to do and I don't believe that Pete is that good a mate of yours now to be one of those people that you'd 'go to the wire' for. But I think you will. I think you'll go looking for this Gavin and the money, because it's a challenge. No, more than that, because it gives you the chance to stick two fingers up at Hillier and show him that you can deal with whatever he throws at you. I've seen this in you before. Never mind what Al would have done, for some reason you want to do more, you're trying to prove something somehow. I don't know who to. Maybe to Hillier, maybe to yourself, maybe to Al even."

He sat down again and the dog relaxed and rested its head back on its paws. I thought about what he said. I'd had the same thought myself once, about proving things and I still didn't know whether there was anything to it. Or I didn't want to admit there was anything to it.

"I don't think so, Mick, I - "

"You can't even see it, Garron. You're a typical ex-pug, trying to find something to fill his time. And when you find something you can do, you're not happy with it. You want out of the life; I'm telling you you'll be back in it within three months."

"Won't happen, Mick, if I can sort this out, I can - "

He broke in again:

"You don't get it, do you? You won't be able to control what happens. You thought you were going to sell Hillier a way out of this for you and Pete and he squashed you. You can't compete, except at a brute force level and with Hillier you can't do that either, because he has too much hired muscle. You're out of your depth."

There was a silence and I stood up. There was too much tension running in me now to sit still, but I noted that the dog stood up with me, still blocking the doorway. Mick threw it a hand signal and he settled down again.

"All right, Mick, you may be right. And maybe Pete isn't as good a mate to me as you or I was to Al, so maybe I shouldn't put myself on the line for him. Maybe I won't," I finished off, half to myself.

"Think about it, just think what you could lose, by doing this. You don't owe Pete anything. He tried to set you up, for Christ's sake."

"I know, Mick, I know, but I made it worse for him by trying to get him out of it."

"That's just Hillier talking. He was putting pressure on you. Pete was dog food before you went to him with this scheme."

Dog food. What Mick didn't understand was that strange feeling I'd had when Tony had been telling me that I should help Pete. Nobody should be dog food.

- *Careful, Garron, people are chewed up and spat out every day.*

- But not people I know, people who mean, or at least meant something to me.

- Think about Tony, or Mick, or Jenny. If they were in trouble, you wouldn't think twice, but you're thinking more than twice about Pete. Admit that you're not doing this for him and it'll all be much easier.

- Except that I'd have to admit there's another reason and maybe Mick is right and -

" - to do what you're going to do."

Mick's voice broke in and drowned out the conversation I was having with myself. I hadn't done that zoning out and talking to myself thing in quite a while and I didn't like it happening again. I suddenly wanted to get out of the flat, to get out somewhere where I could just do what I was going to do. Which was pretty much what Mick had seemed to be saying to me. He was looking at me again with a cross between a concerned and an exasperated look.

"You're right, Mick," I said, "I'm stupid. I don't know what I'm going to do, but I appreciate that I can come here and get a bollocking from you. Someone's got to be able to tell me when I'm being a jerk."

He almost smiled at me.

"Piss off, you idiot," he said and gave the dog the signal to let me out. He followed me to the front door. "But piss off carefully," he added, as he closed it behind me.

*

I went after Lewis early the next morning. I didn't know if he worked or not, but I wanted to be there in time if he did. Going for him was a risk, but a calculated one. I had no idea whether there was anything to connect Lewis with Briscoe's death, anything that would have put the police on to him, but I didn't think so. Whatever had happened would have been down to Gavin, not Lewis, especially the state Lewis had been in with his leg. It felt a little strange thinking of them by their first names, almost like friends, but that was how it had to be. I couldn't keep referring to them as Donald Duck One and Donald Duck Two.

My call with Hillier had been brief. I just told him I would get the money and like he'd agreed, anything over forty thousand would be mine. I'd only thrown that in for a bit of bravado, a gesture to the thought that I was doing this for my own financial purposes, but I wasn't fooling him or myself. He wanted an update in a week. If I hadn't finished this in a week, I wouldn't be finishing it at all, so that was fine.

The question with Lewis, was whether to get to him inside his bedsit, or when he came out of his building. I needed to know two things from him. Had he told his partner in crime what had happened to him and if he had, was Gavin aware now that I knew where he lived? It would be easier to talk to him when he came out of his home, but not if I then had to damage or subdue him. If he got away from me, I wouldn't be able to find him easily if he didn't go back to his room and even he wouldn't be that thick.

As it happened the decision was taken for me. I was parking up near to where Lewis lived when he walked out of the building turned left and walked straight past my car. I couldn't front him now, I'd wanted to do that right outside his house, backing him against the door. But I could find out where he was going and whether there was a better place. He was walking with a limp still and he had some kind of protective shield over his nose and plastered to his face. He didn't notice me and I parked up. Checked the residents' parking times and settled in to follow him at about thirty yards. Tailing someone on your own isn't too easy, especially if your mark would recognise you, but I didn't have too many choices here. The main factor would be whether Lewis was expecting to be followed and whether he was going anywhere suspect, or simply following his daily routine. He stopped into a newsagent's and came out with a packet of cigarettes and a red top newspaper. I couldn't see which one from where I was. Was this just a trip to get a paper, or was he on his way somewhere? He carried on, so either he actually held down a job, or he was an early starter for a meeting somewhere else. It would be too much to hope he was going to meet Gavin, but you never knew. A few minutes later, Lewis reached a bus stop and waited. If there hadn't have been an early morning crowd I would have been in trouble here, but there were fifteen or so people waiting, so I just hung back until the bus arrived and then boarded next to last, five or six passengers after Lewis. He went upstairs and I squeezed myself to the back of the bus downstairs, where I could see when he got off. Oh, for the old Routemasters where you could jump on and off almost at will. All of the new buses have proper driver operated doors, much safer I'm sure, but not so good for tailing people. I'd have to make sure he didn't nip out at the last minute at a stop.

Lewis didn't reappear from upstairs for about twenty minutes, by which time I had cramp in one leg from avoiding standing on various people's toes and I also knew all about the grandchildren, nieces, nephews and associated friends and enemies of the two elderly ladies sitting to one side of me. Then, at a stop, he suddenly seemed to shoot out of the bus last in line and I had a choice, to risk being right behind him, or to lose him.

I followed quickly almost bumping into the back of him in the rush to get off the bus before the doors closed and as I stepped onto the pavement, I turned immediately and walked away, not sure even if he was following me, or if he was going the other way. I walked fifty yards or so, past a couple of small streets and turned into the first shop I could, a greengrocer's and looked back out. No-one there. I stepped back out again, ignoring the shopkeeper's questions as to what I wanted and looked back down the road. Not there. I walked back up towards the bus stop, past the two small side turnings. The second was a cul-de-sac and there were a couple of work units at the far end. Lewis was standing outside one of them with his back to me talking with another man. I walked on and walked back again two minutes later. Both men were gone. They hadn't come out of the turning, so either this was where Lewis worked, or he had some business here. I walked part way down the road until I could see the office front, calling itself 'C&H Engineering' and a passageway that led behind the office maybe to a workshop at the back. I wondered what sort of engineering they did. C&H sounded like central heating, but that would have been too easy and there was no Corgi registered sign. There was, though, a phone number on the signage above the office and I made a mental note of it and walked away. After twenty minutes, I finally found a phone box. There used to be dozens of them, public service and all that, but now there seem to be far fewer, the advent of mobiles I suppose. Again, great for most people, but not so good if you don't want your number coming up on a network trace. The other annoying thing about public phones, is that where you can find one, the odds are it won't be working. On my second try I got lucky and called C&H's number, asked for Lewis.

"Hang on a minute," a man's voice said, "he's only just come in. I'll get him for you. Is it business or personal?"

I told him personal and not to worry if he wasn't to hand, I'd call him later and hung up. So now I had a work place, if not a pattern for Lewis. If I needed to, there were now two places I could pick him up. Question was, how best to get him alone. If I blew it I might not get another chance.

The obvious place was his bedsit again. I thought about whether to go back to my flat and get the gun. I didn't like carrying it around unless I needed to. But this time I might need it. Not so much for Lewis, who probably wouldn't want to have his nose broken again, but maybe for Gavin. The problem with carrying a gun is you tend to rely on it and that restricts your thinking. It's too easy to just 'pull the gun'. And you should never point a gun unless you're prepared to use it. I couldn't threaten Lewis with a gun unless, in the end, I was prepared to shoot him with it. Which I didn't think I should have to do to get what I wanted.

His mate though would be a different proposition. Although I'd not seen his face, he'd been perfectly calm during the robbery at the card game and he'd been the one to pull the trigger on the shotgun, blowing a man's chest into fragments without a moment's hesitation. Odds were that he'd killed Briscoe as well and even if Lewis didn't hang on to his gun, I was willing to bet that Gavin had. So I trekked back to my flat and took my Smith and Wesson 686 out of the top cupboard in the kitchen where I kept it loaded with a full speedloader next to it behind the cereal boxes. Yeah, I know, but without digging a hole in the floor which might go into the shop underneath for all I knew, there was really nowhere to try to hide it and if anyone serious came looking, they'd be better at looking than I was at hiding the damn thing. I worked on the principle that nobody knew I was in the flat and that hopefully, I'd get out of the place if anyone did. As yet, I hadn't used the gun for anything and Castle, who'd supplied it to me, had told me it was clean, but if I ever did use it, I'd ditch it straight away and get another one. Of course, since I was getting out of this whole way of life, I could ditch it anyway. But not until I'd faced the shotgun thief.

*

I decided to take the easy option and sit in my car outside Lewis' flat until he came home. He didn't do that until well after the pubs closed at eleven 'o' clock. It could have been worse. With the new open all hours rule, he could have been there all night. There was a certain sense of déjà vu as I saw him round the corner weaving slightly and I waited until he'd passed the car before getting out and following him up the steps to his front door. This time though, he was a little more drunk and was having trouble with his door key. I offered to help and he seemed quite pleased until he looked up and saw who it was. There was a moment of confusion on his face and then his eyes widened in recognition and he tried to push me away and run. I hit him a short left into his ribs, not very hard, but what I thought would be enough to stop him moving. I must have misunderstood how drunk he was, because he dropped to his knees, gagged a couple of times and then threw up on the steps. I only just got out of the way in time. I didn't think he was in a position to fight, but I didn't want him to try in case he got puke all over me, so I grabbed his hair from the front and pulled him forwards on his knees. Not much, just enough for him to be off balance. With my other hand I unlocked the door.

"We're going inside now, see? If we meet anyone, I'm helping you in 'cos you've had a few too many. I'm sure it won't be the first time that's been seen here."

He couldn't nod as I had his head, but I reckoned he'd understood. If someone's hurt and you want them to move, you've got to keep the pressure on and keep them focussed on what you want them to do, 'keep walking,' 'keep moving' and so on, so I told him to get up and kept on at him. 'Walk in', 'through the door', 'keep moving', all short commands, but constant. I let go of his hair as we entered, that would take a bit of explaining if we bumped into anybody, but I was happier to do that once we were inside the house. I took hold of his arm instead, staying a little behind and to the side of him. It wasn't in any way a restricting hold, but I'd get a moment's notice if he started to move for me and in any case I thought he was still recovering from the punch. There may have been a psychological thing going on as well, because it was almost as though he accepted that he couldn't fight against me, that I had this hold over him. I'm sure it would have been different if he'd had a shotgun in his hand, but unarmed, he was a beaten man.

We stopped outside his door and he physically slumped against the wall.

"What do you want?" he said.

"When we're inside," I replied. "Not out here where walls have ears."

I motioned for him to go in ahead of me and I followed.

156

"Need a drink," he said.

"It's your place, you know where everything is."

But I stayed close to him, didn't know if he'd got scared since I'd last been here and got any kind of weapon into the place.

He poured himself some water from the kitchen tap and turned to face me. The glass could be used as a weapon, but in his current state he wasn't up to that kind of thought process. I was glad he was drinking though, the smell of vomit was still on him.

"One question, Lewis, did you tell Gavin what I did to you?"

He didn't answer.

I sighed a little theatrically and said: "Lewis, you know I'm prepared to hurt you to get what I need, so why go through all this? If I tap you lightly on your nose, that protective plastic will break and they'll be doing reconstructive surgery on you. And, it'll hurt like hell. So just answer me, did you tell Gavin what happened?"

He nodded.

"Did you let him know you'd given me his address?"

He shook his head this time, but I didn't know whether to believe him.

"Call him now, tell him you need to talk to him, you've seen me hanging around your work today and you need to talk to him."

"He won't go for it."

"Don't give him a choice. Say you're coming round and hang up. Where's your phone?"

"You took it, you bastard, last time you were here."

"Oh yeah, you're right, well here's 20p, we'll go use the phone box in the hall. I think I'll come with you though, don't want any mixed messages."

He didn't want to call, but he did. I noted the number he dialled and I was close enough to hear most of both sides of what was said. Then I told him he was coming with me, which he also didn't want to do, but he was beaten by now and we both knew it.

*

We drove there in silence. I wasn't inclined to talk and Lewis was far more concerned with the cable ties that were digging in his wrists and ankles. I'd been generous and secured his hands in front of him, but if you sit someone in a car next to you while you're driving, you give him the opportunity to crash both of you if he wants to, so I used another tie and secured his wrists to the handle above the passenger side window. I didn't want him swinging around at all. It made wearing the seat belt a little tricky, but then he shouldn't have waved a shotgun in my face all that time ago.

Gavin lived with his girlfriend in a tower block near to Shadwell. Given it was nearly midnight when we got there, I assumed that she'd be around, but hopefully asleep. Thing was though, I didn't trust Lewis, or Gavin, or anyone connected to them, so I also assumed this was a complete set-up.

I parked up in what once could have been a decent car park and Lewis complained that I couldn't leave him in the car on his own.

"Well, actually I can," I replied. "Besides which, I don't believe for one moment that Gavin and his girlfriend are in flat 1406. I reckon you gave me the wrong flat number, but probably only by one or two numbers. Then you could tell Gavin what had happened but also tell him that you didn't give him away. You see, I think you're stupid, but I credit you with some sense of self-preservation at least. So I also reckon that Gavin said, 'if that bastard comes round again, then give me a bell and tell me'. What do you say, Lewis?" I leaned into him a bit. "Is that the way it was? Gavin now expecting me is he? Got his girlfriend outside on lookout, has he?"

"You're mad," Lewis said, but it was unconvincing and he didn't say anything else.

I got out of the car and checked the gun in my jacket pocket. It's strange how quickly you get used to carrying a gun. I remembered the first time I'd carried my own gun, only a few months ago. It had been burning a hole in my pocket then and yet now I felt as comfortable with it as I would probably ever be. As I walked across the wasteland that passed for a car park towards the block entry, I reckoned that the fact I was comfortable with the gun might be to do with the surroundings. I wasn't likely to get pulled by the police here at this time of night. If I was in Oxford Street, I might be a little more worried about carrying.

There was a small group of lads off to my right nearer to a second block, but they kept their distance and there was no-one hanging around too close to where I'd parked. Hopefully the sight of someone actually sitting in the car would keep the skells away, but if it didn't, I'd pay Tony for the car out of Gavin's money. A couple of girls were getting out of a taxi by the block entrance, obviously the worse for wear, stumbling a bit and gig-gling. I didn't think either was Gavin's girl. Too much to organise getting the cab, using another girl for cover and she'd have to be a very good actress to pull off a drunk job like this one. But they were useful cover and I followed them in.

What I didn't understand was why I wasn't scared, why I didn't have that tension, the light-headedness, even the adrenaline rush that I should have had. I thought back to Smith and the nerves, no, let's face it, the fear that I'd felt during the time that I'd had to face up to him. None of that was here now. It was just as it had been sitting in Hillier's office, refusing to tell him about the girl that was causing him trouble. I was detached again, feeling nothing. A blank. And as I thought about it, I realised that I'd been like this for a while. The shooting at the spiel; I reacted, but not with fear. The same for the trouble with Hillier's boys, in fact most of the jobs I'd had recently, I couldn't remember feeling scared. Even when Hillier had turned this particular scheme around on me, it hadn't scared me, only removed that sense of detachment for a while and replaced it with a sense of my own stupidity. I tried to generate some emotion, but there was nothing. You might think that would be good, but fear gives you an edge sometimes, as long as it isn't paralysing, doesn't make you freeze. A fear of what can damage you can keep you alive. So here I was now, walking into a closed environment to take on a shotgun robber who almost certainly knew I was coming. And I didn't feel a thing. Not fear, not worry, not adrenaline, not even what I needed, that cold fire burning inside, which might give me an edge. Detached was good, but I'd gone too far and that was dangerous.

But I couldn't manufacture the feeling, so I had a choice. Walk away, which wasn't an option, or carry on and stop worrying about something I couldn't do anything about.

The foyer led into a corridor where the ground floor flats started. Before that, to the right, was the lift, a scratched and graffiti covered stainless steel box. The stairs were next to the lift and as I looked towards them, I saw the door there closing. If it was Gavin there, he couldn't know it was me walking in, unless he recognised me from the card game, weeks ago. I didn't think he could be sure of that and I was partially shielded by the two giggling girls. More likely it was the girlfriend sitting there with a mobile, reporting on anyone who came in.

I followed the girls into the lift. One of them, the taller, slightly steadier one, hit the button for floor eight at the second attempt and said: "Where you going to then?" in a fairly drunk voice. This set the other one off giggling again, so I leaned over and pressed 9. I wanted the fourteenth floor, but I wasn't going to advertise it.

"Cat got your tongue, then?" the tall girl said, "too good to talk to the likes of us?"

The lift was about six foot by three foot, so we were fairly close together and the alcohol fumes when she talked were just about knocking me sideways, but I remembered one of my two lines of French just in time.

"Pardonnez-moi, Mademoiselle, Je ne parle pas l'Anglais"

The shorter girl dissolved into hysterics again, while the taller one stared dumbly at me.

"Bloody foreigners," she said as they got off at the eighth. "I hope you fall down the lift shaft!" she called out as the doors closed and her friend collapsed laughing again. I wasn't quite sure why she hated me, or foreigners in general that much, but having her remember me as a foreign man who didn't understand English would be good.

The lift stopped at 9 and I pressed 12, 13 and 14. I reckoned if I got out on the twelfth floor and the lift stopped at the thirteenth as well, I'd be able to leg it up to the fourteenth before it arrived. Hopefully, Gavin would be standing there expecting me to be in the lift and I'd get the drop on him from the side where the stairs opened onto the hallway. That was the theory. If he wasn't there, then I'd have to think again. I was sure 1406 was the wrong number and I didn't credit Lewis with any intelligence beyond shifting the flat number by one, so I could always knock on a few doors with a gun in my hand. But that would be inviting trouble and witnesses if I picked the wrong one.

Twelve opened and going up the stairs I tried to get a balance between rushing and keeping quiet. That wasn't so easy. The place was quiet and my steps echoed. I hadn't thought of that and it could be literally fatal. I slowed down, I had to and as I got towards the fourteenth floor I could hear the bell on the lift as it arrived and the doors opened. Taking the gun out of my jacket pocket where I'd been holding it as discreetly as I could, I slowly opened the door to the hallway. There was no-one there. I stood still for a moment. The doors on the lift had closed. I walked over to them and stood facing the hallway. What now? I could start banging on doors; 1405 and 1407 were the obvious ones, or I could go back down to the foyer and see whether or not the movement I'd seen by the stairs really had been a lookout. The flats would still be there later, the lookout might not be, although I couldn't understand why there would be someone on guard downstairs and then no-one up here. Unless my friend Gavin was now tipped off and standing with his shotgun behind the door of one of the flats with his eye to the spyhole, waiting for me to walk past. I didn't want to be doing that for the hell of it, so I turned round, pressed the button for the lift and as the doors opened threw myself forwards at him, deflecting the gun to the side as it went off. The sound was ringing in my head and I could see plaster dust everywhere, from the hallway behind me, but I'd been quick enough and he'd missed. He was trying to bring it round to fire again, but I wasn't going to let him do that and a shotgun, even a sawn off, is useless in a close-in fight and unless he stopped thinking of it as a gun and started using it as a club, then it was going to be a waste of his effort.

I'd pushed him against the back of the lift and partway onto the floor with one arm halfway round his neck and the other on the inside of the gun and I was going to finish him in another couple of seconds, because he still had both hands on the gun and didn't want to let go of it. The doors of the lift were trying to close and re-opening when they hit my right leg and I pulled it in because I wanted to use my knee on him and the doors closed on us.

As I scuffed the knee strike, he got the message and he let go of the gun, bringing his left hand around in a series of quick punches to the side of my head, but they were light strikes and it was all right until one of them caught the side of my temple and his ring or something scraped down by the edge of my eye and the blood started to blind me. He wasn't trained, he wasn't strong, but he'd had the advantage of surprise and had fallen into a better position, but then I found my leg between us and got enough purchase to push him away. There wasn't much room in the lift and someone must have called it, because in the split second that we were separated, it started moving downwards and he stood upright and launched himself at me, maybe realising that he was on a time limit now because he'd wanted to shoot me with no-one around and quite obviously there was the possibility that whoever had called the lift might have seen him here before and know who he was. But this was more my type of fight now and as he reached for me, I hit him a hard palm strike with the base of my right hand into his face, grabbed his jacket at the collar with both hands and pulled him round, smashing him back against the wall of the lift and nutting him perfectly, feeling his nose break and then swinging him round into the doors, disorientating him again and going for the knee strike to the groin, missing but landing hard on his leg. The lift was still going, so I pinned him with one hand and hit all the floor buttons that I could reach. The last thing I wanted was to have the doors open where there were other people and have to clear out and leave him. What I wanted, was to get Gavin back into his flat and get the money. He was falling to one side now, so I finished it with an elbow strike, my forearm landing on the side of his face, deliberately not targeting his head, because I wanted him mobile, not unconscious and then I pushed the shotgun away from him with my foot and let him slump. Blood was leaking onto my jacket collar and shirt now and I was blinking it out of my eye. The doors opened. I couldn't see which floor it was, but there was no-one there so I dragged Gavin out and pulled him round to the side, through the door and into the stairway. I reckoned there would be fewer people there at gone midnight. He started to try and push me away again, but there was nothing to it and I shoved him down one flight of stairs for effect and then followed him down.

The gun. I'd left the bloody shotgun in the lift. I held my sleeve against the bleeding next to my eye to try and stop it. It wasn't spurting, but there was enough to drip and it was annoying me. I suddenly remembered my own gun in my jacket pocket and panicked for a moment in case it had been knocked out during the fight, but it was still there and I got Gavin's attention by pointing it at his face, waiting for him to focus on it and then pulling the hammer back.

"Where's the money?"

His face was a mess and he was exhausted, but he was conscious and he knew what I was asking him.

"There's none left."

I said evenly: "Don't play me for a fool, Gavin. I'll spell it out for you. I'm sure, given the shotgun blast, that no-one is out on the fourteenth floor checking on what happened, but I'm equally sure that someone will have called the police. Your gun, with your prints on it, is in the lift where whoever pushed the button will have found it by now." As I spoke I felt that familiar cold edge coming back to me. The cold burning that put me in control. I said to him: "I'll put a bullet through your knee and leave you here for them to find. Then I'll take your flat keys, find the right flat and take most of the money. You'll go down for Briscoe, they'll find the rest of the money and you won't walk properly again."

He was breathing hard now, not just from the physical exertion and the pain, but also because he saw that I would do it.

"There's no money left. I mean it! You can shoot both my fucking legs off, there still won't be any money!"

"He's telling the truth!"

A girl's voice, coming from the stairs below. I looked round and a plumpish, dark-haired girl appeared, struggling up the stairs.

"You bastard!" she shouted as she reached Gavin and knelt down next to him. "What have you done to him?"

"Nothing compared to what he wanted to do to me," I replied. "Where did the money go?"

"I'm not going to tell you anything about - "

She stopped when I knelt down next to her and put the gun against Gavin's right knee.

"We used it," he said quickly.

"What?" I said. "All of it? How much was there? Fifty? Sixty thousand?"

"Yes, all of it, fifty-six thousand pounds and there's none left."

I looked at them, the pain in his face, the defiance in hers.

"I don't believe you. It's too much for you to spend in this amount of time and still be here in this place." I took aim at his right knee again.

"It's true," the girl shouted, "we used it as a deposit on a house out in the countryside."

That brought me up short. I couldn't keep the surprise out of my voice.

"You put it down as a deposit on a house?"

"Yeah," Gavin said, "what's so strange about that?"

I stood up and lowered the gun. It was too stupid not to be true.

"You just went into an estate agent and got a mortgage and put fifty-six thousand down as a deposit in your own names."

"Yeah, that's it. I can show you, in the flat. I've got the agreement and everything."

I shook my head. "It's so dumb, I almost believe you without checking, but I have to check. It's too much to leave to some street punk's word."

"You'll have to help me up," he said.

"No, you'll stay here. She can take me."

"I'm not having you take her anywhere, without - "

He was trying to get up, so I kicked him in the face and he started bleeding again. The girl screamed and I waited 'till she had quietened down and then I spoke to her, ignoring Gavin.

"Listen to me. Look at me and listen to me, because we haven't got much time. Someone's found your boyfriend's gun by now and that will go to the police. They'll tie it into a dead man and you'll never get to enjoy your country cottage. You've got to get him out of here, or get him safely into the flat and I won't let you do either until you've shown me proof. So you come with me now and maybe you can get him out before the police arrive with vans, dogs, armed response and the fifth light infantry."

She didn't move.

"It's that or I shoot him in the leg and he goes to jail, those are the choices."

She looked at Gavin lying back on the floor. "Stay here and don't try to move," she said to him, "I'll be a couple of minutes."

She ran up the stairs and I followed her. Gavin wasn't going to be moving very far and he was unarmed now. I wasn't sure what floor we were on, but we reached the fourteenth after a few flights and I stuck the gun back into its loop in my pocket as I followed her through the doors, past the lift towards their flat. The wall opposite the lift was a mess where the shotgun blast had struck and I had a brief vision of what it would have done to me. There was no-one about, but the clock was ticking. The girl went to number 1407 and opened it up. I was right behind her, not giving her time to reach for any possible second weapon they might have stashed. She went into a living room and moved towards a table.

"Hold it," I said. "Sit right down there in the middle of the floor. Don't touch anything, don't reach for anything."

"But it's right on the table there."

"And I'll get it," I said.

And there it was. A bloody lawyer's letter confirming them as owners of this property in the middle of nowhere and confirming receipt of fifty thousand pounds cash, etc.

"Where's the other six," I said.

"What?"

"Don't be stupid, girl. This letter says fifty thousand, so where's the other six?"

She started stammering a bit. "We used, I mean, we need to have - "

"You don't need anything any more than anyone else. Now where's the other six?"

For a moment she didn't say anything and I thought I'd have to remind her what the situation was, but then she said it was under the bed and I pushed her in front of me into the bedroom and shoved the bed to one side and found a shoebox with notes in it.

"How much is there?"

"I don't know," she said, "four thousand maybe."

I didn't believe she didn't know, she looked like the type to know down to the last note, but it looked like enough to be whatever they had left, so I tucked the box under my arm and started out of the flat.

"You can't just take it," she said, "that's for us to start out again."

I didn't bother to answer and after a quick check of the corridor, I headed back to the stairs and started down at a quick jog. As I passed Gavin on what I now found was the tenth floor, he said:

"Is she all right? What did you do to her?"

I didn't answer him either, just carried on down and as he saw the shoe box, he shouted 'Bastard' after me and I wondered if he'd work out that he needed to be quiet for a while.

On the second floor I covered the blood by my eye with one hand and cut across the corridor at a purposeful, but not hurried walk and went through the fire escape door to the outside metal steps. There was no-one about yet, although I could hear sirens away in the distance. They might be coming here, or they could be just passing. I wasn't going to stay to find out. The eye didn't seem to be bleeding anymore, which was good. I didn't want to have to stop off to get it stitched up.

The car was still there and so was Lewis, I opened the boot, chucked in the shoebox and took out a Stanley knife. Lewis flinched when I opened the door on him and he saw the knife, but I just cut the cable tie securing him to the handle above the window and dragged him out of the car.

"You just watch your back, mate," he shouted from the ground. "Gavin and me will be looking for you, we'll never stop looking for you!"

I thought that was a particularly stupid thing to say in his position, so I kicked him in the gut to take his mind off looking at the car number plate, not that that was linked to me at all. They probably wouldn't have the knowledge or the connections to track me, but they had managed to get shotguns, so it paid to be careful. As I drove off, I thought the sirens were getting closer, but I was out. I was a few thousand to the good, but not enough for Hillier. I'd think about that later. Right now, distance from the scene was the thing to concentrate on, so I went home.

*

Back in my flat I cleaned up and washed the scum of the evening's work out of my system. The cut opened up again, but at least I could clean it properly and it wasn't too bad. I stuck a pad on it and a plaster and let it be. There was no point in calling Pete, I had nothing good to tell him and I wasn't sure there was any point in calling Hillier, but at the least I needed to let him know that there wouldn't be any money. Maybe I could work off a debt to that amount for him, but I knew in reality that was a non-starter. I wouldn't work for him and he wouldn't want me to, not close up anyway. Maybe I should call Pete first. If he was still working for Hillier, he'd need to clear out and I should give him a chance to. It was nearly one 'o' clock in the morning and I didn't know whether Pete would be awake, but if not I guessed his mobile would be off, so I dialled his number and he answered quickly.

"Pete," I said, "listen, it didn't work. I had an idea, but now - "

"It's all right, Garron, I'm at the club. Mr. Hillier said to put you on to him if you called me. He's upstairs now."

"Pete, you need to clear out of there! I can't help you now. Once I tell Hillier that I can't deliver what I said, your neck will be on the line again. Don't pass the phone to him, just get out of there."

"Don't worry, Garron, it'll be OK. I'm a good worker for him, he's not going to hurt me now."

The guy was an idiot. A prize ten ton idiot. But before I could argue any more with him, Hillier was on the phone, the rough barrow boy tones still at odds with the quiet voice.

"Did you get it, or not?"

"Not enough." I was thinking fast, but nothing was going to help.

"Whatever you got, bring it here." He paused, then: "No, not here, you're still not flavour of the month here. I've got a pub in East London," he gave me the name, "bring it there tomorrow night about eight. There's a doorway to the side goes up to the first floor. I'll see you there."

"Mr. Hillier, do you think I'm stupid? Do you think I'm going to walk into one of your places of my own free will and think that I'm going to walk out again?"

He sighed. "Garron, I don't think you're stupid, but I don't usually like to knock off too many people, especially in my own establishments. I'm not going to kill you. You tried something that would have benefited me and it didn't work. You don't want to fight and I can't make you, but your mate Pete is a good worker here now and he's a good spotter in the club for drugs that aren't mine. I think I can use you occasionally as well, for some of the more intelligent work I need and I know you won't like that, but you won't have a choice. I'm not going to ask you to do anything that you won't do, but you're going to work for me. How much money is there?"

"About four grand," I said.

"Okay. That's the first payment. We'll discuss the second tomorrow night. If you're worried, bring someone with you, maybe your friend Mick."

I couldn't tell if there was any kind of veiled threat in his words, but he knew I wouldn't drag Mick into anything.

"Just have Pete there and in one piece," I said. "I don't want to work for you at all, unless it's on my terms, but for the chance of working this out, I'll be there."

"I said, Garron, that I wouldn't ask you to do work you wouldn't agree to, don't make me repeat myself. I'm not negotiating, I'm telling."

He hung up and I tried not to think about what was going on. Out of the life! Some bloody chance. But this wasn't going to happen. I'd go to the meet, I'd bail out Pete, listen to Hillier and then I was going to cut out. I didn't need any of this anymore and I didn't need to stand on pride over this. I'd talk to Jenny and we'd decide what we wanted to do. I wasn't scared of Hillier, I knew that and a part of me was even a little surprised by it, but I had the chance of another life now and I wasn't going to blow it, either by taking him on, or by working for him.

*

London.

Bloody London.

You can walk from one road with property worth upwards of half a million sterling and within two streets, you're in a council estate. And they wonder why people reach out and take what isn't theirs. It's wrong, but in some way it's understandable. If you grow up in a place where you've got nothing, confronted by the sight of what seems to be everything, then something's going to give. And once it does, there's no going back, not for most scum. You might as well try to rehabilitate a hyena. When something preys on the weak, or on the outnumbered, or on those unused to violence, they get a taste for it. You think you're going to change human nature? In a few maybe, in a very few. And try too hard and one of the others will slip through the net. And someone else suffers.

Hillier's pub was on the corner of a cruddy street in a cruddy area that bred poverty like bacteria. And the skells were out to pick the bones. I'd driven in, but I didn't park up. Not there. I drove a few roads away, parked just off the biggest street I could find and got the bus back. If I had to get out of the pub quickly, it'd be just as easy to do it on foot than by trying to get into a car and start it up with a bunch of heavies right behind me. The bus stopped a couple of hundred yards from the pub and I walked the rest. Eyes tracked me from doorways and again I wondered if I'd misjudged things, if I should have brought the gun, but I dismissed that thought. Even if it might scare away a couple of the locals from an attempt at a mugging, walking into a meeting with Adam Hillier while carrying a gun, wouldn't get me very far. A posh car drove past me and I should have twigged it then, but though it was out of place, I didn't. There were two of Hillier's bruisers outside the pub and although I didn't recognise either of them, they knew me and directed me to the doorway on the left which led to a flight of steps. I didn't like the smirks on their faces, but now wasn't the time to do anything about it.

It should have been.

At the top of the stairs was a face I had seen before, one of Hillier's lads from Snazz, suited up like there was something going on. I started up the dirty steps past the walls which were shedding their light green paint. The man at the top looked at home here. Maybe pubs like this one were where Snazz's muscle graduated from. Knowing Hillier, there would be other similar places around London. I waited for the snide comment from the man, but he said nothing, just pointed through the door at the top of the stairs. I knew the moment I walked in that I'd been suckered. Question was, how would I get out of it.

The place was a large gym area, with a shabby boxing ring bang in the centre. The ropes were loose and the padding on the ring posts was mostly missing. Around the room were maybe fifty to sixty people, mainly men, but there were a handful of women attached here and there. Behind me I felt, rather than saw, a couple of Hillier's boys block the doorway. For a brief moment I thought of turning and going for them, breaking out, but there was the other one on the stairway and the two outside.

174

Hillier broke off his conversation with a group of men and walked towards me.

"Now," he said, "you're not going to embarrass me in front of all these people, are you?"

It was a warning, but he could stuff it.

"I won't fight," I said. "You can beat Pete to a pulp in front of me, but I won't fight like this."

"Oh, you will," he said, then changing tack, "where's the money?"

I handed over the bag. "Just over four grand," I said.

"Good. It's your purse money. Winner gets three grand. Lose, you still get a thousand. Now, Garron, you know that's bloody good money for a fight."

"Especially as you haven't had to put it up."

"Oh yes, I know that." He took his eyes off me for the first time and looked behind him. "Lot of important people here, Garron, lot of connected people, lot of money changing hands. You're quite a draw. Everyone wants to see if you've still got what it takes against someone that they know can fight." He turned back to me. "And this lad of mine can fight, make no mistake."

I wasn't going to. I'd been at unlicensed fights before and I knew that the best of the fighters weren't pub brawlers, but hard disciplined fighters, many of whom could have been pros if their lives had worked out differently. Sometimes you'd see young kids slugging it out in an unlicensed fight, but the good fighters, the ones that built reps as fighters not just as hard men in their local areas, they were the ones blessed with natural movement, natural power and if they trained, fitness as well. As a professional, I would have expected to take an unlicensed fighter over a six or ten rounder, on stamina and speed as well as skill, but I was nearly three years out of the game and although the skills were still there, the stamina and maybe to a slightly lesser extent the speed, were gone. I could still punch above my weight, but only if my wrist held out. It was all academic anyway. I wasn't going to fight.

"I hope you haven't spent these people's entry money yet, 'cos you'll have to pay it back."

"Don't be an idiot, Garron, don't you think I know you don't want to fight? Don't you think I'll have covered that?"

And that was the problem. Hillier knew I'd say no, but he wasn't worried by that. He took my arm as thought to guide me forwards and I shook his hand off. I don't like people touching me, even when they're not as dangerous as Hillier. He didn't put his hand on me again, but he said:

"Easy, son, I just want to introduce you to a couple of your old fans."

I followed him further into the room and people moved aside to let us nearer the ring. Everyone was looking at me and I didn't like it. It was as though they were all in on the joke, but I hadn't worked it out yet. Then I saw Pete standing by the ringside.

"What's he doing here?"

"You've got to have a second, Garron, someone to pick up the pieces, someone in your corner that you can trust."

He didn't quite laugh as he said this, but it must have been close. I stopped walking.

"All right, Hillier," I dropped the 'Mister' and I could see he didn't like it, but I was fed up now. "You want me to talk to someone before I go, I can do that. Who is it?"

"Ah," he said, "I lied. I just wanted to get you further in and get Billy here behind you."

I turned round to see Billy. He wasn't a young man anymore, he was probably pushing forty hard and he wasn't that tall, maybe an inch more than me, but he had a neck like an ox and shoulders to go with it. This wasn't some young kid I could take lightly. His stance, the way he held himself, all said he knew what he was about. He smiled at me. Not an arrogant, or a threatening smile, just a smile.

"All right there, Mr. Garron," he said in a quiet voice. "Saw you fight a couple of times at York Hall. Couple of good wins as well. Never thought I'd have the chance at you though."

For a second I nearly turned away, but then I thought better of it. Billy was genuine, irrespective of what his boss was.

"Billy," I said softly, "I'm not fighting today. I haven't fought in nearly three years. It's not my game anymore."

"Yeah, I know, but Mr. Hillier calls the shots, don't he. He says fight and we fight."

Hillier broke in: "And that is what I do say, Garron, I say the fight is on."

I looked around. All these people expecting something from me that I couldn't deliver.

"Forget it," I told him. "I know that if I walk out of here, you'll have your boys take me apart, but it'll be the wrong sort of fight for your punters and you won't get your money from them. All bets would be off as well. So maybe I'll take that option. Painful, but it stuffs you up."

"Yes," he said, "I thought of that one. You see I've explained to the people here that you're not a willing participant in the night's events. I've told them there are two possibilities. One is you glove up and get in the ring for the real thing, rules and everything and the other is that you try to leave and Billy will be trying to stop you. You simply won't be able to leave unless you get through him. That makes it a free for all, a real unlicensed scrap, where only one person ends up standing. Could be a much quicker fight of course, but the bets stand either way."

He stepped back and motioned for everyone else nearby to do the same. There was a collective intake of breath from the crowd.

"Your call, Garron, glove up, or take Billy as he is. He's your way out. The door's behind him. Or should I say through him."

I looked at Billy and he shrugged back at me. He had maybe two and a half stone on me and while a little of that may have been excess, most wasn't. He was wearing jogging bottoms and a sweatshirt, his balance looked good and he wasn't hyping himself up in any way. He looked like what he was; a hard man who knew how to fight. If I went through with this, there was every possibility that I'd lose.

I kept my eyes on Billy, while I spoke to Hillier. Not that I thought Billy would go for me, but it was the right place to be looking, show him that he didn't scare me.

"Suppose I just don't fight, Hillier, suppose I just stand here and don't fight?"

"Well, in that case, Garron, I would lose my money, but you would lose much more."

There was no pretence at hiding the threat, the people here wouldn't be worrying about that. They'd come to see a fight and if I didn't produce, they wouldn't care what happened to me.

"Your boys take me outside, would they?"

"I wouldn't even ask them to go outside."

"Lot of witnesses," I said in a louder voice.

"No, Garron, there are no witnesses here. None at all."

That was the end. I had no other arguments and the crowd were pressing forwards, waiting for the move I would have to make. I looked at Billy and made a fast feint with my shoulders as though I was going to go past him. He didn't flinch or step back at all, but snapped into a stance, not a complete boxer's stance, but not a martial arts stance either. The nearest thing I'd seen to it was maybe Jieishudan, or Jeet Kune Do, either of which, if he was good at it, wouldn't be a lot of fun to take on.

I relaxed and smiled at him and he didn't smile back. He wasn't sure if I was kidding him and going to try something on the back of the smile. False sense of security and all that. When I didn't, he relaxed again and realized what I'd been doing. Sounding him out. Seeing how jumpy, how reactive he was. He grinned at me then.

"Nice move, Mr. Garron, but did it help you?"

"It helps, Billy," I said. "It helps me to know that you're not a mug."

The crowd had drawn closer when I'd moved and I had to make up my mind what I was going to do. I knew Hillier wasn't bluffing. If I just refused to fight he'd have his lads stamp me into the ground and I'd be letting them do it. I might have the satisfaction of ruining his fight night, but I'd be in no state to enjoy it. If I survived at all. I thought about that for a moment. How far did my sense of detachment go? Did it extend to giving up and allowing myself to be beaten to a pulp, or worse? It would be an interesting experience, not to fight back for once...

I snapped out of it. It wasn't the pain that would stop me doing that, although no-one wants to be hurt, but I could damage Hillier in better ways than stopping his show by lying down. Also, I owed it to Jenny not to arrive back in a body bag, or to not even arrive back at all. That was strange, having to consider someone else in the equation, but not bad, I thought to myself, not bad.

I looked round at the group of sick watchers. Were they any worse than the people who went to the legitimate fights? What did they want to see, a boxing match, or a free-for-all? More to the point, what would suit me better?

Too much thinking, not enough decision making. Hillier was giving me time, but that wouldn't last forever. Billy was a tough nut, no question and I wasn't sure that with his weight and power advantage I would be able to take him out in the ring. When I was fit and in training, without a damaged wrist and hand, I would have done. No doubt about it, at least that's what I told myself. I'd had the professional's speed and fitness levels and a good degree of skill as well. But I wasn't sure about here and now. If I took the 'out of the ring' option though, the fight would be bloodier and there would be more opportunity for him to use his weight advantage. Maybe I'd be able to hurt him quicker, but I was under no illusions, Billy may or may not be a boxer, but I was sure that he was at the least a competent street fighter and possibly a lot better than that. An unlicensed fight in the ring is usually four two-minute rounds, not longer than that, as unlicensed fighters don't do the stamina training that the professionals do. A free for all wouldn't last as long. But it would last until one of us didn't get up, whereas in the ring, the fight would be over at the end, even if we were both standing. It might be the safer option. If there was a safer option with Billy.

"Come on, Garron," Hillier's voice cutting in, "what's it to be?"

I looked at Billy again, standing there, comfortable in the role life had given him.

"All right, Hillier, glove me up. Let's see what your boy's got." I winked at Billy, trying for the psychological angle. His expression didn't change. It didn't matter to him how I wanted to fight, his job was the same.

Hillier turned towards the ring.

"Get them ready. The fight's on."

There was a swell of conversation as the people repositioned themselves around the ring. Pete came rushing over.

"I swear, man, I didn't know. He just asked me to be here, I didn't know about all this, I swear it."

"All right, Pete, it doesn't matter now. If I've got the puff, I'll keep away from him for four rounds and if not, I'll get beaten to a pulp and you'll have to get me home."

For a moment he looked worried for me rather than for himself.

"You really think it'll be that bad?"

I tried for a winning smile and failed. "Yes, but we'll find out, won't we?"

I walked past Pete to the ring. A thickset man with a skinhead cut was looking at the posts on the ring.

"Don't tell me," I said, "If there's too much padding gone, we're going to call it off."

He raised his eyebrows and grinned at me. "No," he said, "but I might stuff a couple of shirts in there as well."

He held out his hand and I took it.

"Rob," he said, "Robbie to my friends."

Pete who had followed me up said: "All right there, Robbie."

"And you can call me Rob," the man answered without looking at him. Pete deflated and shuffled a couple of steps back.

"Saw you fight a few times, Garron, thought you might go a long way. How's the wrist going to stand up to this?"

He knew his stuff, this guy. Most people said 'hand', but he knew it was the wrist that was the problem, even though it was the broken hand that people had been talking about.

"It'll be all right," I said. I didn't know whose side he was on and I didn't want anyone thinking I'd be favouring one hand.

He shook his head. "I'll be taping your hands up, Garron, yours and Billy's and I'll do it best as I can, but it's bandages and it's only going to help you up to a point. Got a couple of gum-shields as well, not custom, like you were used to, but clean enough."

"You in my corner then, Rob?" I kept off the 'Robbie' bit, I wasn't a friend that I knew of.

He laughed again. "No, son, I'm the ref," he said and went off to deal with Billy's hands.

Pete was still standing by and wanted to know what he should do.

"I don't know, Pete, find some bottled water, a clean towel and some grease. See what Rob's got." I walked off.

"Where you going?" he called after me.

"I'm going to empty my bladder before I stick a pair of bloody boxing gloves on my hands," I shouted back without looking round, "unless you want to sort that problem out for me later?"

He said nothing of course and a path cleared in front of me through the thrill-seekers as I walked to the gents. Conversation seemed to stop as I walked past and carry on again as I moved on, but it didn't bother me. The decision was made. I just had to live through it. And still there was that sense of detachment, which wasn't good. This was a fight, but I wasn't up for it in the way that I always had been for my amateur and then pro fights. This just seemed like another thing to do. I thought about this on the way to and back from the gents and then as I got to the ring, I saw Billy without his cut off sweatshirt on and started to realise what I was getting into. His arms, shoulders and chest were huge. Not body builder muscled, but naturally big and thick with the power that comes from daily work, not a daily work out. He was carrying some weight around his stomach, but not that much and it just leant an air of solidity to him that couldn't be ignored. I took off my jacket and pulled my T-shirt over my head and knew that although I was fit still and although I hadn't lost too much of the muscle around my upper body, I was now a slightly heavy middleweight and I looked like a stick insect next to Billy. But there wasn't much I could do about that and I knew that if you kick a big guy in the groin, he'll go down as quick as anyone else. Okay, I couldn't do that here, but it made me feel better to think about it. Maybe I would've been better going for the free for all, I was at least as dirty a street fighter as the next man and maybe I'd have done better on those terms. I turned away. I'd never worried about what any opponent looked like in the old days and I wasn't going to now.

-Yeah, said the little voice, *but they were all within your weight range back then, weren't they?*

I shut that out and got into the ring. Still nothing. I had to generate some energy from somewhere, some movement. I loosened up, stretched off, aware of everyone looking at me, measuring me up, *'has he still got it'*, going through their minds, *'what can he do'* and I thought, sod 'em. I still had my jeans and trainers on and Rob came over with a couple of pairs of shorts and a protective cup.

"No boxing boots, son, but you'll need a pair of shorts. Can't have you fighting in jeans with a belt on, can we?"

I took the black pair and didn't bother going back to the gents, just took my jeans off and put the cup and shorts on over my own boxers. Not perfect, but not much else I could do.

"I'll do your hands now, Garron," he said and moved me into a corner. As he wound the bandage round, he talked to me.

"Don't worry about home crowd stuff, there's a mixed group here, some of 'em will even be rooting for you and I'll call it as I see it, but there'll be some rough stuff going on inside and I won't be stopping that. They expect blood here and they're not worried about straying a little from the rules. Nothing too obvious, but I'm warning you. Protect yourself on the breaks and don't expect low blows and heads to be called unless they're so blatant they can see 'em outside in the street."

I muttered a thank you and he carried on.

"Don't need to thank me, son, I've got no more help to offer you, but you should know this. You're an ex-pro and when you were a title contender, over ten, twelve rounds, even with the weight difference, you'd have taken Billy. You'd have moved around him and picked him off, bloodied him up and tired him out. In the end, if he didn't catch you, you'd have taken him. I saw you when you were right up there, close to the British title fight. You had the speed, the fitness and the shots, but you also had something else. You had the 'edge', the hardness to take a fight and make it work for you. But not now. No-one keeps that." He finished the left hand and asked me how it was. I flexed and it felt good, though not as I remembered it from the pro arena. He started on the weakened right hand.

"Billy here," he went on, "he's a natural fighter. He's got natural strength and power and he moves well. He can last four rounders at two minutes a round and you're not in training. You probably don't have the power to hurt him and you're not psyched up for this." I started to protest mildly, but he cut me off. "You're not," he said, "I can tell. And sooner or later you're going to throw a punch with this and find out whether it can take it." He looked up from the hand for a moment. "Or worse still, you're not going to throw the hand at all 'cos you're too worried about it and then you'll have no chance."

He stood back from me and looked at his work. It was a bit thicker than the left hand, with some extra support for the wrist and when I flexed it also felt okay.

"So, little or no chance then," I stated.

"I didn't say that, I'm just telling it as I see it."

Problem was, he wasn't wrong that I could see anywhere down the line. I changed the subject a bit.

"Nice heavy gloves, I hope."

He shook his head. "10oz, son, that's all."

I sighed and put my hands up for the gloves. Pete had them, but Rob took them off him and pulled them on for me. They were old lace up style and once they were on, Rob taped over the laces. I was going to ask him if he'd done the same for Billy, but I reckoned he had and I didn't want to piss him off by questioning his fairness. I tried the gum-shields and one was better than the other, though not perfect and I stuck with that. I'd forgotten about the cut near my eye, but Rob reminded me by pulling off the plaster that was covering it. Nice target for Billy to work on I thought. For a brief moment I wondered what Jenny would say if she could see me doing this. Probably tell me to beat the guy's head in, but that would be an emotional response, not a rational one. Maybe that was what I needed, more emotion, less rationality. But that didn't work either. If I got too into this, Billy would punch my lights out. Rob had moved away and Pete was talking again.

" - the water and I got some vaseline from the guy in the other corner."

It wasn't a jar of the stuff, just a smear in some tissues. Luxury. I hoped the guy who'd dug it out of the jar had clean hands. Even more, I hoped I wouldn't need it. Pete was like a kid trying to be useful, but not getting it right. It would be rude to tell him to clear out and besides I needed someone to hand me the water between rounds, but Hillier obviously wasn't too worried about getting me any real help. I was there to fight and he'd managed that. Anything above that, he wasn't interested in.

I moved to my corner and looked across the ring. It was all very quiet in the gym, very unlike a scheduled fight and Billy looked calm and at ease. I wondered if I looked the same to him. I didn't think Rob would call us into the middle for instructions, it wasn't that kind of a fight and as I stood there and a part of me registered the stupidity of it all, I realised that like it or not, it was going to happen. I had to get out of the weird zone I was in and into fighting mode. I tried to think what Al would have said. Strange that, thinking about Al's advice instead of what my old trainer might have said. But that was it. I wasn't a boxer anymore. If anything, I was more of a street fighter. I felt like shouting to Hillier to get the gloves off me and to go bare knuckle, but that was just emotional think again. I was an ex-pro, this was another job. With, I reminded myself, a three thousand pound payoff for winning and a grand for just being here in the ring. So snap out of it and get ready.

I fired a few jabs out and felt okay, rotated my upper body to loosen up some more and threw a few combinations as well. Ready or not, this was all I could do.

There was an old bell attached to the side of one of the ring posts low down at floor level, but it obviously had nothing inside it, because now we were ready, someone simply picked up a hammer and hit the thing. I felt Pete pat me on the shoulder as I moved out of the corner, a pointless gesture if ever there was one, but I guess he thought he had to do something.

Billy came out from his corner slowly, probably wanting to find out whether any of my professional skills had survived nearly three years out of the ring. His stance was good, hands high and chin tucked in and he moved easily for a wide man, with an economy of effort that said again that he knew what he was doing. My game plan was simple enough. I had to jab him around, make some openings, look after my right hand and make sure he didn't land anything on me with those big fists. He was an orthodox lead, left hand forwards and I did the same, weighing up the disadvantage of knowing that I didn't want to land a big right hand, with the advantage of using my undamaged left hand far more if I led with it.

As we closed in the middle of the ring, I feinted a left, drew his hands slightly and threw a second, real left jab at his face. My range was a little off, not surprisingly after all this time and it only scuffed him. He fired back a straight right, which I took on my forearms and which sent shockwaves through to my shoulders. The man had a punch like a mule's kick. I knew this crowd wanted a tear-up, but I was going to stick and run if I could. I had always been able to take a punch, but this guy was heavyweight division, even if he wasn't at the heavier end of it. Taking one of those at full power was going to hurt. I tried to find a rhythm, get into the kind of zone where your body knows what it is supposed to be doing and gets on with it, leaving you to make decisions above the basic ongoing level. But it wasn't that easy. Billy was a natural fighter. He moved easily and he cut the ring down as well as most pros that I'd seen. It was obvious that he'd had some training, but more than that, he had natural talent.

I kept moving, throwing the jab out, more times than not catching Billy on his gloves, but having to back pedal as he angled in on me, manoeuvring himself into range for his own punches. The crowd were fairly quiet, unusually so for an unlicensed fight, but then it occurred to me that these people knew who I was, or had been, as that young college guy had said. They weren't expecting a war, they were looking at whether their man would be able to take out an ex-pro. They wouldn't object to blood and guts, but Hillier had probably sold this to them as a real academic exercise, aficionados only.

188

While I was thinking all this, Billy hit me. It was a straight left, not his most powerful punch, but enough to rock my head back, split the skin under my right eye and make me realize I had to concentrate. I knew there was a cut, because I could feel a little dribble of wet on my face and I was surprised, because I'd never been one to cut easily. Of course usually, I fought people two and a half stone lighter than Billy.

He kept coming after me and I feinted left again and threw an overhand right that I expected him to block, but he didn't. It caught him high on the left of his head, no damage done, but a little hope in the way that he hadn't been able to get out of the way. He threw a flurry of punches back at me in response, but I covered up, taking the weight of them on my gloves and arms, which hurt, but not taking them where they would hurt most.

The bell rang and we stopped and looked at each other. Billy grinned at me again. It had been a feeler and we both knew it. I was starting to breathe hard, but not too much and he knew that he had the weight of punch to hurt me. What I didn't know was whether he could change gear at all and up the pace. A lot of unlicensed fighters only have one real way of fighting and they keep on fighting that way. I could adapt. In the pro days, I'd had trainers to help me with tactics. This time I had Pete.

"Good round, mate," he said as I sat in the corner on an old stool. He threw water in my face and said, "keep the jab going in his face and watch out for his right hand."

"Shut up, Pete," I said

"I'm just trying to help."

"Well help by shutting up. And stop throwing that bloody water in my eyes!"

He stopped, but looked really hurt. "What do you want me to do then?"

"Get a clean towel and gently put it on the cut. Not so as you open it up more, but so the edges get pushed together. Then push hard on it."

"No clean towel," he said, "I've got some clean tissues here if you want."

I sighed. "Yeah, Pete, use that and then whack some Vaseline on it."

Feeling pleased with himself, Pete sent me out into the second round with another pat on the back and the instruction to 'keep my hands up'. I'd have turned round and hit him if I hadn't had to concentrate on Billy. But I was happier now. I felt looser and I'd decided what it was that I was going to do. It was no use reacting to Billy's style. I had my own style and with the note of caution that I didn't want to get into a brawl which I would lose, I had to set the agenda. If I had the puff to do it, I was going to take the fight to him.

I came out at speed and flicked a double left hand jab at Billy's face to keep his guard high and then drove a low right hook into his side. It was like hitting a slab of meat. He hardly moved although it was a good shot and instead fired a right at my head which I ducked inside. We clinched and his head drove into my face. Not exactly a butt, the crowd might say, more a continuation of his natural movement. Which was what it was supposed to look like. But instead of moving backwards away from him into the punch that I knew he was shaping for I stayed in the clinch, feeling the sharp pain of the butt fade slightly and hooking again for his left side. That's one thing about hitting meat. Just when you think you're not getting anywhere, you suddenly crack a bone inside. It hadn't happened yet, but it would if I kept on at it. I hooked again and a third time and then at last Billy dropped his left arm lower to protect his side, so I whipped a fast right hook over his glove into the side of his head. It was the first punch to bone that I'd thrown with my right hand, but it felt good. The bandages were giving enough support to the wrist for the moment and in a four rounder, it might even hold out. Billy wasn't really hurt by the hook, but he'd been out-thought and he didn't want to clinch anymore this time. He pushed me away, more easily than I thought he would be able to and moved forwards again. I could hear a few isolated shouts now from the crowd as they and we, warmed up into it. A few 'come on Billy' calls and even one for me. Billy didn't need too much encouragement though. He was grinning at me through his gum-shield, but I knew that he wasn't as happy as before. I reckoned most of his opponents would have reacted differently to what had just happened, both to the butt, moving away from it into the waiting punch and also to being in a clinch with a man as powerful as Billy was. That's the thing about a good pro-fessional though, even a good ex-professional. He's been through most of it before and he can think as he goes. Not by conscious thought either, but automatically. I may not have hurt him too much, but he hadn't got to me and he'd have to try something else. If he had anything else in his game.

He walked onto me and I moved backwards, jabbing him as I went, making sure he had to keep his hands up as his defence, not allowing him to throw the big swinging punches he wanted to. I didn't know how long he would put up with this before he lost patience, or simply decided to take a couple of shots in order to get to me.

It wasn't long. He reached forwards with a jab of his own and stepped in to get his big right hand in range. With most of his opponents it may have worked, because jabbing on the retreat as I was doing is not so easy and getting enough power to stop someone like Billy is difficult. Most times he would walk straight through a weak jab and land his own punch. But I'd trained over a period of years how to punch going backwards, getting my balance right and the power into the strikes and I landed a straight left and then switching stances briefly, a straight right bang in the middle of his face. I might not have got away with the switch in a British title fight, but here it worked fine. It stopped him short for a second and blood started to trickle from his nose and I decided to go to work on the blood 'T', the t-shaped area of the eyes, nose and mouth that won't usually knock a man senseless, but that will bleed, hurt and swell up.

I rammed another left jab into Billy's face and followed with a right cross behind his guard, moving closer, waiting for him to try to clinch and then slamming two more hooks into his body. He was going to try the butt again and he did, but I rolled with it and although it made contact there was no damage done. He grabbed on to me and I took a short rest, head tucked in and arms protecting my sides, only a couple of seconds, but it used up some time. I was feeling looser now and the moves were beginning to flow with more fluency and some speed. My stamina was going to be a problem though, but either I let up the pace and allowed Billy back into the fight, or I had to hope I was going to last another two and a bit rounds.

As we broke from the clinch though, he let fly with an overhand right that caught me high up on the side of the head.

My head rocked sideways and blackness seeped in at the edges of my vision, but not all the way and I found that I'd covered up automatically and moved into him again, rather than away, as the blackness receded and clarity returned. It was a shot I would never have been caught with three years ago, but one that had enough power to slow me down. This time as I went to clinch he pushed me away, trying to keep me at enough of a distance to throw more of his hard punches, but I rolled inside his lead arm and hung on while my head cleared. My legs seemed okay, although a little heavy and the fact that I was thinking about that told me I was weathering the punch. Which was about the time that he butted me again, not hard enough to put me down, but enough to open up the first cut properly and I could feel the skin tear.

I was at last getting into the fight though and the butt annoyed me enough to jerk me out of my detached state of mind. I'd been fighting a bit on autopilot, I had to engage a bit more and I did that by staying in the clinch again and by getting angry and ramming a left uppercut into Billy's throat. You can't get a clean shot like that easily with the gloves on, but I got some of it right and he gagged slightly and moved back a step, so I whipped a chopping right hand over his guard at a downwards angle just above his left eye and split his eyebrow open. The blood poured out of the wound, but no-one was going to stop this on cuts, so I switched to southpaw and snaked a couple of quick jabs into the same place. The bell rang and we stopped and looked at each other for a few seconds, before turning back to our corners. The left side of his face was covered in blood from the eyebrow and they'd never stop that flowing, but I wasn't in great shape either, breathing hard now, too hard and too heavy legged as I made it back to my stool.

"Bloody hell," said Pete as he poured water, too much water, into my mouth, "you really copped him then. I thought you said you'd be in trouble here, you'd get hurt."

I didn't bother answering him, didn't bother telling him that Billy was cut, but not hurt, not in the way that a really big punch slowed you down. Anyway, I was too busy to talk, too busy trying to breathe and realising that the cut under my eye was worse than I'd thought. I could feel it burning now and the ooze of the blood was hot on my face, but not, I thought with a good feeling, as bad as old Billy's cut. That was straight over his eye and running into it. I wondered as I sat there how good his corner was, whether they'd be able to stop any of the flow and also whether I could get up off the stool for the next round. Then I realised I was bleeding slightly higher up on the side of my face, just next to my right eye. I didn't remember getting hit there, but it was where old Gav had caught me with his watch or his ring the previous night. It hadn't needed stitches then, but it probably would now.

Someone hit that bloody bell again and Pete forgot the gum-shield, until I reminded him and then I sat for a moment longer before hauling myself off the stool. This was round three. I had four minutes to last. Four minutes minus that second I'd just cribbed.

Billy came out like a whirlwind, arms swinging but, I noticed, held a little lower between swings than in the first two rounds. I back-pedalled again, but then stepped in with a straight left, working for the blood section again, feeling the punch land hard and moving away again. The watchers were getting noisier, but this still had the feel of being unreal, almost like a low key training session in front of an invited audience, except that it was hurting more and the blood was flowing freely.

We traded a few jabs in the centre of the ring and I took a couple of hard shots on my arms and shoulders again. I was going to ache like hell when this was over, but better the bruises on my arms than the punches taking my head off. I was controlling the fight now, keeping him at the end of my jab and stepping in, not at will, but fairly freely to throw harder punches at his face and some hard hooks to his body. Sooner or later, the body punches were going to tell. I knew I still punched above my weight, it was just that Billy was well above my weight.

And then, as we clinched again, he rolled off to the side, a move he hadn't done before and one I would have thought was outside his range and popped a right hook into my side. I caught some of it on my arm, but the rest caught me almost as far back as my kidneys and the pain flared and wind went out of me. I hung on to him again automatically, but this time he was ready and pushed me away and came straight back in and I covered up, trying to heave some breath into my lungs and stop the constriction there. But as I did, he came wading in and I took a huge shot on my upper left arm, that all but paralysed it and the breath started coming again and I slammed a desperate straight right into his face catching him full in the mouth and then tying his right arm up with my left which seemed to suddenly be all it was good for.

The bell rang and he pushed me away and I weaved slightly back to my stool, my breathing sawing in and out now, the pain still there and colouring everything.

"You could have gone down there, mate, no-one would say a thing." Pete again, trying to help I suppose, but I was angry now and I knew why. When I'd fought I'd been able to be angry and cold at the same time. 'A calm rage', Al had called it, but I couldn't recreate that now. I was too detached or too angry, but not cold, not clinical and that was what I was missing. I concentrated on that feeling, tried to get it back, while all the time Pete yakked on and the pain continued and my breathing steadied.

I couldn't do it. I couldn't get to it. And that made me mad as well.

One round. One round to get through and then I'd laugh in Hillier's face and walk away with my three grand. Because I was winning. The few heavy shots he'd landed had hurt, but overall, points scored, damage inflicted and so on, I was winning.

"Pete," I said and my voice was hardly there. "Pull the edge of the tape on the glove, get the edge up a bit and fold it back on itself."

"What?" he said, looking at me like he hadn't understood.

"Pull some of the tape up that's on the wrist of the glove, on the inside, yeah, that bit. Scrunch it up a bit and leave it with an edge of the laces out, but not so bloody obviously, you pratt!"

"What is it, mate, what are you doing?"

"He's been butting me for three rounds, I'm going to get even for it."

The hammer again and I stood up with something that felt like a vice around my lungs, blood leaking down my face and lead in my legs. But although his corner had patched him up, he was still bleeding, from his mouth and most of all from his left eyebrow. And I was going to pop that wound open again like a water balloon. That and his left ribs. I was going for that and I was going to get there.

Unless of course he hit me again.

His corner had done a reasonable job on his eyebrow, but it was swollen up and dripping into his eye. He was holding his left hand higher trying to protect it and I had to bring that guard down if I could.

The crowd was shouting again now as Rob waved us forwards, but there was no touching gloves for the last round. We came together in the middle of the ring and I blocked the straight right he put out and stuck a left jab into his face and a right hook into his low ribs. The punches were coming from me naturally now and I knew that my balance was right and the power was there and this time he flinched as he took it, but he still swung a big right hand that I had to move away from.

And I was tired. He may have been hurting, but I realised that I was going to be too tired to keep shifting away from those big swings and if he caught me with one of them, too tired to stay upright.

He was throwing punches in ones now, no combinations as he laboured a bit and tried to close in on me. I let him come and threw a left uppercut again, missed and as his head came in again threw a soft right to his head and dragged the scuffed tape and the laces on the inside of my right glove across his split eyebrow. It popped open further and bled into his eye. He couldn't see from there now and I slammed another two shots into the same place and then stepped out before he could grab onto me.

He was in deep trouble now, blinded by the blood in one eye and unable to chase me down across the ring and all I had to do was keep away from him for another minute, but my lungs were heaving now and I was too tired to run and although I couldn't generate that cold anger that I used to feel, that 'edge' as Rob had called it, I was angry. Not at Billy, but at Hillier for manoeuvring me into this and I was too far gone to rationalise it. I was angry and there was someone to hit. So I moved forwards, not blindly, not in a red mist, but professionally, jabbing out the left and picking the shots. They were only in ones and twos, though, I hadn't the energy to move faster or throw combinations and fatigue, together with the number of heavy punches I'd blocked with my arms and shoulders was giving me enough trouble in just keeping my hands up.

So far, my right hand felt good and the wrist was holding up okay and maybe it was that, or maybe it was just tiredness that was the reason why I threw a full blooded right hook at his jaw and caught him too far back, hurting him, yes, but also sending a shockwave of pain through my wrist and making me pull back straight away. Billy simply wasn't a good enough boxer for this fight, but he was immensely strong and seeing me pull back, he surged forwards again throwing another couple of punches, the second one catching me in the chest and sending me back against the ropes. He piled in after me, but again the automatic reactions cut in even after three years and I turned him on the ropes, landed a couple of counters and tried not to throw up from the bile in my mouth that was a result of the last body punch. I thought for a moment he was going down, more from loss of balance on the ropes than from the power of the punches, but he was too strong and I was too tired to keep throwing the punches and then he pushed himself off the ropes as someone hit that beautiful bell.

It was my fight, no doubt about it, but that can mean nothing in the world of underground boxing and I wondered how strong Rob would be if he got the nod the other way and then I wondered why I cared. This fight meant nothing. I was out of training, injured and tricked into the fight, so why the hell would I care if some jerk thought I'd won a four rounder.

But I did. So how much stupid pride did I have inside me? And how much trouble had that cost me in the past? And now?

I stood in the middle of the ring, too tired to move as Rob walked over to me and raised my hand. There was a cheer from most of the crowd, but I wasn't focussing on them. I wasn't focussing on anything. I'd come to a full stop. I wasn't sure I could even make it back to my stool on my own and Pete didn't seem to be near enough to help. Billy was dripping blood in his corner and he pushed his second aside and walked over to me. For all the blood and swelling, he seemed in far better shape than me.

"Good fight, Mr. Garron," he said, his voice thick and slightly indistinct and I wasn't sure if it was his voice that was the problem or my hearing. "I thought I'd have too much power for you, but you've still got the speed and the moves."

I didn't trust myself to speak too much, but I told Billy that he was one of the toughest people I'd ever seen in a ring and that if he'd have started early enough, then he could have been a good pro. He liked that and said it had been a pleasure fighting me, which is exactly the sort of cock-eyed statement that fighters come out with after they've been beating each other to a pulp, so

I told him that I couldn't say the same because it had hurt too much and we touched gloves and he climbed out of the ring to shouts of encouragement. Pete had appeared from somewhere and I told him to get the gloves off me and to get me home, but Rob got there first and took the gloves.

"Nasty piece of rough tape hanging off there, son," he said, but that was all he said and my conscience wasn't going to bother me about it. "Fought a good fight," he went on, "but you made hard work of it, you should put in some roadwork, make some good money at this, 'specially fighting out of your weight."

"Wrist won't take it," I said, giving him an excuse he could accept.

He unwound the bandages and looked at my hands which were shaking slightly.

"I'll get you some ice for these," he said "and the doctor will stitch you up."

"You've got a doctor here?" I asked. "You can't have, he'd get struck off for doing this."

"He already has been, son, he already has been. This is my gym, Garron, it's on Mr. Hillier's property" (and I noticed that even Rob referred to him as 'Mister' Hillier) "but it's my gym and if he wants fights here then I tell him there's got to be a doctor."

My legs were locking now, so I sat on the stool and various people came up and said 'well done' or 'good fight', or some other dumb comment. Rob brought a bucket with ice in it and I stuck my hands in one at a time, swapping them over when it got too cold for me. Pete was keeping out of the way, but I caught sight of him a couple of times which was good, because someone was going to have to drive me home. In fact, I thought, he could go get the car now, because it would be too easy for someone knowing I was walking out of here with cash to take it off me in my current state. I beckoned him over and told him where the car was.

"Keys are in my jeans," I said, "when you get here, stay with the car outside. You got a mobile?" I wasn't thinking straight and I couldn't remember whether he had my number, so I gave it to him. "Just call when you get back, stay with the car and leave the engine running."

He turned to go and I said: "Pete, you can drive, can't you?"

"'Course I can," he said, walking off.

The doctor, as he was called, came to look at me, jabbed a local anaesthetic in somewhere and cleaned up the bleeding. He was a youngish guy and I wondered how Hillier had got his hooks into him, unless he was just a fight fanatic that Rob knew. He asked all the right questions and stitched up the cut under my right eye and then put a couple of clips into the cut next to the same eye.

"You can get these taken out at your local GP if you want to, or if you call Rob, he can get me to meet you and take them out." He gave a half smile. "All part of the service," he said bitterly and I thought again about exactly what he was doing here and about the fact that I didn't have a GP to go to. "You're better off than the other guy," he went on, "I can't stitch that eyebrow, he's going to have to have that put back together again properly, which means a hospital visit."

"How do they organise that, then?"

"Oh, there'll be a cover story all worked out, with witnesses, don't worry about that. There have been a few hospital cases in this room, I can tell you." He stood up. "If you're having trouble breathing you'll need an x-ray on the ribs on your side, but if you've got some minor damage there, then there's not much they'll do for that. You know what it feels like, so if you're happy that it's no worse than a hairline crack, then you can leave it at that. But you are going to be sore as hell tomorrow and for a while after that."

"Thanks, Doctor," I called after him, but he didn't acknowledge me and went back to Billy who was standing up outside the ring, with a towel pressed against his face.

Rob came back over and asked where I wanted to clean up. I didn't, I just wanted to get out of there. I was covered in sweat and blood, but I wasn't going to hang around to take a shower, so he got a wet towel and wiped the blood, mine and Billy's, off my arms, shoulders and chest and then helped me get my shirt over my head and my jeans back on. I didn't do the belt up. I was dog tired and a little light-headed and I was still sweating, but I wanted to get out of there as soon as possible. I wanted to get what was left of me back home.

Hillier came up and that was a good thing, because stupidly, I'd forgotten about the money.

"Good fight, Garron and I expected no less."

It was odd. Even though he was a villain, even though he'd backed me into this fight on his own terms, yes for the profit that it might have given him, but also I felt, almost to prove to me that he could, that he was able to manoeuvre me around which I didn't like at all, even after all that, he was still personable. Dangerous as hell on a hot night, but personable.

"Sorry, you lost your money, Hillier." I wasn't putting the 'mister' back on for him now.

He laughed. "Lost money? Not me, son. I made a packet on you."

That got through to me, tired though I was.

"You bet on me?"

"Oh yes. Billy's got quite a rep as you might imagine and once people knew this was on, it was a hot ticket. An ex-pro and a bloody good one, but out of training and carrying the injury that ended his career taking on a natural fighter with a big street rep who's got three or four weight divisions on him. I could have got media coverage for this if I'd wanted to go down that road, but that wouldn't have done and I'm happy with the entrance money from the punters and the betting." He leaned in a little closer as though he was telling me a secret. "This lot might not look like much, but they pay top dollar."

"But you said you bet on me. Against your own man. I don't get that."

"Listen, Garron, I thought you *could* lose, but I didn't think you would. Billy's good, he's probably tougher than you are and he's certainly a lot bigger and stronger, but he doesn't think on his feet, he's one paced. I just thought that you would be too good for him. And I didn't want to underestimate you either. For some reason, you get things done and I thought you'd get this done as well. There were plenty of others who didn't agree with me. So, given that I didn't have to fund either you or Billy for tonight's work and that's big money for a fighter to take home, plus I've seen a cracking fight as well, I've had a good evening all round." He lit a cigarette, turned to go and then looked back again. "Garron, don't worry about the money. No-one will follow you out of here."

I believed him, but I had another question.

"Hillier, what if it had been closer, what if Billy had been a little up at the end, which way would you have had Rob call it?"

"You've got me wrong, Garron," he said. "Rob calls it as he sees it and I don't question that." He gestured around him at the people who were beginning to leave. "Do you think this lot would stand for it, if I did?"

He turned, walked away from the ring and was soon in friendly conversation with two men who looked like they were in his line of business and I wondered just how much people *would* stand for, if Adam Hillier changed their rules for them.

My mobile rang and it was Pete. I told him to stay downstairs and wait for me. I looked around at what was going on. People were still standing around in small groups although many had left during the time that I'd been sitting with the doctor and with Rob. I suppose the bets and markers had changed hands and there was no reason to stay. Billy had gone off to the changing rooms with the doctor and someone else. No-one was talking to me, although there were a lot of glances in my direction. I didn't like that. I'd been happily out of the public eye for a while. I didn't want underground rumours spreading about me and that would be what would happen now. This fight would get re-told in the pubs and gyms, chinese whispers would get to work and in six months time I'd hear about the fact that I'd fought with one hand tied behind my back against a seven foot tall super-heavyweight who broke both my legs. Talk is always going to happen. I just don't like it happening to me.

I stood up. No, I tried to stand up and failed. A little while ago my legs had been locking out, now they were like rubber. I tried again, holding onto the sagging ropes and managed it, but I couldn't get out of the ring without help. Surprisingly, it was one of Hillier's tame gorillas that came over. I recognised him from Snazz, but it wasn't the one I'd tangled with, or one of the others I'd seen in Hillier's office.

"Need a hand, mate?" he said, taking my weight as I ducked under the ropes and thought about the step down to the floor. "That was a tough fight," he went on, "bit of a mismatch on the weight, wasn't it?"

"You noticed that, did you?" I answered, more to keep the conversation going while I needed his help, than because I wanted to make the point. My side was killing me, my hands were sore, my head hurt, I had no idea what my face looked like and my legs weren't working. "Do you think you could help me get out of here?" I asked him.

"I'm not supposed to leave the door, really," he said, sounding a bit worried.

"Yeah, but that was to keep me from doing a runner, wasn't it?"

He brightened up at that. "That's true, didn't think of that."

I didn't point out that his boss might have wanted him inside for other reasons as well, just took his support getting down the stairs. He didn't introduce himself, just talked about the fight and how he wouldn't get in the ring with Billy unless there was enough money to retire in it for him. He was quite helpful really, helped me into the car and everything and didn't seem to hate my guts as much as the others of Hillier's boys. Once I was in the car, I mentioned that to him.

"Well," he said, "Bob's a bit of an arse really, probably deserved you thumping him. 'Course, if some of the lads were here, they might not agree with me. You know, you've got to stick up for your own."

I agreed with him completely. Problem was there was only me nowdays to stick up for me. And Jenny, I thought. And Jenny.

Pete got in the car and asked me where I was living now to take me home and I nearly told him and then I nearly gave him Jenny's address and in the end I asked him to take me to the car lot. I didn't think Pete would drop me in any trouble now, I didn't think there was any more trouble he could drop me into, but I just didn't like giving out addresses.

"You're not going to stay there are you?" he asked.

"No, just a drop off point for my girlfriend to pick me up. She's working tonight and I'm going to need some help moving around. When she's finished her shift she can pick me up from there."

As he drove away from the pub, I tried to twist back to look at it and failed because of the jolt of pain that went through my neck. Quite a drama played out there tonight. Garron's last fight. But then, I'd thought my last fight had already been and gone. Maybe for once I'd be right this time.

*

Pete drove back to Tony's car lot quickly and on the way he must have called Tony and asked if he could meet us there and open the office. I say must have, because I didn't hear him. I was that tired that I was drifting in and out of sleep. The only thing that stopped me was the pain if I moved too much in the wrong direction. I was vaguely aware of London passing me by and I was struck by the thought that some of the people we were driving past might have seen me fight a few years ago. And also by the knowledge that I'd just picked up more money in one night, than many of them would see in a month. Careful, I told myself, that's a dangerous thought to run with.

I'd planned to sit in the car outside the lot until Jenny came for me, but it was better to be inside. The only problem was having to put up with Tony telling me what an idiot I was and Pete going through a commentary on the fight as though I was Superman and Billy had been Captain Caveman. I called Jenny at the restaurant and asked her if she could get a cab and pick me up when she'd finished working. She asked me if I was all right, 'cos I sounded terrible and I said, that yes, I was all right, but I looked a mess and she shouldn't get a shock when she saw me. Of course she then said she'd leave work and come right over straight away, but I told her to wait and finish the shift, otherwise she might not have the rent money and the rent collector would have to exact a terrible revenge on her. I think the fact I made a joke of it reassured her and she said she would see me later and rang off.

Tony said he needed to get back and I should lock the door and put the keys back through the box when I left, but Pete said he would be waiting around with me, so he would do it. Very responsible I thought, maybe Pete was turning over a new leaf. Before he smoked it, that is.

He was pretty quiet though, which was unusual for Pete and given he was now off the hook with Hillier, I reckoned he should be a bit more lively. Then I wondered if maybe he was coming down off something, but I was too tired and aching too much to worry about it, so I just stayed slumped in Tony's chair and we sat in silence.

Then he jumped up and said: "Sod it, you've just won your comeback fight, we should be celebrating!"

I nearly laughed, but it hurt too much and came out as a snort and before I could say anything he'd gone, out the door and away. About five minutes later he was back with a couple of cans of Strongbow and some Special Brew.

"You're still a cider man, right?"

I nodded. "But I shouldn't be drinking in this state, I'll be on painkillers later to sleep."

"Ah, don't be daft, a couple of cans isn't going to hurt you and you always used to have a drink after a fight." He popped a couple of ring pulls, handed a can over and raised his own. "To you, mate. You still got it!"

It was infectious. His mood was infectious. For a while it was just like having the old Pete back again and I'd downed most of the two cans before I started to feel light-headed from the drink and the reaction to the fight mixed together, but I told myself it didn't matter. I wasn't a fighter anymore, there was no training to go back to and in any case it was going to take me a good week to ten days at least before I was even going to start feeling better again, so what the hell!

Pete was talking about the old days, about seeing my early fights and him getting thrown out of a community centre once where I'd been fighting at an amateur meet because he'd been shouting for me in a fight and ended up winding up the local lads. It was relaxed and I began to relax as well and I almost forgave him for the series of events that meant we were sitting here at all. I wasn't doing most of the talking, but I reminded him about a couple of the gigs he'd played and the laughs we'd had and it almost broke the good humour. He seemed almost sad thinking back on it, like it was okay if he picked the memories, but not if someone else did. Maybe it was okay to look back at how I'd wasted my life, but not at how he'd wasted his. So I tried to get back to the present.

"Well, I've got to say that it hurt, but at least you're out of hock to Hillier."

He shook his head. "Not really, mate, I owe him a packet."

I couldn't believe it.

"How can you owe him money, Pete, what have you done, bought your drugs on credit?"

He put his head in his hands. "I bet on the fight."

"But I won the fight, Pete, I won it."

He didn't say anything and finally it dawned on me.

"You bet on Billy, didn't you?"

He didn't look up.

"You actually bet on the other guy." I couldn't believe it.

He still didn't look up, but he said; "Man, you were so sure you'd get a kicking, I just went with what you said."

I couldn't think of any reply. Not betting on me would be one thing, but actively betting on someone else to beat my head in seemed a little out of order. It had a funny side really. Hillier had bet on me instead of his own man and Pete had bet on Billy instead of me. I was hurting and aching and light-headed and slightly drunk on almost no alcohol at all and it seemed funny enough. It wouldn't seem the same way to Pete when Hillier came to collect.

"How much?" I finally asked him.

"I can't tell you," he said.

"Come on, Pete, how much? A hundred? Five hundred?"

Then he said: "More like five thousand."

That stopped me short. "Five thousand?"

He started pacing around the office, which was no mean feat given how small the place was.

"I just saw the chance to make a killing. I mean, you told me you were going to get a kicking, you said it yourself and I thought, how often do you get the chance to bet on something like this, where the guy himself says he's going to lose."

"I didn't say I was going to try to lose though!"

"I know," he said and he seemed completely dejected. "It was a dumb thing to do and now I'm going to pay for it."

"Man, I just got you out of trouble, I know it wasn't how I expected to do it but it happened anyway and now you're right back in it." I started to get up and everything hurt, so I gave up and stayed sitting down. "All right, Pete, I've got three grand here, that should be enough for the first payment and then you're on your own. I can't help you after that."

I'm not even sure why I would offer him the money except that the point of the fight had never been the money and it seemed crazy to have gone through all of this for him to still be in the shit. But then he surprised me. Even in my battered state, where things weren't really making sense, he surprised me.

"No, Garron, I'm not taking any money from you. You won that and I lost it because I was stupid. I shouldn't have bet on anything at all, but certainly not against you."

"Oh, I don't know," I broke in, "it would have seemed like a good bet to me as well, before we got going."

"That's not the point, man. You tried to get me out of this and it's my fault I'm back in it, so it's for me to deal with it."

I was impressed. Maybe this really was a step towards Pete taking some responsibility. He wouldn't be taking any more steps though, once Hillier had broken his legs.

"That sounds great, Pete, but now that you want to grow up, you can do it after you've paid off Hillier. Take the - "

"No."

I didn't have the energy to argue, but I said: "Don't be stupid, Pete, you can't get out of this with Hillier so easy."

"I've already been stupid, haven't I? And sooner or later, I'm either going to have to start doing things for myself, or I might as well give up."

There was a determined edge to his voice which I couldn't remember having heard in him before. Certainly not recently and maybe only years earlier, when he'd quit London and gone up north to get into the music scene up there.

"Sooner or later, yes," I said, "but not now, Pete. Not with this."

"Yes, now. Yes, with this. You stood up for me when I shouldn't have asked you to and I'm not going to have you do that again."

"Pete," I reasoned, "I appreciate what you're saying, but right now, this is just plain crazy. Even more nuts than making the bet in the first place."

He sighed. "Maybe it is, but it's right. Come on, Garron, haven't you ever done anything stupid, anything really dumb that you felt you just had to do?"

And I don't know what it was, whether it was fatigue, or pain, or the fact that Pete was finally sounding more like his old self, or the alcohol, or maybe just the rush of what was almost relief at having survived the night, but I told him. And to him it meant nothing, but God, it was a dangerous thing to have done and I realised later, that even if no damage had been done, I had lost my grip for a while.

"You killed someone?"

It was a question, but I could tell that he believed me, didn't need any confirmation, it was just his way of absorbing the information.

"Two people actually, but one was self defence, so I reckon it doesn't count in the same way."

"Wow! Who were they?"

"Man called Smith, would you believe and someone that worked for him. Couple of low life criminals and killers who got what they deserved."

"Yeah," said Pete, "but killing them...how did it happen?"

"I'm not going through the details, Pete. You asked me if I'd ever done anything stupid that people thought was stupid and in fact was stupid, but seemed right at the time and I told you. Now I'm going to tuck it back where it belongs, in a black hole where I don't go. And so are you."

"Oh yeah, totally, man."

There was a silence and then he said: "Funny thing is though, it doesn't surprise me."

"Oh, well, that makes me feel just great! I'm an unsurprising killer!"

"No. Well, yes, in a way."

"Okay, I think it's time to leave this conversation, before one of us drunk people says something that can't be unsaid."

Which is why there was little conversation going on a few minutes later when Jenny knocked on the door.

*

There was a predictable, but kind of comforting explosion of concern when she saw me and I had to explain with a shortened version, what had happened. At least it broke the silence that had fallen between Pete and me.

"You said you weren't going to fight." She turned on Pete. "This is your fault, isn't it?"

"It's not his fault, Jenny, he didn't know Hillier was setting me up."

"But," Pete cut in, still working on his new role as self-flagellating martyr, "it is my fault that you got into it in the first place."

Jenny was looking at me with real concern and I thought for a moment that she was going to cry, which was when I realised that I hadn't looked in a mirror yet properly, only the reflection in the office windows and I was probably a hell of a mess. She pulled herself together though and asked me if I needed a hospital, but I said no. I just wanted to get home. She had the cab waiting still, so I tried to get up and only just made it. My legs were beginning to seize up now and shake, both at the same time. Nothing to worry about, just a muscular reaction, but I had to get back home and collapse. The alcohol, although it had only been two cans, hadn't helped at all and in fact I was beginning to feel a little nauseous with it.

Jenny tried to support me and Pete also helped and somehow walking was more difficult than it had been coming out of the pub earlier.

"Christ, Garron," Jenny said, "you really are a mess. You've got dried blood all over you."

"It's not all mine," I said, which actually wasn't the best comment to make, but she didn't complain, just said: "Did you at least win?" and I grinned at her, which hurt even more and said: "to the tune of three grand" and shook the carrier bag, as Pete chipped in about how good I was and I shut him up. He was trying to be helpful, but I didn't need the ego build up and neither did Jenny.

We got out to the cab where the driver didn't want to take me. I promised him a healthy tip and told him to get us to Camden High Street. I didn't like the idea of the driver knowing where he'd collected me from, in case he decided to report a beaten up man as a pick up, but he was a mini-cab, not a black cab and I didn't think he would. In any case, I wasn't going to give him my actual address and he just dropped us near the tube station. I could walk from there. With help.

Pete had offered to come with us, but I didn't want him to. I'd offered him the money once more and he'd refused it as I'd thought he would and he hadn't said much else. That worried me a bit, but not enough to take my mind off the pain I was in. Maybe I should have gone to hospital, but all they would have done would be x-ray my ribs and wrist and check out the stitches. What I needed most was rest and I could get that better at home. Couldn't get a brain scan there of course, but nowhere's perfect.

The stairs were tricky, but once inside I got to the bathroom, propped myself on all fours under a slow shower and Jenny cleaned the blood and sweat off me. Bed was next and although it was hard to get comfortable, I found a position where the things that hurt most were not being lain on. From experience, I expected the various parts of my body to start causing trouble in stages now and that was what began to happen. My wrist started to throb and the stitched cuts pulsed. My ribs were painful and my arms and shoulders where I'd blocked most of Billy's punches were aching and sore. I took a double dose of painkillers and promised Jenny I'd wake her if I needed help during the night. Then I tried to sleep. The fight went through my head time and again and Pete's stupidity in betting against me and for such a big amount also crept in, but I was dog tired and soon enough I dozed off and the body took over its age old task of healing itself.

*

I woke in the morning with the familiar hurt that I thought I'd left behind years ago. I was okay until I moved, but then the pain flared up and I actually shouted out loud. That brought Jenny in from the kitchen where she'd been eating breakfast, trying to be quiet for my sake. Luckily, as I only had a mattress to sleep on which lay directly onto the floor, getting out of bed wasn't too difficult, but unluckily that meant I had to get up from the floor to stand, which wasn't too easy. Jenny had to help me to the toilet to wee and I was relieved that given the pain around my side and kidneys, there was no blood in my urine. I didn't pass that relieved thought on to my human zimmer frame

215

though, I reckoned she had enough to deal with, without that pleasantry. I couldn't hardly raise my arms and my hands and wrist were sore as hell, but as Jenny pointed out, I was moving which was more than she thought I'd be doing. And thinking about it, I remembered what it had been like after a couple of the hard pro fights that I'd had, once having to eat liquidised foods through a straw for a week because I couldn't move my jaw properly to chew and the time I was bruised up so badly that I couldn't hardly breathe. This was no worse than those occasions, the only difference was that back then I'd been in peak condition and now I wasn't. Jenny was sympathetic but sensible, pointing out that if I'd been in a car crash or fallen off a ladder, I could have been in a far worse state and although I thought for a while that that was a little unfair, she was quite right. As long as there was no internal damage, then I just had to rest up and I'd be okay in a couple of weeks or so. I did have a splitting headache though and I was tired after sitting up for ten minutes, so I eased myself back on the mattress and continued the healing process.

We didn't talk much about what had happened and for all Jenny's talk of not wanting me to change and not telling me what I should be doing, I got the impression that she wasn't too happy about the reasons for me being in this state and maybe she thought I could have avoided it. I was wrong though. After a couple of days, when I looked worse, but was beginning to feel a bit better I asked her about it straight out.

"No, I just don't want you to be hurt."

"That's it?" I asked, "no, 'it was a stupid thing to do', or 'you could have avoided it somehow'?"

She looked at me like I was mad.

"You told me you were suckered into it. You told me you couldn't get out of it and you got through it the best you could. So," and then she smiled at me, "unless you're lying to me, in which case I'd up and leave, then why would I be upset about that. I'm upset you're hurting and I don't want that to happen again, but nothing more than that."

"But you're not even bugging me about applying for jobs and stuff like that."

"Garron, in your condition, no-one is going to employ you. It's not even worth thinking about until you can shake hands with someone, or at least go out without a pair of dark glasses and a limp."

She was right of course and I settled into a recovery routine that involved being looked after and cooked for, playing a few games of scrabble, which she bought for us to 'improve my mind', reading some of her books, which she brought over from her bedsit and was something I'd never been much into and watching a fair amount of daytime TV, which was rubbish except for the old films which were sometimes on in the middle of the day. She didn't go to work for the first couple of days I was home, but then we reckoned I was okay to get to the loo on my own and she went back to the restaurant. She was staying with me though, not at her home and we both began to get used to that. I also got to spend more time with the cat, which pissed him off no end, but I was the one that paid the rent, well worked for it at least, so he had to lump it. After a week I was still stiff and aching, but the only real problems left were my hands which were still sore and my wrist which ached badly still, but which I was at least able to move.

I had to call Mick and tell him I couldn't collect the rent but I only missed one week and he said that was all right. By the second Sunday, although I couldn't drive, I was okay to walk and I got Tony to drive me around the route and I hobbled out where necessary and collected the envelopes. Jenny came with me 'in case,' she said, 'there was any trouble'. I couldn't talk her out of that, it was the condition that she made for me going at all and when I pointed out that Tony was there, she said nothing but held her ground. She and Tony hit it off pretty well when they met, considering that the circumstances of rent collecting don't make for usual social interaction, but she clearly didn't trust anyone else to look after me. Half way through the round I asked her just what she thought she would do if there was any trouble and she pulled an illegal electrical stun gun out of her jacket pocket.

"What the hell are you doing with that?" I asked her.

"Well, a girl's got to look after herself."

I was stunned into silence. At last I said:

"Where did you get that from anyway?"

"One of the girls at the restaurant got hold of one to keep behind the till for those dodgy Saturday nights when there could be some problems and we can all borrow it occasionally if we need to, or if we're going back late at night."

"Jesus," said Tony, "remind me to tip well if I ever eat in a Mexican restaurant again."

"So, you just carry that around with you?" I asked.

"If I think I might need to, yes." Then she added; "I took it on our first date, actually."

Tony collapsed in fits of laughter and nearly drove the car off the road.

"You did what?" I asked.

"Well, I didn't know you and one of the girls who saw you when you turned up at the restaurant that first time thought it would be a good idea to take this along. You know, just in case."

I was speechless again.

"I didn't bring it on our second date," she added.

"I should bloody hope not," I said as Tony broke up again.

The night was otherwise uneventful, but it did leave one question. I'd been too busy recovering to worry much about Pete, but Tony brought up the fact that he hadn't seen him around since the night of the fight and although he'd spoken to him on the phone, that had been a few days ago and now he was just getting voicemail. Jenny didn't say anything, but I could tell she didn't want me to follow that up and in my current state I didn't want to either. I was worried though. I told Tony about Pete owing money to Hillier and why and that I'd offered him the three grand towards it, but he'd turned me down. Also that I'd taken that to be a sign he was getting a sense of responsibility back again.

"Maybe," he replied, "but he was also dumb enough to bet money he didn't have with someone like Hillier." He sighed. "Maybe he is sorting himself out. This girl he's lodging with, I think they may be together now and she might be straightening his head out. Look, I'll call him again and just ask him to get in touch, let us know he's all right. If he doesn't answer his mobile, then I can always call the club and ask for him."

I shook my head.

"Don't do that, Tony, leave the club alone. There've been enough of us caught up with Adam Hillier, I don't think anyone else that knows me should get involved. He's got a way of controlling things that somehow draws people in and it just seems to happen. If you don't get a response from Pete, then I'll check it out...from a distance," I added, as Jenny started to say something.

"How can you do that from a distance?" she asked.

"I can do it, don't worry."

Tony left it at that and Jenny seemed to, although I knew she'd come back to it later and after Tony had dropped us back in Camden, as near to the flat as he could since he knew the address anyway, she picked it up again.

"I just don't want you to get hurt."

"I know."

"Is that all you can say about it?"

I was lying on the mattress. The night's work had tired me out more than I had expected and it might have been a bit rude, talking up to the ceiling, but I wasn't going to get up again.

"I'm not going to get into trouble, Jenny, for several reasons, but for one in particular. Pete's not going to let me. He wouldn't let me help him with the money, which was an easy thing to do and he's not going to let me do anything else. You heard what Tony said, he thinks Pete's growing up at last."

After a while she said:

"I've lied to you."

I didn't know what to say to that, so I kept quiet.

"I said I wouldn't ask you to change anything," she went on, "I said I wouldn't ask you to change, but I don't want you to get hurt again."

She came over and sat down on the floor next to the mattress.

"It's for selfish reasons. I'm just finding something with you and I don't want to lose it. If you get involved with Hillier again, it might be even worse than now, he might - "

"Easy, Jenny," I cut in. "I don't need to see Hillier again. I don't need to see Pete again either, unless he's straightened himself out and I don't intend getting hurt again if I can help it."

"But you said that before."

"Yes, I did, didn't I, but now it might be a little easier to keep to it."

"I'm not asking you to stop everything, you know, just to stay out of this."

"I know. That's fine. That's what I'll do. That's what I want to do."

She took a deep breath and lay down next to me, but facing away. After a while I nudged her.

"Don't fall asleep yet," I said.

She rolled over propped herself up on one arm and smiled down at me.

"Why not?" she asked.

"Light's still on," I replied, "and I'm in no fit state to get up and switch it off."

At least that drew a laugh.

*

Nightmare again, but this time I stayed in it until Smith's face had embedded itself so deeply in my consciousness that the image remained with me as I shouted and woke myself up. I'd been getting better, so what was it? I could be out now. I could walk away from the life, but I couldn't shake this. What was I looking for? Absolution? Justification? Forgiveness? Forgiveness from a killer who would have finished me without a second thought, without regret, without remorse, without conscience.

I snapped out of it and the room came into focus. That was it, of course. I still had a conscience and that was the problem. Jenny was still asleep, so maybe I hadn't shouted out loud, just screamed inside my head. I was cold, the sweat was cooling on me and I got up, bits of me aching still and sat on a straight chair at the table.

Conscience. I had one, or at least I had one about some things and that was bad. Or, if I was changing my ways, was it good? I looked back at Jenny lying on the mattress. To be with her, maybe I needed a conscience. Maybe I needed to be that sort of person. I thought back a few years. Did Al have a conscience? He never seemed to worry about anything that he'd done, but that might have been just front. Or perhaps he really was so sure what he did was right, that thoughts like this never bothered him.

So on the one hand I was struggling because I was too detached, but then I was struggling to sleep because I wasn't detached enough. I wanted to be able to turn on that cold, burning sensation that I used to have when I fought, but I needed to ditch that if I was going to have any kind of normal life.

-You had a 'normal' life for a while before and you chucked it.

-No, I had to change it to deal with Smith and that situation.

-Call it what you will, you made the choice.

Bloody mind working against me again, but sitting here my pulse rate was returning to normal and although I didn't want to sleep yet, I was okay. A few weeks ago I'd have been reaching for a bottle, but I didn't seem to need that now. The dreams would come or not, I couldn't control that, but I hadn't got to react to them by diving into a hole each time. I wasn't going to get any sudden revelation about what was happening to me or how I was dealing with it, so I would do what I usually did. Break everything up into pieces I could handle and get on with them. Right now, I was content to sit for a while and when I was ready I'd go back and lie down again, next to Jenny. I didn't need a drink to be able to do that.

*

I called Pete a couple of times over the next few days and left voicemail messages. At last I left one that said if he was still alive and trying to protect me from Hillier by not returning my calls, then he'd better speak to me soon, or I'd just go round to the club and front Hillier anyway. That was a bluff. I didn't want to confront anyone at the moment. I was still sore, my ribs were at the least bruised badly and it was quite possible that there was in fact a hairline crack there, as the doctor had said, given that they were still aching. If that was the case, I knew from times past that they could be hurting for six weeks. On top of that I was having trouble closing my right hand completely without getting pain in my wrist and that was worrying me more. Pete wouldn't know it was a bluff though and later that day he called me back.

"They worked me over because I couldn't pay." His voice was indistinct and it occurred to me that he might be in a worse state than I'd been after going four rounds with Billy.

"How bad?"

"Bad enough that I can't work, which is dumb because he still wants the money, but I can't work to pay him off."

I didn't bother explaining that paying the debt off wasn't the only thing Hillier was interested in. Having people know what happens to someone who doesn't pay up is also useful every now and again in Hillier's line of business. I didn't think Pete had worked this one out yet. It was also possible that the whole line that Hillier had fed me about Pete being useful around the club, might have been just that, a line to use while he worked out how to get what he wanted out of me, but there was no way of knowing.

"What are you living on, Pete?" I asked him.

"The girl I lodge with, she's not pushing me for the rent."

"What about the drugs?"

"She's not pushing the drugs either." It was a poor attempt at humour, but it made me think that he would be okay. "I'm rationing myself, but it's not easy. I'm going to have to get money from somewhere soon. To be honest, Garron, this girl will buy for me if I need it."

"She's buying for you? You're lodging with an addict?"

"No, but she knows where she can get stuff. She only uses soft drugs herself."

"Only," I said.

"Don't judge me, man, I kept you out of this."

"Yeah," I said, "but for what?"

He didn't reply.

"Pete, what are you going to do when Hillier comes back for the money?"

"He won't come back, he knows I don't have any."

"That's not going to stop him. Does anyone else know about the bet?"

"What do you mean?" he asked.

"I mean, was this a 'quiet handshake' bet, or a loud 'in your face' bet?"

He thought for a moment. "I guess it was pretty public. You mean he can't afford to lose face?"

"He can't afford for people to know that someone welshed on a bet with him, not in his position."

"Christ."

"Yeah, Christ."

After a while he said: "What do I do now?"

"Take the money I offered you, ask him to work off the rest. Either that or bugger off up north again and lie low, hope he lets it go."

"Do you think he would?"

"Don't know."

There was the sound of another voice from his side and he said something that I couldn't hear.

"Who was that?" I asked, more to fill the gap in the conversation than because I wanted to know.

"My landlady. Well, sort of my girlfriend as well if you haven't worked it out already. Why else would someone put up with me?"

I had wondered about that, but I didn't comment since I couldn't see anyone with half a brain being Pete's girlfriend either. Instead I asked him what she thought about what was happening.

"She's not happy. She works at the club as well, behind the bar, so she knows a little about what Hillier's like."

"And Hillier knows you're living there?"

"Yeah, he does."

"Let me give you the money, Pete."

"No."

"You're being stubborn."

"Yes."

"If you won't take the money, then clear out."

He didn't say anything to that. Then:

"I'll work something out. Don't phone me, Garron and don't go to Hillier. I'll call you when I've sorted this out."

"Don't do anything stupid, Pete. We didn't get this far to have you thrown into the river by some thug for a debt we can pay half of now."

"You can pay half of it. I can't. I've got to do things for myself, Garron, not keep passing things over to others. Hillier's not going to kill me. He knows you and Mick and he knows it could get messy."

I didn't say anything. I couldn't tell Pete, but the truth was that if he was taken out, killed, I wouldn't go looking for Hillier out of some revenge motive. Pete didn't mean that much to me anymore. I'd wanted to keep him alive and unhurt if I could, Tony had been right about that, but I wouldn't put myself in any kind of danger for him if he was dead. The other thing that I knew was that Hillier wouldn't worry about me at all if he decided to work on Pete. He'd shown that already.

Pete interrupted my thoughts. "I'll call you," he said and cut the connection.

*

"I like Tony, he seems like one of the good guys."

"He is," I said. "I grew up with him and he's managed to keep his nose clean and build his own business. Considering what the rest of us have managed not to do, that's pretty good going."

We were sitting at the table in the flat and I was healthily not thinking about Pete, or Hillier, or anything to do with them. What I was considering was the fact that I'd have to get someone to look at my stitches soon and take them out. I wasn't with a GP, but I'd go to one of the walk in medi-centres that were springing up all over the place. I certainly wouldn't be going back to Rob's doctor. The less connection I had with those guys, the better I'd feel. I was also thinking about the fact that Jenny was paying rent week after week, but spending most of her time here with me. I just wasn't sure about pushing the relationship further and whether she would want to keep her own bedsit. I didn't want to ask the question if the answer was going to be no. And I wasn't even sure that I wanted to give up my space, but so far we'd been good together and sooner or later it would get to the stage where it would be rude not to ask her to move in. Just for now though, a conversation about Tony seemed an easier option.

I was wrong.

"So what else did you two get up to then, in the bad old days?"

"There are a couple of stories, I suppose, but Tony kept out of trouble and after he met his missus, he was absolutely legit. She wouldn't let him out half the time."

"Do I get to meet his wife and kids?"

"Maybe one day, but Marie isn't too keen on me. She thinks I might drag him into trouble, which is unfair, because for a long time before he met her, I used to get him *out* of trouble." I shrugged, forgetting that it would hurt. "I can see her point though. He's respectable now and I'm still working the edges."

"Well, that may change if you turn up with me in tow."

"I hadn't thought of you being 'in tow' anywhere," I said, "and she is very protective of Tony." I pushed my thumb down hard on the table to illustrate.

"Being protective of someone is not the same as being under the thumb," Jenny said.

I shrugged again, knowing this time that it would hurt, but figuring it was less tiring than discussing Tony's home life further. I didn't get off that lightly though.

"So there's Pete, who isn't really a friend anymore and Mick, who I might meet and Tony and his family. Anyone else?"

I thought for a minute. There wasn't, which was a bit depressing really.

"Not to mention," I said. "There used to be, but I kind of lost touch with people. Lot of hangers-on at one point. There's Sean McGuire of course," I went on, "you'd like him and his wife would love you."

"What about Al?" she said, "I've heard you mention him."

I sat back in my chair.

"Al's dead, Jenny. He was killed a while ago now and I still don't know exactly how. But yes, Al was a friend."

"I'm sorry," she said.

228

"So am I, but it is what it is." I tried the smile again. "He'd have thought you were great, but I don't know if you would have taken to him."

"Why not?" she asked.

"Because he was a bastard. I'd have a good laugh with him and I learnt a lot from him and he would be absolutely the person you'd most want to have around if you needed help, but he was capable of being a real bastard."

"How come you were such good mates with him then?"

"I don't know, Jenny. Maybe because there's a part of me that's a bastard too."

*

I got the call two days later. It was Pete and he sounded finished, defeated.

"Garron, I need to talk to you and it has to be now. I know it's late, but it has to be now."

"You can't talk on the phone?"

There was a hesitation, then: "No."

All right, Pete, I'll meet you at - "

"No, you'll have to come to me. I'm in Finsbury Park."

"What, the actual park?"

"Yeah."

"Which bit?"

"Call me when you get here, I'll let you know."

He hung up on me and I tried to work out what exactly it was in his voice that had disturbed me. Resignation? Defeat? I didn't know, but as I picked up my car keys, it occurred to me that he could have been standing there with Hillier right next to him. Would he be setting me up? But why on earth would Hillier want to set me up? Besides which, Hillier was the sort of guy who would come at you direct, not through someone else. All the same, I went to the kitchen and opened the cupboard where I kept the gun, before deciding that I was being overcautious. Pete hadn't sounded right, but I didn't really want to be wandering around Finsbury Park with a gun in my pocket. I debated whether to call Jenny, but she was working and I didn't want to disturb her just to say I was going out. Telling her I was going to meet Pete might not go down too well either, so in the end I just scribbled her a note and left it on the table.

Finsbury Park is a hole of an area in North London, near where Arsenal play and where Pete and I shared the lock-up that he'd stolen half my furniture from. The park is a focal point for joggers and other less reputable groups and the local paper generally keeps track of what has happened there, or at least what has been recorded as having happened there. Right now, it's being 'rejuvenated', which means the alcoholics will have somewhere nice to leave their empties.

I left the car a little way away from the park itself and struggled out from behind the wheel. Driving had been manageable, but not comfortable; any sharp turns and it was painful to manoeuvre and even keeping my arms up for a protracted period of time made them ache. I made a mental note that next time I borrowed a car from Tony I'd ask him for power steering. It was still light out, even though it was late and it was a warm evening. Summer had finally come to London.

The station is a main connection for the underground and overground train networks, so there are usually people about and even at this late hour, business folk would be waiting on the platforms. Outside though, it was mainly the locals hanging around. It's a busy area and the shops were still open; convenience stores with junk food, newspapers, cigarettes and booze being the main offerings.

At the edge of the park I dug out the phone and called Pete. He sounded drunk, but that might have been the further result of one of Hillier's goons smacking him in the mouth again. He told me he was in the middle of the park at the small brown pavilion and told me to hurry. I didn't like that.

"What's up, Pete?" I asked. "What's wrong?"

"Wrong?" he said and almost laughed. "I haven't got much time, Garron and I need to talk to you now. You need to hurry up."

I needed to ask the question, so I said: "Pete, one word answer, are you alone there?"

This time he did laugh and I realised that he really was drunk. "Oh, yes," he said, "I'm alone all right. Don't worry, Garron, I'm not setting you up, but you have to hurry."

I didn't know what he meant, but I was aware that running through the park dressed as I was might get me stopped by any passing policeman. If I'd have been thinking straight, I'd have brought an old briefcase with, or something that marked me out as a commuter, rather than a possible loiterer. I'd got ten yards into the park when this thought got the better of me and I turned around, found the nearest open newsagents and bought a paper. Not great, but something to carry, something to be holding and it's surprising how often a small detail like that can change the way someone views you. Basic cover is better than none at all. I'd delayed a bit for Pete, but not by much and not by as much as if I was stopped and searched.

I went in through the Finsbury Gate. Like I said, they're trying to make the park a communal area, but if I had kids I'd still not let them roam here on their own. There may be tennis courts now and playground areas, but there are still too many guys sitting against the trees with White Lightning cans in their hands for it to be child friendly. Although of course, the winos are also part of the community. Just not too well integrated.

I could see the pavilion from the entrance. It was just before the kids playground area, which at this time of night would be full of teenagers hidden in the climbing structures, sniffing their aerosols, drinking their booze and smashing the bottles for a laugh, leaving the glass everywhere for the young kids to fall on the next day. I didn't see Pete though until I got up close. He was sitting propped up against a wall rocking gently with several cans of special brew lying on the ground next to him. He didn't look good, but the bruising on him wasn't new and I wondered what had prompted this latest binge.

"Drunk and disorderly in a public place? You'll get yourself pulled for this one day, Pete."

"Be quiet and listen to me, Garron, I haven't got long." His voice was quiet and I had to strain to hear him. In fact it was so low that I squatted down on the ground next to him and noticed that he was breathing slowly. His eyes were closed and he was still swaying and I started to get worried.

"I screwed it up, Garron. I wanted to keep you in the clear and I've fucked everything up."

"Screwed what up, Pete?" I spoke gently to him. "Whatever it is, we can sort it out. But you don't look too good. Maybe I'd better get you home."

He gave out a short laugh.

"Oh, I'm going home all right, I'm going home and it feels good right now."

I started looking to see if he was injured somewhere, maybe bleeding and I couldn't see it, but there was nothing. Nothing except the syringe on the ground behind him.

"What have you done, Pete, what have you taken?"

"Don't worry about that," he said, "I need to tell you something, I need - "

"Pete," I cut in, "What have you taken? Jesus, tell me what you've taken, I'm going to call an ambulance and we'll - "

"Garron!" he shouted and it took an effort. "For once, just listen. If ever we were mates, friends, please listen."

He was looking at me and I saw his eyes had changed, the pupils were tiny and I started to panic about him dying on me, before I remembered that he was a seasoned addict and knew what he should be taking.

"One minute, Pete and then I call the ambulance."

"One minute," he repeated, "okay. Don't know where to start, how to say this." He took what for him was a deep breath. "Girl I'm with, was with, Jane, she heard me talking to you on the phone, asked who you were and I told her you were the guy from the fight. She knew about that. I told her and she works at the club. She asked if you could help me and I said I wouldn't ask you. And then...and then I said it was a shame really 'cos you'd just told me you were a killer and that might solve a few things."

I took a deep breath. Idiot! Me as well as Pete. But I couldn't say that to him now. Later I'd wreck him for it, even though it was my fault and I should have known better. Talking was getting more difficult for him and I was about to interrupt him to call the medics when he went on.

"She asked me who you'd killed and I told her it was some villain called Smith, had to be a false name, but she never said anything. Then she says, she's going to get me off the debt with Hillier and goes out. I didn't ask her how. I didn't get the chance."

"All right, that's enough talk now. I'm calling an ambulance for you."

"No, mate, you're not. Because I'm dying here and I've done it to myself and you've got to listen to me so as I get one thing right before I pass out."

"What do you mean you've done it to yourself?"

"Big dose of heroin, mate, into the vein, more than usual and I'm going to sleep soon. No pain, never could stand pain. Waited until you called from outside the park to do it, so as I could talk to you before I pass out, but it won't be long now."

He was still rocking and his breathing was slower. He looked like he was beginning to sweat a little.

"Pete, I'll get an ambulance, get you to a hospital. You can be all right. I'm no expert, but OD-ing on heroin takes time and they can do something about it."

"Takes a lot less time if you're stuffed full of alcohol, mate."

I looked at the empty cans.

"I've planned this, Garron, I decided to do this, don't shit on my party."

"Why, though? Because you told this girl about me? So what?"

"So, she goes to Hillier, tells him she'll trade info for my debt. He says it'll have to be good and she tells him about you killing Smith. Here's the crunch, mate. Smith used to work for Hillier."

I felt things cave in around me. Ice snatching at the pit of my stomach. Smith used to work for Hillier.

"Somehow," Pete went on, "Jane knew that and she traded it for me. Except when she came back she threw me out. Told me what she'd done, told me she'd helped me enough and threw my stuff out of the flat. Said she'd got what she wanted and I meant nothing." He turned to look at me and it threw me because his pupils almost weren't there anymore. "Don't you see, Garron, I meant nothing to her. It was all for nothing. Getting sorted, getting work, trying to do the right thing. It all meant nothing."

It suddenly hit me where I'd heard the name Jane before. The woman who set up the brawl in Hillier's club. The one causing the trouble. The woman whose brother had died. She'd simply walked into the club and got herself a job there. No more fights, no more trying to disrupt things, she'd just sat there and bided her time. Maybe she'd thought she'd find out something on Hillier to turn over to the police, but he'd be too smart to leave any evidence of anything for the hired help to see. And instead she'd stumbled on me. Probably without even knowing who I was, that she'd even met me. She must have known the name Smith from when her brother was working for Hillier. And perhaps she didn't even think I would bring him down, perhaps she just wanted to stir things up, but she'd know by now that Hillier wouldn't be able to let this go. If someone had taken out one of his men, then he'd have to come back on it and that would put him in direct confrontation with someone who was, in Pete's words and my own, 'a killer'. For the woman that I had met, set on revenge of any kind, that would be a good enough opportunity. I wasn't sure what to do, or how to deal with this, but in the meantime I had to get Pete to a hospital. He'd stopped rocking now, which I took to be a bad sign and I started to panic.

"Pete, I'm getting an ambulance now. Can you hear me, Pete?"

"No ambulance, Garron." His voice was so small now I had to lean in to hear what he was saying, ended up supporting him. "I want it to finish now. I want this all to end. I'm too tired..."

"Pete," I called his name again, trying to get him to respond and he did, a few more words came out.

"Don't, mate, please don't get anyone, just stay here, just for a few minutes..." And then he said: "Hey... do you... remember... that time when we..."

He didn't get to the end and I took my jacket off and put it on the ground, laid his head on it. He was still breathing, although shallowly and I picked up my phone to call 999 and stopped. If I did, there would be a record of the number. It wasn't registered to me, but if it was traced, all the other numbers I had dialled or that had dialled me, would be available. Jenny, Mick, Tony, Hillier and certainly Pete, would all be there. I didn't know what the data protection act would make of that, but I wasn't prepared to find out if I had another alternative. I picked up Pete's phone and realised the same thing applied to that one as well, it certainly had my number on it for a start and what's more, it would be listed as the last number that had dialled in, so

I got up and ran for the nearest person I could find, choosing the young woman over the businessman and asking her to please call for an ambulance, there was someone passed out, maybe dying by the pavilion and I had no phone, telling her she didn't have to get involved, I would stay with the man, but would she please make the call. She did and as I heard her giving the instructions to the operator, I was running back to Pete, lifting his head off the floor onto my knee and then cursing myself for forgetting the basics, that's what panic does for you, but that's no excuse and turning him as quickly as I could into the recovery position, checking he was still breathing and then staying with him, feeling as emotional as I could remember in a dog's age as I thought about the friends we had once been and wishing to God he could have finished his sentence about whatever it was he had remembered us doing and wondering in a moment of clarity whether I was really upset about Pete maybe dying, or about what had happened to all of us since those times past.

I heard the ambulance before I saw it and I didn't understand why it had taken so long, maybe someone else dying, a pillar of the community, not a thieving junkie, or maybe someone being born, a life beginning with all its chances and possibilities, instead of one ending, where the chances had gone and the possibilities had petered out, heard the sirens while I sat there helpless, as helpless as I'd ever been, with my hand on his cold forehead, failing to work out why things happened the way they did and as the ambulance pulled into the park, I wished Pete untroubled dreams and left him there for them to find with a note I'd scribbled to say it was heroin and alcohol and it had been about twenty five minutes, maybe thirty, remembered to take his phone with me and stopped before the exit of the park to look back and see that they'd found him.

It would be something to say that I swore vengeance on Hillier for this, but that wouldn't be true. Pete was someone who had been a friend once, but no more. The hurt I felt was something that had been missing in me for a while, the hurt for another human being in pain and maybe Pete had brought that back to me, but even more, the hurt was for myself and I was at least able to recognise and admit that. The truth was basic. I was in trouble now and if I read Hillier correctly, he would be looking for me. He might not realise that I knew it, but that would be my only advantage. I hoped Pete didn't die. I wanted him to live and clean himself up and retire to the country and live happily ever after. But more than that, I wanted to do the same myself.

*

Jenny was at my flat when I got back there and straight away asked me what was up. I was clearly losing my touch. Time was, no-one would have been able to see that anything was up from looking at me, but she could. So I told her about Pete and I told her what she didn't know about the detail of the job I'd done for Hillier in his club and about the fact that Hillier would now almost certainly be looking for me.

"You can't know that," she said.

We were sitting on the two straight back chairs at the table and the flat, which had seemed like a sanctuary before, seemed to now be just a small oppressive room.

"I can know it, Jenny, I know his type and I've begun to know him as well. Maybe if he thought that it was just between him and me, that no-one else knew about it, then he might pass it off, but if there is any possibility that someone could find out that one of his people was taken out and that he knew who had done it and hadn't done anything about it, then it would be a loss of face and a loss of prestige, a challenge even."

"But does anyone else know?"

"This woman knows and she'll have made sure that Hillier's lads know about it and that will be enough. They'll want to be sure that one of their own would be looked after, or his killer tracked down, in case it happened to them."

"What is that, some kind of macho group thing, or what?"

"It's a confidence thing, but yes, it's a group thing as well. 'We all stick together and look after each other'. That helps if you're working in something which may turn violent."

She got up and closed the curtains. It was almost dark, but she did it because she needed to move, needed to have something to be doing, rather than sit opposite me with nothing to say. She turned from the window and asked the obvious.

"What are you going to do?"

I sighed. "I don't know. I really don't know. If he comes for me, well, he can't, because he can't know where I am. Unless he pressurises Mick, but I don't think he'd do that." I suddenly wasn't so sure. "At least, I don't think he'd do that. He's more likely to try to - "

My mobile rang. I answered the call and said: "Yes."

"Garron? It's Hillier."

How did he have the number? When had I - the time I'd got Pete to drop off the money back to Hillier. I'd taken him round and called from the car. And he'd noted the number down and stored it just in case. So he knew it was me and I'd go along with it. The only advantage was if he thought I was in the dark. So carry the call, but don't make it easy for him.

"How did you get my number?" I asked him

He laughed. "Be surprised what I can get when I need it, Garron. Now listen, I've got a proposition for you, something I'd like to discuss. Can we meet up? Go through it?"

My mind raced through the possibilities. He couldn't be genuine, he couldn't be. He suckered me into the fight with lies and he was doing it again now. I'd turn him down, make him work to find me, if he could. But then the longer this went on, the more he'd expect Jane to have told Pete. No, he'd have told her, warned her, not to do that. But he couldn't be sure. So if I wanted the surprise element, I'd have to move quickly. I couldn't work this all out in my head, it was too complicated trying to second-guess the guy.

"I'm not interested, Hillier, I've fought your fight, I'm not interested in anything else. I just want out and away from you." Sign of weakness, backing away, but true at least. Maybe he'd let it go.

Some hope.

"I'm not asking you to fight, that's over and done with, but I can make you some quick money for a short term agreement. Nothing you wouldn't be happy doing. It's advice I'm looking for, not action."

Didn't believe him, too many explanations, too nice, out of character and he'd set me up before. Jenny was pacing up and down, knew who this was, couldn't sit still and I was sweating, felt trapped. I couldn't control the conversation, couldn't talk my way out. I didn't know the best thing to do.

"I'm sorry," I said, "I've had enough of this kind of stuff, I'm taking a long break out of London and when I come back, if I come back, I'll be working a different side of the street."

There was a silence, then he said:

"But Mick will know where you are, won't he? I, we that is, can always ask Mick where to find you."

Whether it was the words or the tone, the implication was crystal. I didn't need confirmation, but I pushed for it anyway.

"He won't know, Hillier, we're not that close. I don't send him a postcard every time I go on a day trip."

"I'm sure he will, Garron, I'd make sure we ask him carefully in any case."

No implication then, a straight threat. And he knew that I'd caught it. There'd be no point if I hadn't. What to do? Get angry? Or go along with it? Make sure he didn't think I had any clue as to what he might want from me. Like my head on a stick.

"Do you always get what you want, Hillier?"

He laughed again. "Usually, Garron, usually. Now I need you to come to one of my businesses - "

"What, now?"

"Yes, now. I've got a deal I'm clearing tomorrow morning first thing and I need your advice on it tonight."

"It's nearly ten 'o' clock, Hillier," I said, more for the look of the thing than for any other reason. I didn't expect him to change anything, he'd mapped this out in his own mind, had thought through any objections I'd put up and had reasonable answers for them. What I didn't know was whether he had any idea that I knew he wanted me dead. And that was my only card. So I was going to give in, but not before I'd made all the appropriate noises.

Jenny had stopped pacing and was looking at me with an expression I couldn't read. Maybe it was better that I couldn't.

"It's business, Garron and business doesn't stop at any particular time of the day. I've got a carpet warehouse in the East End, off Brick Lane." He gave me the address. "How soon can you be there?"

It would take me maybe twenty-five to thirty minutes to get there, park up and look around, certainly if there was any traffic, but I wanted to be there well before he expected me, so I said maybe an hour and told him I'd leave straight away. Of course that could have been pointless, he could have been sitting in the warehouse already.

"I'll see you there, Garron," he said. "Don't worry, I won't keep you long."

I'll bet not, I thought, but the conversation was over.

I could feel Jenny looking at me and I couldn't take her gaze. Her question when it came was more of a statement.

"You're not going to meet him?"

I didn't answer her, didn't know how to say it.

"You think he wants to kill you, to murder you and you're thinking of going to meet him."

At last I said: "I don't have a real choice."

"Yes, you have a choice. You can sit it out, he doesn't know where you are, or we can leave, get out of London, go somewhere else."

This time I looked at her. She had an expression on her face that was half disbelief, half non-understanding and I didn't blame her. She deserved a straight answer, so I gave her a straight answer.

"Hillier will take it out on Mick if I don't go to him. If that happens, either Mick would, under let's say, 'pressure', give out this address, or if I'd done a runner, he'd simply have nothing to trade and be in worse trouble."

"Call Mick, tell him what's happened."

It would, of course, seem like a logical thing to do, but that's not how it works.

"I can't call him. I can't put that onto him."

"Maybe he can clear out as well."

"He can't. He just about manages to get from his flat to the local pub and back."

"That's not your problem."

"Oh, it is. It is my problem."

She came over and knelt down in front of where I was sitting.

"We could just get away," she said, "vanish for a while. I can get a job anywhere in a restaurant and you can pick something up."

"Some cash in hand job that doesn't leave a trail anywhere?"

"Yes, I'm sure - "

I put my finger on her lips, stopped her talking.

"Jenny, you don't understand. There are maybe three people in this world I couldn't abandon. You, Tony and Mick. In the end that's what this is about. I thought I was fireproof. I thought I had no ties. No-one knows about you, Tony's a step away from people like Hillier and I thought Mick was too well protected, but I was wrong. I can't call Mick, because even if he said, 'clear out, son, I can look after myself', I wouldn't be able to. I couldn't put that on him. In the end, if I haven't got that, I haven't got anything."

"But you'd still have me," she said. "Isn't that enough?"

Hell of a question and I thought before I answered it.

"I'd have you," I said, "but I might not be able to live with myself."

"But if you go and meet this man, I might lose you."

"If I run and something happens to Mick, I'll be no use to you or anyone."

She got up and walked to the window, looked out through the curtains she'd just drawn.

"It's a bit like my Mum. That feeling that I'm not enough."

"It's not like that at all," I said. "I'm not abandoning you, I'm not turning away from you. I'm trying to do the right thing."

"But you might not come back," she said, still staring out of the window.

After a moment, as the realisation of it struck home, I said: "No, I might not come back." Then I got up and went to stand behind her. "But it won't be for lack of trying."

I put my hand on her shoulder, was going to turn her round to me, but she didn't respond and I took my hand away and went into the kitchen, reached up into the cupboard behind the cereal boxes and took out the Tesco bag with my gun in it. I checked it was loaded, slipped it into the loop in my jacket pocket and put the full speedloader into the pocket on the other side which still had a lining in it. When I turned round, she was standing in the doorway to the kitchen, watching me.

"I didn't know that was there," she said.

"Well, I don't advertise it and you don't eat cereal," I replied, thinking that I should have told her at some point that there was a gun in the flat and would she be angry about that as well.

"You're right," she said, "it's not the same as with my Mum, but it's still not easy to take. With all I said about not wanting you to change, not expecting you to do anything different, I still didn't think that you'd be walking out to meet someone that we know wants to kill you. And now I see you loading a gun. It...it's not easy."

I walked over to her, but she still didn't want to be held, turned away to the other room.

"Are you going to kill him?" she asked.

"If there's nothing else I can do," I said and a part of me noted how matter of fact the statement was. I'd killed before and it had almost unhinged me. It had caused me sleepless nights and driven me to look at what I had become and now I was stating that I was willing to do it again without a flicker.

Not willing, I caught myself. Prepared to, but not willing.

Maybe that was important.

I'd followed her back into the main room. The cat had come in and was inspecting its empty food bowl. Maybe we were domesticating him too much by feeding him. If he wanted to kill, he just did, no second thought, whether for food, or for survival. Should I be that different? This wasn't about monetary gain, or territory, or status. This was about staying alive. Didn't I have a right to stay alive?

"It's not real," she said, "standing here talking about it like this, it's not real."

I had nothing to add to that, so I kept quiet.

"I want you to come back to me," she went on, still not looking at me. "I need you to come back, but I don't know if I can deal with it. It won't just be him, will it?" she added. "There'll be others there."

"Maybe," I said, "I don't know."

"Yes, you do know," she said quietly.

I looked at my watch. I needed to be moving and I needed to keep the state of calm going that I seemed to be operating in at the moment.

"I have to leave now," I said.

She turned at last and handed something to me. The keys to my flat.

"I can't sit here," she said. "I can't sit here not knowing whether you'll be coming back or not. I can't stay here. "

"I'll call you. When - "

"No. Don't call me. I have to think about this. About the fact that even if we come through this, it could happen again. Another set of circumstances, another problem, another friend of yours in trouble. So don't call me. Let me be."

She picked up her jacket and left. No slamming doors, no histrionics, just honesty. The honesty that said she didn't know how to handle this. Few people would be able to and I certainly didn't know what to do to help her with it. There was no play-acting here, as there hadn't been all through our relationship. It had been too important for that and it still was. But Hillier wouldn't just go away and I didn't have any other ideas as to how to deal with him. Force a standoff, if I could, work out a truce if it was possible. It all depended on what he wanted, none of it was up to me. If I could have run and left Mick safe, I think

I would have done. Maybe not a few weeks ago, but now, with Jenny, I would have gone. But I didn't have that option, Hillier had closed all the doors. Including maybe, the one that now separated Jenny and me.

I put her keys, maybe the spare keys now, down on the table and stupidly, said goodbye to the cat. Like he would understand. But he was the only one around and I was prepared to take cold comfort where I could.

*

I sat in the car and switched on the radio, switched it off again. Did I want silence or noise? Turned on the cassette, got Led Zeppelin, *Gallows Pole*, but I could do without that image, so I turned it off again. I'd been here once before, driving to a confrontation and I'd been lucky. This time I couldn't see how to plan for what might happen. Hillier would be in his element. His element, I thought, not mine. I was out of my depth in another man's world. How many people would he bring with him? Enough to be sure, but not too many witnesses. Five in all? Six? It was too many. If there were five or six, it would be too many. I didn't have enough bullets to miss six guys a couple of times each. Would he search me? Would he have someone waiting with a gun on me as I walked in? I didn't think so, but there was no way to know. Professionally speaking, that would be the right thing to do, but it didn't have the class that Hillier would want to portray. I'd walked into the supposed meeting with him at his pub unarmed and he'd have no reason to think I'd do any different this time. Unless of course he thought I knew why he wanted to see me. And unless he was worried about my having killed Smith.

My head was now working too hard. I tried to think about the fact that if Hillier knew the circumstances of Smith's death, he'd know that he'd been shot with a gun that was found there and maybe he wouldn't think I had another second weapon. Or it all hinged on whether he thought Jane would have told Pete what he'd done and Pete would then have told me. Couldn't answer that one. In fact I couldn't answer any of them, I really didn't know what I *could* do, but I knew I couldn't leave Mick to Hillier, so I'd have to play it as it came. And if I was killed...well that was it really, I wasn't sure anymore. I knew I didn't want to die, but if I did, then I did. Which was weird. And I started to wonder whether I really cared for Jenny enough if that was my attitude, but if I didn't, then there wasn't any hope for me at all, so I had to.

And I did. But this scenario existed outside of that relationship, not that it was bigger or more important, it was just there. Something that had to be done, not out of any macho stance, but because there didn't seem to be any way of not doing this and living with it. And no, I didn't want to be killed, I really didn't, but I was able to accept the fact that it could happen and carry on. Which was also weird. And in the back of my mind, hiding away as though I didn't want to examine it too closely, was the thought that although she had walked out, given me the keys back and all, I still didn't think that we were over. Or maybe I couldn't think about that possibility while this still had to be dealt with. One crap thing at a time, Garron, you can't cope with more than one crap thing at a time.

I hadn't switched on the ignition yet and I could sit here for eternity working this through and getting nowhere right up to the time that Hillier's lads tracked me down street by street to this spot and emptied two dozen rounds through the car window into me, or I could start the car and drive to Whitechapel.

It took an effort, but I turned the key.

That made sense really. The body tries to protect itself. If you're falling over, the body tries to regain its balance automatically. You may still fall, but your brain instructs your body to fight it. I reckoned that if you were driving to be shot and killed and you knew it, your hand might not want to turn that starter key.

I drove out of Camden down the main road towards town and then turned left onto Euston Road towards Kings Cross. I suddenly felt very tired. I think someone once said that if you were tired of London, you were tired of life. I looked around me at London passing by. I was tired of everything. But I wasn't ready to give up on life yet. Problem was, I didn't have a plan. I didn't know how things were going to go. I was just hoping to play it as it came, which wasn't the best plan in the world. I think that in the back of my mind, I thought I would be able to reason with Hillier, to argue that whatever had happened between me and Smith was just between me and Smith and no-one else, but the front of my mind was screaming that I was an idiot and I should go in with my gun out and ready to shoot. I was near to Euston Station by the time I'd decided to compromise. I'd leave my hand on the gun in my pocket and if anyone tried to search me I'd fire straight away. Other than that, I'd try to talk, at least until I could see that it wasn't going to help.

Past Kings Cross and I remembered how when I was a kid that station used to be, in my child's mind, the gateway to everywhere. We didn't go to Heathrow, or any of the airports, so as a North London lad, the stations were the way we all thought we would get out. Jump on a train and go anywhere. If you could afford it and they hadn't broken down. I had the fleeting thought that I could do that now, get a ticket and disappear, but the same reasons that I'd said no to Jenny were still there.

Pentonville Road - associated forever with the prison, okay a women's prison, but still a lock-up. I'd killed and I was on the outside. Maybe I shouldn't be. Maybe what was going to happen tonight was God, or nature, redressing the balance, showing me that I couldn't take a life and get away with it. But I wasn't a religious man and if there was morality behind this, then Hillier and Smith were both as guilty as me, if not more so. If I had to kill to survive, I didn't see that as wrong. I had worried about it before, but this time, it passed me by. With Smith I had worried about whether I could kill. Now I knew that I could. This time it was more about whether I would have the opportunity before I myself was taken out.

Why wasn't I worrying about it? Was it the detachment again, or did it really not bother me? Was it true that having killed once, then it was that much easier to do it again? And if I really wasn't worrying about taking another life, then why had I had such trouble sleeping during the past few months? None of this made sense. A psychologist might tell me that there was no reason why it should, but I wanted to know. Was this different somehow? Had Hillier pushed me to a point that Smith had not, or was it because in my own mind I thought that I could have avoided confronting Smith back then, but not Hillier now?

This was too much to think about, but I also remembered that when I'd driven to meet with Smith that time, I'd lost it a bit, had a bloody panic attack on the way and yet this time I was calm. Detachment again. Control some would call it, but I didn't think so because I wasn't having to try to control it, I actually was calm.

City Road, council accommodation and not far from the million pound bonus boys of the City. How London survives without imploding is a mystery. Something to do with the English character perhaps, or just general human nature.

Past the eye hospital to the Old Street roundabout and once past that I hung a right down towards Shoreditch and then on to Commercial Street and Whitechapel. I was running parallel to Brick Lane now and I cut across lower down to park up on one of the back streets above Whitechapel Road. I locked the car up and thought about the fact that the last time I'd been here, I'd been shopping for a gun. A gun that was in my jacket now and that I hadn't to date fired in anger. If I was going to survive the night, that would probably change in the next thirty minutes or so.

The Royal London Hospital was close by, opposite Whitechapel tube station. I'd been in there before, not for myself, but to visit a friend who'd tried to limbo dance under a bus - whilst driving a car. Not that he knew I or anyone else was there. He was busy communing with his God about whether to have a face to face meeting or not. The fact that he didn't, gave me a degree of confidence in the hospital if I needed it later. Assuming I survived at all.

And that was something to think about. Not only surviving, but surviving clean. Right now, there was no record of me being in the area, nothing to tie me to a place where shooting and killing might occur. A hospital admission anywhere in London, but especially around the corner from the site of a shooting, would be difficult to explain to the police and the chances of me getting away clean were small. But then again the chances of me getting away at all were pretty bad anyway.

I stood for a moment by the car. The sounds of London's East End were all around me and I had to walk away from them to a warehouse where someone probably wanted to kill me.

Crazy.

Mind you, at least there was a history of it round here.

The gun was still in the loop in my jacket pocket hanging down where the lining of the pocket used to be and I closed my hand around it to mask the shape slightly and to stop it swinging around too much. I was still having trouble closing my fist fully without it hurting, but I thought holding and firing the gun would be all right. Besides which, I didn't have a choice.

I walked past squat blocks of flats, closed up shops, a concrete five-a-side football pitch and every so often an off licence, or a takeaway still open, trying for the last few sales that would make it worthwhile. Then I was into the cloth and fabric centre of London. Big warehouses selling huge mass-produced rolls of cloth next to small specialist shops, trying to survive by being the best at something, the fastest supplier, the cheapest, or the one that you'd been trading with for the last ten years and which was the last place in the UK where you could get a line of credit. Almost all of them with metal roll shutters protecting them from the casual smash and grab punk, or guaranteeing their insurance payout against the professional thief.

Hillier's warehouse was set back from the road behind a small car parking area. The sign across the top proclaimed it sold carpets to all and I wondered whether they'd ever rolled a body up in one to transport it discreetly.

For a minute, as I'd started walking from the car I'd had some thought about trying to find a different way in, breaking a window or something, but that wouldn't square with the image of an unarmed man walking innocently in and then talking his way reasonably out and in any case, as I approached the warehouse one of the main double doors at the front was open and Bobby from the club was waiting for me. He waved me towards him and I thought that this was the moment of truth. I would keep my hands in my jacket pockets, one covering the gun, the other the speedloader and hopefully the casual look would work. If anyone tried to search me, I'd pull the gun and take it from there.

I nearly stopped when I reached him at the door. I just naturally didn't want to have him behind me as I walked in and I suppose the subconscious didn't want to go in there anyway, but although I slowed, I carried on past him and he probably thought I was going to make some smart comment and then decided not to.

There was a short 'airlock' type space and another set of double doors and then a large warehouse filled with racks of carpet rolls that formed corridors to the left and ahead of me and stood to a height of two floors. There were stairs at various points around the sides of the warehouse that I could see leading up to walkways around the second floor with offices built in against the far and right hand walls looking out over the storage space below. A ground floor office and reception to the right, a small forklift by the side of the office and Hillier and two of his boys straight ahead of me, the other side of a piece of large green plastic sheeting which had been spread out on the floor. I stopped a few feet short of it and felt Bobby come in and stand behind me. I wondered if there were any more of Hillier's hired hands elsewhere in the building, but I didn't look around or ask. He knew I wasn't a fool and he'd be expecting the obvious question. He looked the part though. Big man in a suit, flanked by his minders, sure of himself and his world. I couldn't see any guns yet, but they would be there. It wouldn't be classy to have them on show yet for the sake of only one man.

"I hope you don't want me to step onto that," I said, nodding my head towards the sheeting. I made no other move. Didn't want to appear threatening in any way.

"It would be easier if you did," he replied.

I carried on the dumb show.

"Just because I won the fight?"

He laughed a short laugh. "You know, I think I believe you, Garron, I think you don't know why, so I'll tell you."

I wondered whether to pull the gun now. Hillier was close to his two lads, I might get a couple of shots off before anyone moved. But then Bobby was too close behind me and he would at the least knock me over before I could finish things and certainly before I'd have got to him. And I did want to get to him. The look on his face as I'd walked in had been a sneer and if I hadn't have had other things to think about, I'd have nutted him there and then.

On top of that, I thought as Hillier spoke, I wasn't a practiced shot to be able to take out three men on the move. I'd almost certainly miss. So I stayed still and waited.

"Man called Smith, Garron," Hillier continued and I stayed deadpan. "I understand you killed him."

I'd thought it was a statement, but it was a question and when I didn't answer Bobby leant in and pushed me on the left shoulder.

"Answer Mr. Hillier, Garron."

I didn't look behind me, stayed in eye contact with Hillier. "The answer is yes, I killed someone called Smith and if you put your hand on me again, Bobby-boy, I'll break it for you."

Hillier glanced past me, presumably telling Bobby to back off and there was no comeback from the man behind me. I'd been working things out as best I could and the way they were positioned now, I didn't have too many options.

"Smith used to work for me," Hillier said.

There was quiet for a moment, then:

"Did you hear what I said, Garron? Smith used to work for me."

"I heard you, Hillier, I just don't know what to say to you. If I'd have known he worked for you I would still have killed him, because he was trying to kill me." I looked him dead in the eye. "He and you are in a tough business. I didn't choose to kill him," and even as I said it, a part of me wondered just how true that was, "but it happened. Smith knew the business and so do you. You don't kill someone for no reason and I didn't know I was treading on your business, so why all this?"

"It wasn't my business. I wasn't involved," he said and for a moment I thought I could see a way out of this, but then he closed it again. "Smith was working for himself. I said he could, but he was still on my books and I have to look after my people. Otherwise they lose faith in me."

"Smith was working for himself, while he was working for you," I said. "I don't believe it. You're not the sort of person who - "

"He was my friend, Garron, he'd been with me for a long time. I said he could branch out a bit, but still pick up a wage from me. And you killed him."

And the timeframe narrowed to zero. I tried to get the conversation going again. I wanted to move when they didn't expect me to, not when I had no other choice.

"How did you find out about this, Hillier? When did you find out about this?"

He ignored me.

"Step onto the plastic, Garron."

"It was that girl, wasn't it? Works in your club behind the bar."

It didn't matter now whether he worked out that I'd known before I'd stepped into the warehouse. I just wanted a few seconds more to pick my own moment.

"It was Jane, wasn't it," I said. "She gave you this info and she got it from Pete and she's also the one that was causing you the hassle in your club, but you don't know that yet. She's played us off against each other, Hillier. Do you like being manoeuvred, because that's what she's done to us."

It wouldn't make any difference, just might have made him think for a minute, but then Bobby chose that moment to grab my shoulder and try to push me onto the green plastic shroud saying: "Come on, Garron, you heard Mr. Hillier, onto the plastic," so I turned slightly to my left to face where he was standing behind me with his hand still outstretched towards my shoulder, took my empty left hand out of my pocket and shot him through my jacket with the gun that I still held in my other hand.

It wasn't a scientific shot, but it hit him in the stomach at close range and he doubled over and fell backwards at the same time and I ran like hell down the first corridor of racks and waited for the feeling of the bullet entering my back, not hearing a thing, deaf in the immediate aftermath of the shot, but waiting to feel that bullet hitting and pushing me even faster forwards, but it didn't come and I took the first break in the racks to the right, while my legs hurt and my wrist screamed from the recoil of the gun and I struggled to get the damn thing out of my jacket pocket as I kept moving.

A shot exploded from my right as my ears cleared and I crossed the next corridor, but nothing hit me although the sound made me flinch and I carried on to the back wall, thought about climbing the steps to the second floor walkway, bottled it and turned left down the length of the warehouse running at full tilt, ducking to the left behind one of the racks and stopping dead. Sound of my own breathing sawing in my lungs. Chest heaving, ribs on fire, my legs and back in agony. I couldn't run anymore, but I couldn't stay here. They would know pretty much where I was. I couldn't be seen because of the stacked carpet rolls, but they'd just flank me and that would be it. I looked up. The second shelf of the rack would give me some height and the cover would be about the same, but at least I wouldn't be exactly where they would expect me. I tucked the gun back in my pocket and hauled myself up to the second shelf and then for good measure, the third. It would have been an easy climb if I'd have been in any kind of condition. As it was, my wrist screamed at me and my shoulders and legs simply didn't want to work. But the adrenalin was flowing, which is another way of saying I was bloody scared and I managed it without thinking about it too much.

I lay flat on top of one of the rolls, a dull orange thing with no pattern and then moved to a darker one. I didn't think there was much use in being camouflaged in a carpet warehouse, but any slight edge could help. And this new position also had the advantage of being to one side of the stack and slightly lower, so my left side was hidden by another roll. From eighteen feet up I could see straight down along the corridor to my right and if I stuck my head up over the top of the stack, a little way to the left as well. I didn't want to move too much though. Lying still I felt safer, movement might be seen.

My mate Bobby was out of view at the end of the furthest corridor away from me, but I reckoned they would have left him to bleed and the fact that I couldn't hear anything might mean he'd passed out. Or died. I also couldn't see anyone else, which was worrying because they'd have to be coming for me. I could wait all night, but it wouldn't take long for them to find me in here and Hillier would want this wrapped up before any of his legitimate day staff turned up.

Movement between the racks in the corridor in front of me. Someone keeping to the side, but moving towards me. I held the gun out to arms length, keeping flat against the roll of carpet and supported my right hand with my left. My wrist was aching again and after a couple of seconds my arms and hands started to shake. I wasn't sure if this was because of the position I had taken up, or because of the physical state I was in, but the stupid thought came into my head that the next time I was planning on having a gun battle with a bunch of gangsters I'd try to arrange it so that I hadn't just been through an eight minute fight with a fourteen and a half stone thug at some point within the previous ten days.

I put the gun down for a moment to try to give myself a rest, but I saw the movement again, took up the position and the next time I saw the figure, fired at it. I was maybe thirty feet away and I missed. Dumb! All I'd done was give him a better idea of where I was. Then I heard something thud into the carpet roll that was shielding my left hand side and I crawled forwards to the end of my section and took a quick glance over the roll to my left. One of Hillier's goons was on the walkway level with me and he'd worked out roughly whereabouts I'd hidden and was taking aim again. He was only maybe fifteen to twenty feet away and I sighted over the roll, steadied myself and squeezed the trigger gently. The noise was huge and the recoil still hurt, but maybe because I hadn't had to extend my reach, the shot was good and he slumped down, blood pumping from his chest, so I must have hit an artery or something vital.

I looked back to where I'd missed shooting the man to the right and ahead of me and he was still there. Hadn't seemed to have moved, but he fired up at me and the noise was there again and I felt something thud into the carpet close to my head, much too close to my head and I thought, this could be it, that was the sighter, this could be it and I scrabbled backwards along the rack, not knowing whether I was making a more noticeable target by moving or not, but knowing that I couldn't stay where I was. And then there was another explosion and it missed me and I thought how strange it was that these sounds which I could hear and which I was taking in my stride now, which I recognised, were actually the sounds of death in the air and if one of

the shots were to hit me I would just stop. No more hearing anything, no more thinking, no more. And I caught myself wandering like this even as I was trying to get out of the way and I
thought, 'concentrate you idiot, concentrate on what you're doing, what you need to be doing' but I couldn't really take it all in.
I was trying to stay alive and I couldn't quite believe it and
maybe that was just as well, because if I'd have realised how bad
my position was, I might have panicked and frozen and been
finished there and then.

Another sound, different, masked by the sound of the
shooting and I risked a look over to the left and saw the forklift
coming down the corridor, nearly at my rack and thought it
must be Hillier driving it, because there was only him and the
man on my right who were still functioning. And again the brain
registered stupid thoughts, like the fact that Hillier could drive a
forklift and know how to handle it and I pulled myself up short
and tried to concentrate again. Fired two shots at the cab over
the carpet rolls, but it didn't seem to have any effect and now I'd
lost track of how many shots I'd fired and when I'd have to re-
load, but it couldn't be yet and I was going to check, when the
forklift turned in the corridor next to my rack and the forks
started to rise. Sound of another shot from my right and the
wind of a bullet past me and this was too close, too bloody close
and then I suddenly realised what Hillier was doing with the
forklift as the rolls on the rack below me were pushed off and fell
to the floor and then the forks came higher and I took a last shot
at the man on the right and swung myself off the edge of the
rack I was lying on, holding on to the bottom with both hands so
that the drop would be only about seven or eight feet and that
was when the carpet rolls on my rack went tumbling down and

for the most part missed me until I was caught by one a glancing blow and I fell down on top of them, the last one landing on a pile next to me and slipping sideways, coming to rest half across my left leg.

I looked to the right and saw the man I'd shot at was on the ground, still moving, but curled up and facing away from me. I must have hit him, but I couldn't see where. I also couldn't see my gun although it must have fallen near me. The forklift stopped and the engine cut out. There was suddenly quiet in the warehouse, where moments before with the shots, the carpets falling and the forklift engine, there had been a maelstrom of sound.

I heard the cab door of the forklift slam and tried to push the carpet roll off me. It felt like it weighed a ton, but it rolled, so I kept pushing at it while I looked around desperately for my gun. Then I saw it on the floor half showing beneath a green nylon looking carpet, only a few feet away, but it was too late, Hillier stepped through the now empty rack from the next corridor, a gun in his hand by his side. Left handed, I noticed, for no real reason.

"Underestimated you again, Garron," he said. "I'm almost sorry to do this, but it's gone too far now."

And that was it. Not like the movies, no preamble, no explanation, no time. Most of all, no time. One moment you're alive, thinking about your next move and then there's no time left for thought, for words, for anything.

He raised the gun and I actually heard the shot, flinched from the impact, before the brain registered that there had been no physical impact. I don't remember closing my eyes, but I must have done, because when I opened them I saw Hillier slumping to one side on top of the carpet rolls, the gun falling from his hand. I looked to the right and there was the girl, Jane, or Nicola as I knew her name to be, standing not ten feet away, both hands holding a gun out in front of her, a terrified expression on her face.

I got my right leg up and used it to push the carpet roll the rest of the way off my left leg. Hillier's gun was on the floor next to him and not that far from me. I moved towards it and the girl moved her aim around so the gun was pointing at me.

"You going to shoot me too?" I asked. "After all I've done for you?"

Gallows humour, but I had little to say and I didn't know which way she was going to jump.

"Shut up! Don't say a word to me." Scared voice, right on the edge.

I shifted into a more upright position, looked straight at her. I wasn't sure she would shoot me, but until I knew she wouldn't, I needed that gun.

"Three words," I said. "He's not dead."

"He is. I shot him. He's down."

I was suddenly very tired. I even broke the golden rule for a moment and took my eyes off her and looked down.

"Not everyone you shoot dies," I said. She was shaking now and the hard facade was long gone. "I'll check him," I said.

She didn't respond and I pushed myself up and across the couple of yards to where Hillier was lying. I was now nearer his gun and I hadn't even lied to get there. He was still alive. Pale, shaking and struggling to breathe, so I thought maybe the bullet had hit a lung, but still alive. He knew I was there so I threw away the rule book completely, turned half away from the girl and squatted down next to him.

"She...with you then, Garron?"

"No, I didn't know anything about her being here."

"Why did she...shoot me...then?"

"She had a brother, Hillier, guy called Stuart. You threw him out of a window, so she says."

He laughed, or tried to. What came out was a sickening sound and blood bubbled slightly out of his mouth.

"Stuart? The junkie...that jumped. We didn't...throw him. We tried to stop him...jumping, but he was off his head. Thought he could...fly. Tosser."

The effort of the sentence had hurt him and he closed his eyes. I owed him one thing more though, from the original agreement.

"She was the one causing you trouble at the club."

He didn't open his eyes, but after a moment said:

"Should've...told me, I wouldn't be here like this now."

"But I'd be dead," I pointed out.

I put my hand on his gun, moved to stand up and he gasped out.

"You've got to kill me, Garron, you...can't leave...me."

I nodded. I knew what he meant. Not just that he didn't want to be left here dying, but that if by some chance he did survive, then my life and those of the people I knew, wouldn't be worth anything. There would be no finesse about it. Tonight had been to the death and I didn't have the luxury of mercy. I couldn't take the chance, however small, of him surviving.

I picked up his gun and hesitated. I'd done this before, but that seemed a long time ago and for all that had happened, on some level I still liked the man. And this was different from the gunfight that had just ended. Murder? Against someone that had tried to kill me and would try again given the chance?

"Do it!" It was almost a snarl, the lips curled and the teeth bared, whether in pain or anticipation I didn't know.

I took aim and shot him twice in the head.

In the silence that followed, there was a noise from the side and I turned to face it.

She was still standing there, shaking slightly, the gun lowered, pointing at the floor.

I didn't know if she wanted me dead as well, so I raised Hillier's gun until she was looking straight at it.

"Let go of the gun," I said.

She didn't move.

Assuming she'd never shot anyone before, she was holding it together quite well, just the shaking and the sawing deep breathing. But I wasn't sure that she might not go hysterical on me and start blasting away, so I said again:

"Nicola, let the gun drop. If you don't, I will shoot you dead."

Her eyes came back into focus and I tensed as she moved and the gun dropped from her hand onto the stone floor.

"Is he dead now?" Her voice was harsh, sounded brittle.

"Oh yes," I replied, "Hillier's dead. And so are a few other people."

"I don't care."

I stepped away from his body.

"Where did you get the gun, Nicola?"

"Picked it up off a dead man by the front door."

RIP Bobby. Rest In Pieces.

"How did you know to come here?" I asked her.

"I knew he had this warehouse and I heard one of them talking about the carpet place. I know their cars. I came here and saw them parked up."

"And thought you'd wander in to join the fun?"

"I wanted to see him dead! I wanted to see it for myself!"

I suddenly felt sick of it all. I lowered the gun I was holding.

"Well, take a good look, Nicola, take a good look at all the dead people you made."

"They deserved it," she said, her voice rising. "They killed my brother. They threw - "

"They didn't kill him," I cut in, louder. "He jumped. He was off his head on whatever and he jumped. That's it. He jumped!"

"Hillier was lying!" She screamed.

"No," I said quietly, my voice sounding tired, even to me. "He wasn't."

And then, quite suddenly, I was angry. Not the cold detached anger I'd been craving, but a hot, dangerous, uncontrolled feeling that rose up out of my gut through my chest and into my throat and then exploded as a shout.

"You stupid bitch! You stupid bloody bitch! All these people dead because you wanted revenge for something that didn't even happen! You used Pete and you used me and you got what you wanted. For nothing!"

And the gun was pointing at her again and it would have been so easy, the little voice telling me *no loose ends - clean it up - she's the cause* and the anger still there, still rising, still rising and then I pulled it back, pulled it all back in, saw at the end of my aim just a stupid girl with no real understanding of what she'd done and dragged it all back in again, but it was hard, a real physical effort to pull back from the edge, because by God I was angry and blowing her brains all over this warehouse would have been no more than she deserved.

But I wasn't Hillier.

I wasn't Smith, or Gavin, or Lewis, or, Lord help me, even Al. I wasn't any of them.

The moment passed and I let my arm fall, the sweat starting out on me again.

Her face was pale, terrified, the blood drained away and I recognised at that moment that she knew just how close she had come to dying.

"Get out," I said quietly. "Out of here, out of London. Find yourself a life somewhere else. Anywhere. If I hear you're in London, I'll kill you. If you think about saying anything about this, then remember who shot Hillier first and why. If you turn grass, then I, or someone, will come looking for you and we will find you. Now get out."

She stumbled backwards a few steps before turning and I heard her heels on the stone floor running to get clear. When I could no longer hear her footsteps, I looked around at the devastation.

Carpet rolls in the aisles, bodies, blood and guns. I wanted to get clear myself, but I had to clean up first. I wiped Hillier's gun with my shirt and put it back in his hands for the prints. Obviously, he couldn't have shot himself, but it was his gun and it would confuse things. I picked up my gun and tried to figure out what to do with it. It was supposed to be clean and I believed the dealer who'd told me that, but if I left it here I'd have to wipe it clean anyway and then it wouldn't make any sense lying there as a spare gun. Although I'd shot people with it, so the police would know there'd been someone else here anyway. This, I thought, is what comes of winging it and not planning things through. Still, I'd had no choice. In the end I decided to take it with me on the basis of leaving as little as possible behind, but I'd ditch it at the first opportunity.

Then I took Bobby's gun that the girl had used and wiped her prints off it. I took it with me while I checked that Hillier's men were all dead. I didn't want anyone left to talk about this night. When I reached Bobby by the front entrance, I gave him his gun back and then checked in the office that the cameras weren't switched on. I didn't think they would be. Hillier wouldn't have wanted any record of tonight.

I stepped carefully around the obscene green plastic sheeting that was still laid out on the floor and checked a couple of times that Nicola wasn't waiting out front for me to walk into an ice pick or a speeding Micra. It was unlikely, but now wasn't the time to be careless. Keeping to the shadows with my collar turned up, I made my way back to my car, doubling back on myself a couple of times just to be sure, but there was no-one with me.

Back in the car I sat for a minute. I should have felt relieved. In one way I was free now, but in getting out from under Hillier's control, I'd moved further into the way of life I'd been trying to get away from. But that had been the only way. Or maybe it had been the only way for me.

I wiped my gun clean and carefully put it into a carrier bag. Tied the bag closed. I kept the speed-loader and unused bullets. I don't know why, but they weren't incriminating of this night's work, so I kept them.

A wave of tiredness came over me, but I couldn't relax yet. The gun had to go and the nearest place that I could easily ditch it where it wouldn't be found was the river. Lord knows how many other weapons were there, but it was as good a place as any to lose a gun. The jacket would have to go as well, since I'd shot through it, but I'd do that later. For the moment it was still cover and the hole wasn't too obvious.

I drove down towards the river and parked up north of it, to the east of Tower Bridge. I could have just chucked the thing in from the side somewhere, but it might not have gone far enough especially at low tide times. So I walked back and then along the bridge towards the middle, but I stopped before the first tower by the traffic lights. A quick check for nosey passers by or cameras, but it was dark and all the cameras were sighted to the middle of the bridge or at the doors of the tower. I waited until there were no cars passing and I was about to ditch the gun when I thought how stupid I'd feel if a boat appeared from under the bridge just as I dropped the bag. What were the chances? But I'd learnt not to tempt fate, so I took a look back over to the west, left it a few seconds in case there was anything actually under the bridge at that moment and then let it go over the side. It's amazing how attached you can get to a small piece of metal, even if it has saved your life. I was genuinely sorry to see it go. What does that say about you, I thought to myself.

I walked back to the car wondering at how calm I was, but knowing - from experience - that the sweats and the shaking would come later, once I let go and allowed myself to think, took the brake off my head. Right now I was still on automatic. Ditch the gun. Get home. Be safe.

I drove back carefully, concentrating on the driving and on trying not to let anything enter my mind, other than the primary thoughts. Get Home. Be safe. But there was one more thing crowding in.

Tomorrow, I thought, tomorrow I'd call Jenny, or maybe tonight, now, just to let her know I was all right. Or at least still alive. Was I all right? I wouldn't know until some kind of reaction had set in and I found out how I was dealing with it. Or not dealing with it. So maybe I wouldn't call her yet. Not for a while. And she'd said to leave it, to leave her alone.

Sense of déjà vu again as I parked up a little away from my place and walked the last bit. I got to the stairs by the shops and started up. As I rounded the stairwell, I saw a figure sitting a couple of steps from the top.

"I couldn't wait at home," she said, "I had to know."

I stopped as I reached her.

"Now you know," I said and my voice sounded like it was coming from far away.

She was looking up at me.

"I changed the rules, didn't I? I said I wouldn't ask you to change anything and then I did."

"You had a right to. You have a stake in this."

She shook her head.

"No. Maybe I'll have the right in time, but not then, not just then."

She got up and took my hand and we walked on towards my front door. As I got the keys out, she asked:

"Was it bad?"

I stopped for a moment and saw it again, not just that night, but all of it, right back to Allingway and that bloody card game, maybe even further, then pushed the door open and turned to look at her.

"Yes," I said, "but it's getting better."

*